When We Meet Again

When We Meet Again

Caroline Beecham

G. P. PUTNAM'S SONS
New York

PUTNAM
— EST. 1838 —

G. P. Putnam's Sons
Publishers Since 1838
An imprint of Penguin Random House LLC
penguinrandomhouse.com

Library of Congress Cataloging-in-Publication Data

Names: Beecham, Caroline, author.
Title: When we meet again / Caroline Beecham.
Other titles: Finding Eadie
Description: New York : G.P. Putnam's Sons, [2021] |
Includes A conversation with Caroline Beecham about When we
meet again and Discussion guide. | Includes bibliographical references
Identifiers: LCCN 2021021671 (print) | LCCN 2021021672 (ebook) |
ISBN 9780593331156 (trade paperback) | ISBN 9780593331163 (ebook)
Subjects: LCSH: World War, 1939–1945—England—London—Fiction. |
Unmarried mothers—Fiction. | Missing children—Fiction. |
Publishers and publishing—Fiction. | Books and reading—Fiction. |
GSAFD: Historical fiction. | LCGFT: Historical fiction. | Novels.
Classification: LCC PR9619.4.B425 F56 2021 (print) |
LCC PR9619.4.B425 (ebook) | DDC 823/.92--dc23
LC record available at https://lccn.loc.gov/2021021671
LC ebook record available at https://lccn.loc.gov/2021021672
p. cm.

Printed in the United States of America
1st Printing

Book design by Elke Sigal

This book is for the Brighton girls—
Amanda, Becky, Gill, Lisa and Vicky—
for your love and friendship

If you cannot read [all your books], at any rate handle them and, as it were, fondle them. Peer into them. Let them fall open where they will. Read on from the first sentence that arrests the eye. Then turn to another. Make a voyage of discovery, taking soundings of uncharted seas. Set them back on their selves with your own hands. Arrange them on your own plan, so that if you do not know what is in them, you at least know where they are. If they cannot be your friends, let them at any rate be your acquaintances.

—WINSTON S. CHURCHILL

People die, but books never die. . . . No man and no force can take from the world the books that embody man's eternal fight against tyranny. In this war, we know, books are weapons.

—FRANKLIN D. ROOSEVELT

Prologue

BRIGHTON, MARCH 18, 1943

Alice woke with a start, seagulls screeching from the gabled rooftop. The dawn glow bled through uneven curtains, illuminating the white wicker crib that stood only a few feet away. She was curled on her side at the very edge of the bed, eye level with the crib, which sat beside the splintered paintwork of the windowsill.

Her lips curved into a smile. She needed to nurse Eadie now, just as the midwife had shown her the day after the birth. Alice tried to ease herself up onto one elbow, but her limbs were so weak with tiredness that her arm wouldn't support her, and she collapsed back onto the pillow. Everything was so tranquil; Eadie must still be sleeping—this most precious time preserved—and all Alice could hear was her own breathing. It was clear that no one else in the guesthouse was awake.

Her lips twitched into a half smile as she wondered if her daughter would always be so calm when she slept; her mother had told her that she'd snored like a grown man.

Alice pushed herself up again, trying to ignore the soreness and discomfort as she carefully swung her legs around and levered up with both hands. With eyes alight, she beamed in anticipation as she tilted forward, ready to see her newborn, her face hovering over the crib—but when she looked down, it was empty.

Her eyes flashed wide in horror, staring unblinking at the wrinkled crib sheet and white crocheted blanket flung over the sides.

The sound of traffic intruded from the road outside as the clock hands carried on their twin journeys, and several moments passed before Alice regained the capacity to think, running her fingers across the place where Eadie's tiny swaddled body had lain.

It was stone cold.

Was her mind playing tricks on her? Could she be hallucinating, even though they had refused her any pain relief?

No, she could feel it in each aching tendon and the viscera of her body, in the thickness of her womb. Eadie had been born weeks early; Alice's mother hadn't arrived by the time the baby came squalling into the world, so her aunt had taken charge, calling the doctor. He had stitched Alice with unsympathetic detachment before telling her to rest and that any questions should be saved for the nurse who would come the following day.

Her aunt had been on hand, helping with hot water and

the constant supply of towels, until the other guests complained there was no supper on the table.

That was it: her aunt must have taken Eadie downstairs.

Alice relaxed as she gathered the white crocheted blanket between her fingers and lifted it to her nose, breathing in her daughter's scent.

Then she saw the handwritten note.

I'm sorry, Alice, but this really is for the best.

She recognized the handwriting.

One

LONDON, NOVEMBER 1942
FIVE MONTHS EARLIER

The baby's face was scratched and dirty, the blanket barely covering its pale unwashed skin. But the haystacks looked as if they could provide some warmth and comfort, as did the Three Wise Men standing nearby—even though one was missing his head. Alice stared at the nativity scene a fraction longer, a smile broadening her lips as she gazed at the infant, fear and excitement blooming inside her.

Shopfronts glistened with Christmas decorations and seasonal greetings, the frosted windows strewn with multicolored tinsel and sprigs of holly, handmade decorations and signs: defiant gestures by Londoners determined to get on with their lives. Alice wished she had time to stay awhile longer, but she had to hurry; it was Monday morning, so they would all be assembled for the weekly meeting, and she would make the speech that she'd been practicing for some time.

More shops and offices were opening as she hurried by, their entrances and doorways crowded with the morning rush. She carried on past a line of steam-filled cafés, only slowing when the storefront of W.H. Smith & Son came into view. A sign above the entrance read, BLACKED-OUT EVENINGS—TAKE HOME SOME BOOKS, and a familiar poster stood propped against the end of the bookstand:

IMPORTANT

Newspapers and Magazines Supplied to order only. The only way to make sure of regular supplies is to give a standing order for all newspapers, periodicals and magazines required, whether these are to be delivered or bought over the counter.

Please give your order NOW.

Alice buttoned her coat as she read, trying to even out her breath, the brutal sting of cold air reawakening her nervousness over what she was about to do. There was no time for second thoughts now, no chance to turn back the clock, so she placed her hand protectively across her belly and carried on into Russell Square.

Above the dark slate roofs, the firewatchers' platforms and terra cotta chimneys, a reluctant winter sun struggled through a sullen sky and the city grew more orderly. Alice headed south toward a Gothic building flanked by taller neighbors, trying not to step on the cracks between the paving stones as she ran through her speech one more time.

The old five-story building creaked as it welcomed her inside. Since the entrance hall was empty, she stood and looked longingly around: at the substantial glass lantern overhead, still hanging obstinately despite the bombing raids; at the black-and-white tiled floor with its worn oriental rug, and the two wingback chairs on either side of the buffet table. An oversized mirror hung above it, reflecting the vase of cascading silk flowers. On the opposite wall, an imposing carved Victorian coat stand resembled an upended fishing vessel full of coats, hats and umbrellas, with Nelson's leash dangling at one end; he was her employer's black Labrador.

She dropped her belongings at her feet, heart hammering in her chest, grateful no one was there to see her disheveled state. She'd caught her reflection in a shop window: her dark-blond hair frizzy in the damp air, navy eyes ringed red with tiredness. Her mother was right, she did need more sleep. For her and the baby's sake.

Her colleagues had told her that lots of people had once milled about in the entryway to Partridge Press: agents, delivery boys, a visitor from one government department or another, or a journalist on the scent of a story about one of their writers. Their offices had once been in Paternoster Row, in the heart of the city, until a tragic night in December 1940 when their building and seventeen other publishing offices had been destroyed, larger ones like Hutchinson, Longman and Blackwood included. The firms had moved to locations around the British Museum and further west, the event uniting the industry as publishers lent each other office space in a show of solidarity. That was when she had joined Partridge, and she still tried hard not to imagine the collective loss of books and artworks. Her company had lost thousands of works and illustrations, and most of their steel and copper engraving plates and woodcuts, and they were still struggling to recover.

She took another long sweep of the hallway, trying to quell her fear as she remembered the day nearly two years ago when she'd stood in this exact spot, an administrator with little knowledge of the industry. How welcoming they'd been, and how like a family they'd become.

On the left of the entrance was the closed office door of the managing director, George Armstrong-Miller, his name engraved in bright gilt script. On the opposite side was the office of his son, Rupert, onetime financial controller and now an engineer in the Royal Air Force. His image, in full uniform with a teasing half smile and a mass of dark hair, commanded attention from his portrait beside the door; his expression was the one that always beguiled people, its playful immaturity making him seem harmless and charming. That look had drawn her in, made her trust him, and given her the ill-conceived idea that she was protected here. When she took a step backward his eyes seemed to follow her, just like when they'd first met and he'd always kept her within his sight. He'd never hidden what he thought of her or been too shy to show it.

Alice averted her eyes and tried not to think of him as she hurriedly backed away, trying to focus on what lay ahead as she recovered her things and climbed the staircase.

The third-floor editorial department was accessed from a helter-skelter arrangement of stairs, with uneven landings pivoting off in all directions. It always felt to Alice as if she were stepping off a fairground ride to be propelled through small doorways, their brass handles far too low down. She held on to the handrail and planted her feet firmly as she climbed, striving to ignore the growing tightness in the pit of her stomach as she passed the production department on the first floor, with its unmistakable chemical reek, then accounts on the second floor.

On the third floor she stood outside the boardroom for a moment to steady her breathing, worried her rapid heartbeat and flushed cheeks might give her away—just as Nelson had, scratching at the bottom of the door.

Alice unbuttoned her coat, letting it fall loosely around her hips, and turned the handle. The door opened into a large wood-paneled room where a meeting was under way, and they all turned to look at her. George was at the head of the grand mahogany table in a haze of cigarette smoke; Tommy Simpson, their bald-headed production controller, was seated at his side; and Emily Dalrymple, the nonfiction editor, was at the other. Ursula Rousson, the fiction editor, had her back to the door, a brightly patterned scarf tied around her neck and her chestnut hair tousled into a hairstyle every bit as unorthodox as her personality. She swung round to look down her nose at Alice, then tutted good-humoredly. "Good morning, Alice," she said, smiling warmly.

"Come in," George said, motioning at the seat next to Ursula. "You haven't missed anything, although I was just saying that we do have some important discussions to get through."

Nelson greeted her with his wet nose, and she bent down to scratch his neck. "I'm sorry I'm late. The bus was so crowded I had to wait for the next one." She quickly looped her bag and gas mask over the back of the chair before she sat down, gathering her coat self-consciously across her lap.

"Can't be helped," George replied in his gravelly voice, "and you're here now." He smiled broadly as he leaned back in his chair, lifting his elbows as he smoothed back his wisps of hair with both hands.

He was the younger of the two sons in the publishing family, and he had a gregarious and generous nature. He'd given Alice an opportunity, ignoring the gaps in her education as if he already knew what other powerful men didn't—that thousands of young women like her around the country were completely unqualified for the roles war had chosen for them but immensely capable, nevertheless.

He leaned forward abruptly, resting his arms on the desk in front of him, which reminded her where Rupert got his habit of fidgeting from. "Actually, we started early because there have been some developments. Tommy, why don't you fill Alice in?"

The boardroom had formerly been a morning room, its ornate light fixtures and oversized windows allowing in plenty of light as well as providing glorious views over Russell Square. Spread across the vast table were several editions of *Bomber Command* and *The Battle of Britain*, their eye-catching covers featuring images that had become all too common in recent months: the faces of actual pilots—the real heroes of the empire—not fictional characters. In the six months following its release by the Ministry of Information, *The Battle of Britain* had sold nearly five million copies to become a surprise bestseller, and none of them—not Penguin nor Hutchinson nor any of the other major book publishers—had been able to replicate the success.

"Rumor has it they're planning a new one on minesweepers," Tommy said, leaning across the table to push the latest edition toward her.

"You can imagine the drama and intrigue in that one," Emily said, raising an eyebrow.

"The truth is, we can't really compete with the Ministry anymore," Tommy said, sounding glum. "We need some big new ideas of our own."

George stood and moved over to the window, leaning his shoulder against the architrave, hands thrust into his trouser pockets as he gazed out onto the grass square.

The others glanced at one another, waiting for him to speak, and Tommy offered cigarettes from a smart leather case. Only Ursula accepted, and as Alice watched him light it for her, she desperately hoped the smoke wouldn't nauseate her now as it had started to. She'd been lucky with her pregnancy so far, only developing a deep distaste for fish and eggs, and since they were both difficult to get hold of, it hadn't been too much of an inconvenience—but most of her co-workers smoked.

George turned to face them. "The public's appetite for books is still growing across all genres, but we don't have the resources to try anything new, that's the maddening thing. Tell them, Tommy."

"Our paper ration has been reduced again." He waited for their collective groan to end. "And since it takes one ton of paper to produce three thousand books—"

"Only if they're two hundred and fifty pages long." Emily clearly wasn't willing to be outdone.

"Well, yes, that's right," he said. "But it still means we can't publish as many titles as in previous years. We'll be lucky if we get five nonfiction and ten fiction books out of our paper stocks this quarter, and that means we can only produce two new titles."

"It's difficult to take risks with only two new titles," Ursula said, with the trace of her eastern European accent.

"Precisely," George agreed.

The knot in Alice's stomach tightened; this really wasn't the day to be telling them that she was leaving, when what they needed were winning new ideas. The public was reading more than ever in shelters and in their homes during blackouts, as were the troops and voluntary services as they waited, and yet here was the publishing industry without the means to produce more books.

Tommy said, "You all know the new rules, that we don't get the paper ration next year unless we get the book sales this year. So, we can't really afford to take risks. We need certainty, and to give booksellers titles they can sell."

"Well, that means more crime and romance, then," Emily said confidently.

"If we want to play it safe, it does," Ursula replied.

The Bookseller published a weekly chart of the bestsellers and the most borrowed books, and they included Agatha Christie, Ernest Hemingway, Daphne du Maurier, Graham Greene and Victor Gollancz, as well as the propaganda bestsellers that the Ministry of Information produced.

"What about children's books?" Alice suggested. "Apparently *Five on a Treasure Island* is proving popular."

"It's just novelty," Emily scoffed. "It's not going to last. Do you seriously think anyone is going to be interested in reading about what four children and their dog get up to in the school holidays?"

"I don't know," George said thoughtfully. "I really don't, but we need to try something."

"Maybe we should publish new fiction," said Alice. "We could take a chance on some new writers. It would be more economical, wouldn't it?"

"I like how you're thinking, Alice," said Tommy, "but now is not the time to be launching authors."

"All right, then maybe we should relaunch the classics," Emily said. "Our most-loved authors, like Penguin did."

George sighed. "Yes, the backlist would have been the answer, if we hadn't lost all the plates in the bombing."

"Oh yes, of course, I'm sorry." Emily looked sheepish. She was as plain-looking as she was plain-thinking, with her short brown bob and knitted clothes that no one in their twenties should be seen in, even during wartime, but Alice didn't hold that against her; it was the frequency with which she said such inappropriate and thoughtless things.

"We do know the MOI books are popular, that they're a new kind of narrative," Ursula said. "We'd be insane not to try to find our own version of them."

"We don't have the same access, though," George said, as he paced the room. "Those books rely on expert knowledge and firsthand accounts from serving officers." He picked up *The Battle of Britain*, tapping the front cover with his finger. "Look, diagrams and photographs from the army—where would we get any of those?"

"Rupert would have known what to do," Emily said under her breath.

"Yes, well, Rupert's not here, is he?" Tommy snapped.

Alice chewed her lip as she tried to put Rupert from her thoughts and decide whether she should tell them about her idea, or just that she was leaving. But the smoke was beginning to nauseate her, and her brain was like wet porridge. It was excruciating: here she was, about to tell them that she wouldn't be working for the foreseeable future, and they needed her more than ever.

Instead, she blurted, "We could get our most popular authors to write on a topic of war, long essays from their point of view—just like Hilary Saunders did."

"That's because Saunders isn't just popular, he's damn good," said George. "He's just done a six-week sellout tour of America. What do the rest of you think?"

As they carried on discussing the idea, Alice picked up a copy of *Bomber Command* and found herself caught up in a story from one of the returning aircrew members, even though she'd read it before. There was no getting away from the fact that these topical nonfiction titles were compelling; when real life became more dramatic than fiction, it was hardly surprising that people wanted to read these types of books. Her gaze fell across the bookshelf that took up the entire back wall, containing an edition of every one of Partridge's books that hadn't been destroyed: the successful crime series, the one-off novels, the how-to's, the breakthrough successes, and even titles that had been returned. There were hundreds of emotions and thousands of brave words and ideas bound inside those covers, and she needed to show bravery now too.

"Well, what about real lives and real voices?" Alice said hesitantly. "They make better storytelling these days."

Tommy looked puzzled. "But we're not in the business of producing propaganda, Alice, which is what these 'real life' books are intended for."

"I know, but I'm talking about civilian stories," she said, "and they are just as dramatic as any Hollywood film, but they're real."

"What do you have in mind?" Ursula asked, leaning forward, resting her chin on her clenched hand.

"Stories from the home front . . . not the soldiers' point of view but the women behind the scenes. The female wardens and the ambulance drivers, the Wrens and the WAAF—we could show their side of the story and that their experiences count too."

"But why would we want to tell the same stories that *Picture Post* and *Illustrated* do?" Emily said, shaking her head. "And why would people pay sixpence for them?"

"These titles wouldn't be like the magazines you read once then give away to your next-door neighbor—they would be books to treasure. The first could include stories of what women and children are doing to cope, how they're helping and being affected." Alice pushed the book back into the center of the table. "Families will want to keep them for their children, to remember this aspect of how we won the war and understand what was sacrificed for them. It's about the women and children first."

"Hear, hear," George said, clapping, "marvelous!"

Alice wasn't sure what had come over her, but it had seemed the right moment to share an idea she'd been thinking about for some time. After all, she had nothing to lose now. "They'll be extraordinary stories of ordinary people," she said, smiling at the thought.

"It *is* rather clever," Tommy said slyly. "We won't need to pay any advances or royalties."

"So, what are we going to give them then, Alice?" Emily asked, with a note of skepticism. "What specifically is the first story going to be about?"

They were all looking at her, expecting an answer. This was far worse than she'd imagined; she wasn't just letting her mother down anymore but also the people she respected and admired, the ones who had believed in her. And she couldn't even tell them why.

"Come on, Alice," said George, "how far have you developed this idea?"

Was there any way she could stay longer, perhaps leave in a few more weeks? She pulled out her notebook containing schematics of the idea, clippings from newspapers that, once investigated and researched, might make for bigger human-interest stories. There were the schoolboys now working as zookeepers, the child wardens, and small children reunited with long-lost parents, but there wasn't nearly enough to illustrate the idea, let alone content for a whole book—not yet, anyway.

Alice looked at her employer, knowing that whatever she said now she wouldn't be able to deliver on; it would be someone else's job.

Everyone's eyes were on her, and she was drowning under the weight of their expectation.

"Well, at least we have something to think about," Ursula

said, coming to her rescue. "We can have a brainstorming session after lunch. There are other things we need to discuss now, aren't there, Tommy?"

"You can make a start now though, can't you, Alice?" Tommy asked. "Draw up a list of possible stories, people to interview."

"Of course, but—" It really was terrible timing, but she couldn't wait any longer; the worrying was keeping her awake at night. "I'm so sorry, and I realize this is awful timing . . . but I'm afraid I can't work on these books. I've got to go away for a few months."

George looked confused. "What do you mean, Alice?"

"My cousin is about to have a baby, and her husband has just been killed." The lie made her throat constrict. When she glanced up, George was glaring at her, and Ursula looked surprised. "I've got to move in with her for a while. She's a mess, you see. Heading for a breakdown, my mother said." Her cheeks burned as the blood rushed to her face.

"What about your mother?" George asked. "Or isn't there someone else in the family who can help?"

"George!" Ursula snapped, narrowing her eyes at him.

"I'm sorry, Alice. That's terrible news, and I'm sure we are all very sorry for your cousin. Please give her our profound sympathies. And there really isn't anyone else who can help look after the poor woman?"

"I'm afraid not, George. It's up to me."

The group's excitement dissipated, and even Nelson rested his head on his paws and lay forlornly at George's feet. The meeting continued in a genial manner, and after some discussion it was decided that Emily would coordinate the work on

Alice's book idea. They would bring in a freelance writer to develop it until Alice came back; it was hoped they could generate some noteworthy stories about women and children on the home front, as well as tales of exceptional romance and bravery from everyday lives.

Just as they were preparing to leave, George addressed them again. "I'll be expecting you all to dig deep into your own lives—think about family members or friends who might have had experiences they've never shared before. You know how people can surprise you." He stared directly at Alice.

She didn't know where to look, but she waited for everyone to leave and caught up with him. "I am really very sorry, George," she said, forcing herself to meet his gaze. "I will try to hurry back, but I understand that you can't keep my job open." She'd no idea what had got into her; there was no possibility of her ever coming back. How could she keep up the pretense in the office, hiding the identity of the baby's father along with her anguish over what had happened? The whole idea was wildly inappropriate, and she couldn't believe she'd suggested it, yet the thought of leaving them all and her job for good seemed just as impossible.

"Nonsense!" said George. "There will always be a place for you here; you know that. And that's the reason why you will have to excuse my selfishness, even though I really am very sorry for your cousin." He placed an arm around her shoulders.

Alice shuddered, bracing herself against his touch; so much about him reminded her of Rupert.

"We'll all be sorry to see you go, Alice, but we understand how difficult it must be for you too. And we value your loyalty to your family. It's only right to keep strong principles during these times." His sincerity made her feel a hundred times worse.

"Thank you, George. I think so too." She forced a smile, wishing things were different and that she could have shared the truth.

Two

At lunchtime Ursula followed Alice into the courtyard. Bundled in her red velvet turban and old sable coat, Ursula was clearly fuming that Alice hadn't confided in her. "So," she said, "this cousin of yours, I don't think I've ever heard you talk about her before."

"Really? I'm sure I must have . . . she's a poor old thing." Alice picked at a corner of her sandwich. "Mum's convinced she's having a nervous breakdown, so we need to be there—for the baby."

They'd settled at one of the wrought-iron tables to eat their lunches, the brittle wind carrying the noise of traffic from surrounding streets. Alice felt oddly unnatural, as if they were actors on a stage about to begin their scene, and not colleagues and friends who knew each other well and did this all the time.

"That's understandable," Ursula said, "but what about you? I can see how upset you are about leaving. It just doesn't seem very fair." Alice felt Ursula eyeing her surreptitiously, as if noticing that something had changed—perhaps even the shape of her belly—and she tried to remain composed, knowing that the more guarded she was, the more suspicious Ursula would become.

"Why isn't it fair?" Alice asked.

"You having to give up work, for one thing." Ursula pushed away her barely touched lunch and pulled out a packet of Sobranie cigarettes, offering one to Alice, who shook her head. "So, you're giving up cigarettes too?" Ursula said flippantly, then placed one between pursed lips.

"Well, of course I'd obviously rather not give up my job, but Mum won't stop working, so I have to."

"Maybe you should let me talk to her," Ursula said as she forcefully exhaled. "You're going to make such a great editor, Alice. And after all my hard work training you . . . I really don't know how you can bear to throw it all away!"

Alice didn't know how she was going to either. She didn't have a degree like Ursula, Emily and Tommy but had learned through reading widely and taking a course at the London College of Printing. After a lot of hard work and determination, she had been hired as an administrator by George, then Ursula had trained and supported her in becoming an assistant editor—much to the horror of Emily, who couldn't understand how on earth this could happen. Ursula had shown Alice how to assess manuscripts, copyedit, proofread, brief illustrators and typographers, and look after the department's ever-shrinking advertising budget; all things Ursula had told her that she'd need to know when her time came to be an editor. Only now that could never happen.

"Well, I'm sure I'll be back before we know it," Alice said somberly.

"It is a lot to ask, though, for you to put your job on hold rather than hers. After all, you're in a profession now, and she's not," Ursula replied emphatically.

"I know, but she doesn't see it that way. She thinks I've only been here for two years, and she's been at the munitions factory for much longer. She won't give it up."

Alice took another bite of her sandwich, trying desperately to hide her watery eyes as she fixed her gaze on a robin that tapped its beak on the frozen water of the nearby birdbath. Ursula watched too as the bird persevered, but she cast sneaky glances at her friend. Alice wanted to tell her the truth, but for every reason she found to share her secret, another swooped down like a magpie to steal the thought. Still, she couldn't silence the tiny voice that whispered, *A trouble shared is a trouble spared*, or the avalanche of other old sayings that sprang to mind. She looked up at Ursula and forced a smile. It hurt to keep the truth from her, but it could hurt more not to. And Alice knew that her friend was keeping a secret of her own, one she might not be inclined to share even if Alice revealed hers.

She forced herself to finish her sandwich, then got up to explore the small courtyard, crunching across the slippery gravel as she examined the ropes of ivy that twisted over the gray flint walls and trailed down the other side. This compact space felt like a safe haven, but soon Alice would only be able to dream about it.

"Anyway," she said with a sigh as she turned around, "Mum says bullets are more important than books."

"Christ, your mother really is a drain and not a radiator!" Ursula said with a roll of her eyes. "Anyway, books have a great deal of power."

"That's what I told her."

Smoke curled through Ursula's lips. "Don't you love earning a decent wage?"

"Of course I do. But you know Mum, she says it's our 'God-given role' to look after family first and foremost. You have no idea how many times she's quoted verse at me."

Alice rolled her eyes, and Ursula smiled. "Go on, which one this time?"

Ursula was always amused by stories of her mother's piety, and the unspoken tension dissolved as the rhythm of their friendship returned.

"The First Epistle to Timothy," Alice replied quickly. "'But if any provide not for his own house, he hath denied the faith, and is worse than an unbeliever.'"

It surprised Alice that she still remembered the verse although there had been years of forced churchgoing for her and her brother, William.

"Oh, dear, you don't want to risk going to hell," Ursula said in a dramatic voice, then smirked. "Well, some of us would never go back to how things were before the war," she added, exhaling heavily.

"Of course I like earning money, but if it's a choice between having three pounds in my pocket and not having a war, I know which one I'd take!" Alice said as she sat back down, gathering her coat around her and shivering.

"You know that's not what I meant. It's just that it's not all bad."

"What about *your* mother?" Alice asked, wanting to change the subject. "You rarely talk about your parents."

"What of them? I told you they banished me to London after I had too much fun at college. Besides, Oxford is too far to travel on my one day off. And there's enough excitement to be had in this fine city." She looked up and smiled, but Alice sensed a sadness behind the mask.

Early in their friendship and after too many drinks, Ursula had confided that she wasn't prepared to hide who she was from her family or pretend she was ever going to change; consequently, they never got in touch. At the time Alice hadn't been sure what she'd meant, but with more life experience, and having met all sorts through publishing, she was now fairly certain that Ursula was a lesbian.

"When was the last time you saw them?" Alice asked.

"A few Christmases ago."

"Why don't you visit them? It's nearly that time of year."

"Oh no, you won't be here for the Christmas party!" Ursula said, taking her turn to change the topic. "How will you survive the season without listening to George's speech or watching Emily fawn over Tommy?"

Alice's heart sank again. It perhaps seemed silly in light of everything else that she faced, but these communal events had taken on more importance in recent years; surviving to another Christmas was a significant achievement for which she was grateful.

"I can live without that, but I will definitely miss our nights out," she said, thinking about their regular drinks in Soho.

Ursula laid her hand on Alice's, and Alice gazed down at

the pale skin and bright red fingernails. "You would tell me, wouldn't you, if anything was wrong?"

"I'm fine, really. Everything's fine."

"You know I'm here, though, don't you? You must tell me if you ever need help."

Alice looked at her and smiled. "I will, and thank you," she said, patting Ursula's hand.

"I suppose at least you won't have to put up with Tommy prattling on," Ursula said as she pulled her hand away.

"And Emily's whining," Alice said, rolling her eyes.

"And what about the interminable boredom of one of Patricia Reece's lunches! That's why you're leaving, isn't it?" Ursula narrowed her eyes. "It's just a ploy to get out of seeing her. Really, Alice, that's a bit extreme, if you don't mind me saying!"

"Yes, I know, extreme but understandable."

They grinned. Patricia Reece was one of their most established authors, and her distinctive style of cozy thriller had generated a strong following, but she subjected Ursula and Alice to long formal lunches while avoiding discussion of her edits.

Ursula finished her cigarette and ground the stub into the gravel.

"I suppose you've heard the news?" Alice said, relieved that Ursula had stopped questioning her.

"About Germany invading Tunisia?"

"No, far more significant than that," Alice said, trying to hide her smile. "The Church has decided that women don't have to wear hats anymore. Can you imagine? How scandalous!"

"Really?"

"Yes. I'm going with Mum on Sunday—hatless."

This had the desired effect: Ursula laughed. If she'd been angry with Alice or suspected anything, then at least she appeared to have forgotten it.

Three

The day hadn't gone as Alice had expected, leaving her with a deep unease, so she sneaked away early—before they could make a fuss of her leaving—and hoped the London Zoo would be the sanctuary it always had been. But this visit needed to be quick and before dusk when it closed, a brief good-bye; she would see the new black swans, finish the journal and get home before her mother worried where she was.

She took her usual route through the North Gate, crossing in front of the Victorian redbrick ticket house, the aviaries and the darkened Reptile House, then along the Broad Walk. London Zoo—or Regent's Park Zoo, as the locals called it—was only thirty-five acres, but it took time to navigate the main garden, and a late-afternoon fog lingered in the air, reducing visibility.

Memories lurked in all the shadowy corners: the chimpanzee tea parties, feeding hay to the hippos and taking camel rides. Her father, Frederick—or Freddie, as everyone had known him—had been one of the keepers when he'd come back from the Great War, and so Alice and William had spent their holidays and most weekends at the zoo. She'd kept coming as an adult, and had even been there the day that Rota the lion arrived. He had growled at the keepers as they'd ushered him from his crate into a walled enclosure, then he'd stood on the highest rock and roared at the sky. But this afternoon Alice couldn't hear Rota or his cubs, and the zoo would soon be closing for the day.

Shivering, she wove her way to the Bears' Den, peering inside to see if they were still awake. She could only make out vague outlines of russet shapes between the iron bars, mountains in a landscape of hay. She carried on toward Three Island Pond; it had been one of her and William's favorite childhood spots, with its colorful tapestry of trees and the flamingos, which their father never tired of telling them were the only birds to feed with their heads upside down.

She walked west, feet crunching gravel down Elephant Walk to the Penguin Pool, her quickening breaths creating clouds of condensation in the cold darkening air. Up ahead, one of the aquarium supervisors, Mr. Vinall, walked out of the Penguin Pool and shut the gate behind him. He was dark complexioned, his black curly hair barely contained beneath a keeper's hat that conjured up memories of her father in the same uniform, the familiar clamor of cage doors and the squeal of trolley wheels as he'd distributed food.

"Good afternoon, Mr. Vinall."

"Miss Cotton," he said, and broke into a smile, "whatever brings you here on such an inhospitable night?" His gray uniform was covered in a white apron stained with fish blood, and as he drew closer the smell grew so potent that her stomach lurched—her visit might not have been such a good idea after all.

"Yes, it is rather cold, isn't it?" she said, taking a step back. "But I want to see the swans before I leave."

The two black swans had just arrived as a gift for Mr. Churchill, courtesy of Dr. Evatt, the Australian minister for External Affairs.

"Ah yes, beautiful specimens they are. But what do you mean, leave? Are you going away?"

"Just for a while."

"When will you be back?"

"I'm not sure yet. In the springtime, I hope."

"Just like the marmots," he said with a smile.

She looked at him quizzically. "I'm not sure . . ."

"They like to hibernate too. But they've beaten you to it—they've already taken to their burrow."

She took a gulp of air. "Yes, of course," she said, forcing a smile.

"Is everything all right, Miss Cotton?"

"Yes, it is. Everything is fine, thank you."

"We'll miss you." He offered his hand then seemed to think better of it, wiping it on his apron and smiling broadly.

What was it that lit up a person's face when they smiled, she wondered, turning even the most incongruous of features into a perfect anatomical form?

"Look after yourself. And stay warm," he said.

"You too."

He walked away, carrying the unpleasant odor with him.

Of course she would try to look after herself, but there was no telling how things would go in the months ahead, in such challenging circumstances. She was certain, though, that she would bring her child here as soon as she could, and she would read the animal stories her father had once told her, along with others she'd written in her journal: stories about the aardvark called Adolf, and the axolotl they'd named Mussolini, and the medal-winning keepers. And she'd included how in *Alice's Adventures in Wonderland*, they used flamingo heads to play croquet, a fact that had caused her endless worry as a child. She could hear her father's softly spoken voice: *"The chief difficulty Alice found at first was in managing her flamingo . . . Alice soon came to the conclusion that it was a very difficult game indeed."*

Alice smiled at the thought as she settled on a bench by the Penguin Pool. She took out her journal and pencil, half-watching the birds as they swam and dived. A keeper was wading through the far end, cleaning up shredded foliage, while Peggy, the king penguin, kept a watchful eye from the platform above. A young penguin launched onto its tummy and ricocheted off the stone wall, hitting the water at speed, much to the chagrin of its mother. Alice laughed and set about sketching the young bird, thinking yet again how much she would miss her visits.

The zoo was a place of hope and optimism, where animals and keepers had battled the odds and survived, and she needed some of that in her life. Everyone said it was a miracle the zoo was still there, that it hadn't been severely damaged in the Blitz. Even though some animals had been shipped to Whipsnade, the country zoo in Bedfordshire, the majority had remained. The closed aquarium had been refilled, its fish tanks restocked. In fact, it seemed as if the zoo's inhabitants were determined to carry on entertaining the tourists and visiting servicemen for the duration of the war at all costs.

She continued to watch the show from the bench—Peggy's conceited stroll up and down the ramp, drawing herself up, and the younger creatures braying—only the penguins' meal of dead fish enough to spoil the memory that she was trying to preserve. Her journal lay open across her lap, almost full, as she added the finishing touches, coloring the tip of Peggy's wing. They were her favorite animal, and their play-fighting with the polar bears had brought them to the attention of the London papers, which wrote about their show, commending it to the capital's visitors as an antidote to the "jitters." But this evening the polar bears had gone indoors, and the solitary column of penguins marched across the rock as though they were characters from a children's storybook and needed the accompaniment of a military marching band. Alice placed her hands across her belly and whispered, "I can't wait to bring you here," before deciding it was time to leave.

Alice woke to a high-pitched whistle and the thudding of slammed doors. It was dark, and she hurriedly grabbed her bags and stepped onto the platform just as the train moved off, the backdraft lifting her coat as it howled through North Dulwich Station. With relief she watched it gather speed; fewer services ran now that most civilian machinery was deployed for war, and she'd have been stuck for ages if she'd missed her stop. Commuters overtook her as they headed for the covered stairway to the street-level exit, but she didn't even try to hurry, too emotional and exhausted. An easterly swirled dust and autumn leaves, and she had to lean into it, her clothes plastered against her as she forged ahead.

The five-minute walk home took the rest of her energy, and she was glad to reach the Victorian terrace house she shared with her mother. The family had moved there when her father had fallen ill before he died, and although that had been nearly eight years ago she still missed their old home in Primrose Hill; Dulwich felt a million miles away from her best friend, Penny.

"Hello?" Alice called as she clicked the front door shut behind her.

The house was dark and quiet and smelled of apple pie and damp carpet. She switched on the light, its small velvet shade illuminating the cream walls and burgundy hall runner, as well as the blistered wallpaper and the watermark that crept across the ceiling like a large ink stain. The décor was dilapidated due to financial constraint rather than neglect, not that any builders would have been available in wartime even if they'd been affordable. *This house might be razed to the ground any day if God desires it,* her mother said whenever Alice complained about how depressing it was. They had made some effort to cheer it up with new curtains and flowerboxes for the windows, but it didn't feel like home without her father and brother. She'd often been tempted to take lodgings with girls in the city but couldn't bring herself to leave her mother alone, and now it was too late for that.

Alice piled her belongings on the kitchen table, grabbed the book she'd brought home as a gift and went in search of Ruth. "Mum, where are you?" she called.

Light spilled from beneath her bedroom door, and as Alice

pushed it open, the pink rosebud walls, the metal bedframe and then the dresser came into view. Her mother's wiry figure was standing on tiptoes on a chair. It was strange to see her in a childlike pose: tartan skirt hitched up, cream sweater stretching across her shoulder blades, head arched backward as her hands probed inside the tall cupboard. Alice didn't want to make her jump, so she waited until Ruth had heaved the suitcase down.

"Alice!" she said, twisting round. "I didn't hear you come in."

"You should've let me do that."

"I don't think so." Ruth picked up the chair and set it back down in front of the dresser. "Not in . . ."

"Not in my condition?"

Ruth pursed her lips rather than smiled as Alice had hoped she might.

"What are you doing anyway? And why haven't you lit the fire? It's so cold."

"I'm helping you pack," Ruth replied as she opened a drawer and lifted out an armful of clothes.

"I can do that, but we don't need to pack yet."

"Yes, we do. You're leaving in the morning."

"The morning! That's not what we agreed." The conversation had been some weeks ago, but Alice remembered it clearly. They'd been in the garden, and she'd been quite definite that she wouldn't go until after the holidays.

"Yes, it is. Besides, there's not much coal left."

Alice shivered at the thought of spending more nights in three sets of pajamas and her overcoat, but she wasn't ready to leave yet either. And it worried her that Ruth hadn't remembered their discussion. Was she becoming ill again?

"Are you all right?" Alice asked with concern, hoping the anxiety wasn't returning. "You've not had any more of your migraines?"

"No, I'm fine," Ruth replied matter-of-factly. "It's simply for the best. You've finished work now, so there's no reason for you to stay."

"It's not what we discussed, though. I said I'd go to Brighton after Christmas. I want to be here . . . with you."

"Best not risk it." Ruth glanced at her. "You're beginning to show."

Alice gently pressed her palms over her belly. She was lucky to be tall like her father; she could carry a bit of extra weight without anyone noticing. "I don't want to be by myself," she said, growing tearful.

"You won't be. And you'll be helping your aunt for as long as you're able." Ruth carried on smoothing out the wrinkled garments with her fingers. She was moving with her usual calm, practiced efficiency, which made it even more troubling that she was reneging on their agreement. "Come on now, you did say you'd be all right on your own. And I'll come down on Sundays after church. Anyway, Hope needs you—it's busy in the lead-up to Christmas."

There was no question she wouldn't go; her aunt was counting on her, although she still didn't know what Hope really thought about her predicament, or what sort of reception she would get, since Ruth had been the one who'd made all the arrangements.

"I don't see why I can't wait a few more weeks."

When Ruth didn't reply, Alice walked over and placed a hand on her mother's arm, but she shrugged it away. "How did you get on today?" Ruth asked tersely as she opened another drawer.

"It was okay," Alice replied with forced cheerfulness.

Ruth wouldn't look at her, and Alice realized, with renewed sadness, that she must still be very disappointed. Was she ashamed of her daughter? Alice wanted to tell Ruth again that it wasn't her fault, but this hadn't done her any good when she'd tried before. She hoped that in time her mother would forgive her—maybe when the baby was born.

"They were sorry to see me go, but I said I'd see them again." A bubble of emotion caught in Alice's throat, and she moved beside Ruth, picking up a garment and folding it, while willing herself not to cry.

"Was that wise?"

"What do you mean?"

"Well, they're unlikely to want you back afterward, are they?"

"I know, but it was harder than I thought."

Ruth's attention was fixed on the small statue hanging above Alice's bed. The eyes of the Virgin Mary were half-closed as she looked down at the baby Jesus in her arms, and it felt as if there was meaning in her gaze.

"You haven't changed your mind, have you?" Alice said quietly.

It had been Ruth's idea for her to stay with Aunt Hope, have the baby and return pretending that it was an invented cousin's. There were so many war orphans to look after now that one more wouldn't create any suspicion.

Ruth looked up, her moss-colored eyes finally meeting Alice's.

Alice smiled at her. "I can't do this without you."

But her mother's expression was cold, and she held her daughter's gaze for barely a moment before looking away. "Are you ready to tell me who the father is?"

"I told you, it won't make any difference."

"It will to me."

Alice's heartbeat quickened as she remembered the first time: his hot ragged breath in her ear, the agony as his cheek pressed down on hers, her initial struggle as he pinned her beneath him, the roughness of his hands. And, as he forced himself inside her, a stinging sensation and the sharp stab of pain. Afterward, her soreness and the strong musk of his sweat as it dribbled down her neck, collecting in the crook of her collarbone when he collapsed on top of her.

"How do you know he won't come for his child?" Ruth pressed.

Even now it was still difficult to think about. Alice would probably have consented if he'd asked, but he hadn't, and it had been too late when she realized what was happening. She should have known then, taken it as a sign of his character that he'd tricked her, but she'd been foolish enough to think he cared about her—that she was the only young woman in his life instead of one of many whom he'd seduced, as she'd later found out.

Alice closed her eyes, trying to dispel the image, to imagine him as he was when she'd first met him: the gentleman everyone thought him to be.

"He won't come for his baby," she murmured. The knowledge that he was no longer in the country was her only comfort.

Outside the wind had worsened, howling along the street as tree branches battered against windows, the same storm that had been lashing the south coast for days.

Her mother moved closer. "God forgive you, Alice. And may he forgive me too, for helping you."

Then Ruth was gone, her footsteps on the wooden staircase echoing noisily through the cold, empty house.

Left alone to finish packing, Alice considered whether she should tell her mother the truth. But while Ruth might believe that she'd fought the first time, would she believe that Alice couldn't resist him the time after that? Or that he'd promised a future for them, before admitting it wasn't one in which she'd be his wife?

Tears rolled down her cheeks as she opened the wardrobe door and pulled the closest garment from its hanger before realizing that the dress barely fit her anymore; none of them did. As she closed the door, Alice caught her reflection in the mirror on the other side—bloodshot eyes sunken in their sockets, her skin paler than usual, its tone uneven, her cheekbones sharp under the harsh light of the bulb—and she was struck by how different she looked, as well as how foreign her life and her body had become. It wasn't just because of what had happened to her but also because she was leaving her old life behind; when she returned, everything would be so changed.

Over the past few years she and Ruth had needed to get used to many strange situations, things that didn't make sense, and this was just as impossible to reconcile.

How can my world have cracked apart to reveal the worst of human nature and the best of it? How do I feel so much hatred and yet have so much love to give?

She'd managed up until now because she'd believed that she wasn't alone; that she had Ruth's love and support, but did she? Her mother's moods were increasingly unpredictable, just as they'd been after her father's and brother's deaths. The prospect of an illegitimate grandchild might be too much for her after all; perhaps she was too mentally fragile to cope.

Alice crossed the hallway to William's room, stopping halfway to check that Ruth was still downstairs. She was moving around in the kitchen, and Alice pictured her as she'd once been, softer and warmer.

Then Alice crept into the darkened bedroom that she wanted to turn into a nursery but that Ruth didn't want touched. It was two years since the destroyer William served aboard was sunk off Norway, and although to Ruth his room was a reassuring shrine, Alice knew that it would never bring her brother back.

With the door firmly closed, she switched on the light and sat on the edge of William's bed, gazing around at the cupboards they'd hidden in and the furniture they'd made makeshift camps from. A locked glass cabinet held souvenirs and their father's gun, with which he'd taught them both to shoot when they'd gone hunting in the countryside. Soccer cards were still stuck to the wall above William's bed: Arsenal's winning team from the 1936 FA Cup Final. He'd gone with their father, returning home more excited than she'd ever seen him before, face lit up, talking twenty to the dozen. The team had only won by one goal, but they were both so exhilarated, which she understood only came from being a true sports fan. Their family dinner that night was a real celebration, as if Christmas had come early. She remembered the occasion well because it was one of their last meals together.

And what if William were alive now? Would he be as shocked and appalled as Ruth, or would he look to punish Rupert; perhaps make him marry Alice? She wasn't sure how William would have reacted to the awful scenes when Ruth had first found out, or Alice's refusal to put the baby up for adoption as her mother had initially insisted she should. Would William or their father have agreed with Ruth that Alice had ruined her life?

Alice spread her fingers across the top of William's eiderdown, feeling the bumps of the well-worn fabric and the damp of the untouched bed, and thought about the day her mother had come up with the plan. Alice had felt disbelief and then warm gratitude flood through her. It had seemed that Ruth's motivation flourished from either duty or the protective instincts of a mother, and Alice had felt relief—that was, until Ruth had looked at her with disdain and said, "Thank the Lord that your father's not here to see you like this."

Four

NEW YORK, MARCH 1943

Theo crossed Astor Place onto Fourth Avenue, enjoying the ease with which he navigated these streets, so much less crowded than the Upper West Side, where he lived. The last time he'd been to Book Row was six months ago; he'd ridden the subway downtown from the Bronx when the Yankees had just beaten the Boston Red Sox to win their thirteenth game. He hadn't worn a suit and fedora, as he did now, but chinos and a leather jacket, his Yankees cap covering most of his thick dark hair, his lean figure making him look like one of the athletes he'd just seen at the stadium. He'd played baseball through college and supported the Yankees since boyhood, when he'd gone to every home game with his pop, and the win that day had felt like a good omen. He'd proposed to Virginia that same night. He still felt like the luckiest man alive that she'd said yes, and while he had business on Book Row he also wanted to get a special birthday gift to give her that evening.

He walked briskly, overtaking the taxicabs and buses that were bumper to bumper beside him, dwarfed by towering office blocks and three-story brownstones. His smile broadened at the thought of seeing Virginia and of her soon becoming his wife. Passing carved stone entranceways, he strode under striped roof canopies, avoiding the rows of wooden bookstands and the metal fire escapes that zigzagged up to the clear blue skies. "Mrs. Virginia Bloom," he muttered to himself. The words had a special cadence.

The view up toward East Thirteenth hadn't changed since he'd worked there as a boy in his parents' bookstore. His father had hawked copies of the classics, while his mother had done two-bit haircuts in the back when business was slow. It was then that he'd read anything and everything he could get his hands on, which accounted for a lot. Not only did it help him academically, but his popularity grew as he was able to answer all his peers' questions about girls—as well as the usual popular and rare books, there was always plenty of anatomy and erotica on hand.

When he neared the corner of East Eleventh Street, Theo caught the aroma of chargrilled meat as Tony's Deli came into view. Just along the street the Brussel Brothers bookstore greeted him with its familiar grids and squares, its rows of shelves backing onto the front windows. Ike and Jack Brussel had been trading long before and after Theo's parents. Ike was a bear of a man who talked with his hands, and he wasted no time jumping up to hug Theo as soon as he walked in. "Good to see you, buddy," he said, releasing him and gripping him by both shoulders as he looked him up and down.

"You too, Ike. How ya keepin'?"

"Can't complain, can't complain." Ike took a step backward. "So, what brings you down here?"

"Looking for a gift, for Virginia. And I heard you had some trouble you might need help with." Theo glanced around. The symmetry of the window display was mirrored inside with its neat ranks of bookcases, and the shop looked and smelled the same as it had the last time he'd visited—the same as ten years ago, probably: ink, dust, promises. And there were still plenty of customers, sitting in chairs or standing, heads bowed, open books resting in their hands. But the once-overstuffed shelves looked a little depleted, with gaps where volumes lay on their sides instead of standing horizontal.

Ike followed his gaze. "Donations for the troops."

"Of course, good for you," Theo said, patting Ike's shoulder. "So, the association—"

"Ah, yeah. Those morons. You'd think they'd have bigger fish to fry, but oh no"—he raised his arms—"they've decided to make our lives a misery."

"Sorry to hear that."

"Take a seat," Ike said, hands on the move again.

Theo sat on the worn leather chair in front of the desk as Ike shuffled through piles of books and mountains of papers, lifting several cold cups of coffee out of the way until he found a wooden cigarette box. He flipped open the lid and held it out to Theo.

"Thanks," he said, taking one before pulling his solid gold lighter from his pocket.

Ike didn't take his eyes off the lighter the whole time, and when he took his cigarette out of his mouth, he exhaled a long slow whistle with his cloud of smoke. "You sure are marrying up."

"Yeah," Theo said. "It was a birthday gift from Virginia, and all she's gettin' from me is a lousy book!" He gave Ike a crooked smile, his small mustache tilting upward.

"So, you set a date?"

"She's got her heart set on Valentine's Day. I'm thinking about it, but it's kind of corny, to tell you the truth. I'd rather just go to the country and do it quietly, but you know women."

"I do. Which is why there isn't going to be a fourth Mrs. Brussel."

Theo laughed, knowing his friend wouldn't be able to help himself if the right woman walked into his store.

Ike asked, "How're Samuel and Madelaine?"

"They're doing okay. Pop's getting some extra help now he's not so mobile, gives Mom a break. He's gained a few pounds since he stopped working." Theo raised his eyebrows. He was making light of the situation; he had learned few people really wanted to know the truth, which was that his father wasn't doing well at all. The doctors couldn't get his insulin levels right, and his swollen legs meant he walked less and less, exacerbating his condition. If only he'd taken notice of the honey urine earlier, or lost weight as the doctors had advised him years ago.

"That's good," Ike said. "I should visit. . . ."

"It's okay, they understand. It was seven days for them too, once. They remember what it's like."

Ike wasn't getting any younger; strands of fine brown hair were combed across the top of his balding head, and his beard was wispy and gray. He wore his clothes loose, but Theo could see that his pants were hitched high around his rotund stomach; it was the sedentary job and the temptations of the area.

"Tell me about the association . . . what are your plans?" he asked.

"You know what cowards those city officials can be. They just got nervous and tried to make us move the stands from the sidewalks. You know we can't do that—it'd be bad for business. Besides, those stands have been there longer than any of us."

Theo already knew the background but also how much Ike liked to chat—he was informally known as the grandfather of Book Row. Over the weekend, Theo's father had told him all about how the labor troubles and worker strikes had made the authorities cautious. Just as Ike said, the New York City authorities had asked the sellers on Book Row to remove their stands. They'd fought back by forming the Fourth Avenue Booksellers' Association, and now they needed help getting things to the next level when the authorities had refused to take any notice of them. These seven blocks between Astor Place and Union Square had been home to more than thirty bookshops since the end of the last century, and there were nearly as many stories about them as between the pages of the books they sold.

"No, that wouldn't be good for business at all," Theo replied, holding Ike's gaze.

He had spent his childhood discovering the landscape of

each shop. He could have told you which one had the best corners for hide-and-seek or the best for browsing. By the age of twelve he could advise book hunters on the best store for ephemera and which ones specialized in history or philosophy. He'd devised his own tour, which took book hunters from shops infamous for their erotic literature to those famous for first editions, then down into the basement of Schulte's store, and to the three-sided balcony where book-lined alcoves were lit by bulbs that browsers had to turn on. Theo had planned it carefully, through a labyrinth that escalated the mystery and excitement accompanying the journey into any new book. Each store was unique, and to Theo, and the others who lived and worked there, Fourth Avenue was a neighborhood made of books as much as it was of bricks and mortar.

"Look," Ike said, leaning forward and resting his arms on the desk, palms clasped together, "I don't want to make a big deal of this when we've got bigger problems, our boys bleeding in the Pacific, but it's important. It's New York's heritage, our history—"

"I know, Ike. I agree. Which is why we're going to do something about it. You leave it to me."

"Thanks, Theo. I appreciate it."

There were a few benefits to working at one of New York's largest publishing houses, and having the ear of some of the city's most influential figures and officials was one of them.

Virginia sat in a booth at the Blue Angel, gray silk dress flowing like a waterfall across her pale skin, diamanté necklace reflecting off the spotlights to create starbursts on the wall behind her. She leaned back in the chair, one hand resting elegantly in her lap, the other playing with the stem of her cocktail glass while she watched the band, legs jiggling with the rhythm.

Theo's desire caught him off guard, and he stood admiring her for a moment, until she saw him and waved him over. He had offered to pick her up from the Red Cross sorting station where she worked, but she'd said she was having a drink with friends and would meet him at the Angel. Now he was beginning to wish they were at home and he had her all to himself, but he knew she'd been excited to celebrate here. It was Max Gordon's latest venue, and they'd been lucky to get a table as Manhattanites flocked to try it. Max's established club, the Village Vanguard, was already a New York institution, where you never knew what mix of poetry, cabaret or comedy you might be entertained by on any given night, but Virginia had said she wanted a new club with new artists to see in her twenty-fifth year.

Theo knew which one he'd rather be at, he thought, as he made his way up the ostentatious staircase, hand running along the decorative chrome handrail, the smell of new carpet barely disguised beneath the oversweet scent of lilies in vases and the heavy veil of cigarette smoke. The band played a Dizzy Gillespie number that he recognized—only twice as loud as it should have been—and the crowd was mixed: at a glance, Wall Street suits and struggling starlets, high-ranking servicemen and the usual uptown socialites. It wasn't his scene, but he suspected that Virginia wouldn't be disappointed. She had a lot to feast her eyes on: men lounging in plush velvet chairs, and women sipping from crystal glasses that waiters kept filled.

And as he wove through the extravagantly dressed crowd toward her table, he wondered if it helped some of them to forget that there was a war on.

"Happy birthday, beautiful," he said, sitting down and placing the gift in front of her. When he leaned close to kiss her, her delicate lips responded, bittersweet with alcohol and lipstick. He sat back and smiled, staring into her dark eyes, then noticed her teasing half smile and the rosy gleam on her cheeks. "What're you having?"

It was too noisy to hear her reply, the saxophone taking over the room as it reached its outro, the musician twisting and bending as he hugged his instrument.

"C-o-s-m-o-p-o-l-i-t-a-n," she mouthed slowly, then moved her lips close to his. "But I'll have another one of those first."

He turned so their lips brushed, and they kissed again. "How's my birthday girl? Has it been a good day?"

"It's been a *wonderful* day," she replied brightly.

"Well, we'd better make sure it's a wonderful evening then too."

"There's just one tiny hitch . . ."

It was unlike her to spring surprises.

"Do I need to order a drink?" he asked.

"Yes, I think you'd better," she said, anxiously tucking strands of her ebony hair behind her ears.

Theo waved the waiter over, ordered another cosmopolitan and a Scotch, then pushed the present toward her. "Are you going to open it?"

"As long as I don't have to give it back?"

"Oh, it's that bad?"

Virginia grimaced then tore open the paper, her face

lighting up when she saw the title, *The Moon Is Down*. "It's wonderful! Thank you."

"It's autographed," he said, as he stretched his long limbs out in the booth.

She opened the cover and read the inscription on the title page.

He'd been pleased to find the signed copy of John Steinbeck's latest novel at Brussel's, since he remembered her brother, Saul, telling him how much she wanted to read it. Theo had met Saul at Columbia, where he'd studied English and philosophy, although his real education had been on Book Row. He'd moved on to business affairs, but his love of bookselling—the grime on your palms, the special requests, the change ricocheting in the register—had never left him.

The drinks arrived, and Theo took a sip as he readied himself for her news. "I thought you could hide Hadley Chase inside," he said with a wry smile.

Chase's book had been taking the world by storm: *No Orchids for Miss Blandish* was a tale of sex, crime and kidnapping that couldn't be read in polite society, but could be concealed behind the cover of another book.

"Good thinking," she said, and gave him an exaggerated wink.

"So, I'm all ears. What's the news?"

"Daddy wants you to go to England. He's going to ask you tomorrow."

"Really? Why?" It was the last thing Theo had expected. He wasn't sure how he was going to decline, but there was certainly no chance he could think about leaving now—even if he could get on a flight, which was highly unlikely.

"Uncle George is having a time of it over there, and with Rupert gone, well . . . he could use an Ivy League brain to help them through a rough patch."

"How rough?"

"Something about being understaffed, paper rations and government restrictions causing all sorts of grief," she said with a forced smile. "Just your thing."

"That's a bit drastic. Surely there's someone local who knows the business better than me."

"That's exactly what I said. And it's an appalling time to be traveling. I told Daddy it's too dangerous, but for some reason he seems to think it will be all right." Her voice cracked. "You'll have to talk to him, darling. See if you can change his mind."

Theo frowned thoughtfully into his glass before taking another swig. He'd worked with Partridge for the past four years, but his other work with the Council on Books in Wartime was reaching a critical stage. In six months they'd be publishing their first book for the troops: the Armed Services Editions would be accompanying men into battle, a paperback in their pockets to comfort, distract or entertain. This wasn't the time to be abandoning his work for the council, but he knew his loyalty also lay with Partridge, particularly since his boss was also his future father-in-law.

"And what if I can't?" he asked.

"I don't know, but you need to try," she said, eyes growing watery. "I don't want us to be apart. And I'm scared for you."

Theo cradled his near-empty glass between his hands, staring into the amber liquid before meeting her gaze. "He's used to getting what he wants. Do you think I should go . . . if he insists?"

"Come on, you know that's not fair."

"Sorry," he said, draining the last of the Scotch then trying to attract the waiter so he could order another. "It's just . . . maybe this is one of his traps. He might be testin' me again, hopin' I'll fail."

Theo had always suspected he wasn't the match Walter had wished for Virginia: he didn't come from money or the district she'd grown up in, and he hadn't been educated alongside her. But when it came to intellect, Walter now surely knew he was an equal.

"No, Daddy knows we're perfect for each other." She moved closer, pressing her thigh against his and coiling her leg around his ankle under the smoked glass table. The two wall sconces behind her framed her in a warm light, making her look even more beautiful and even harder to think of leaving. Sometimes it scared him to reflect on what his life had become, so different to the one he'd imagined for himself. He had never expected to fall for Virginia or be part of all this, so removed from his upbringing, his old circle of friends, but he was unnerved by the idea that it could all come crashing down.

She glanced at him and made a sulky face, pushing out her bottom lip. "I really don't know any more than what I've told you, so please don't ask me anything else. I just couldn't keep tight-lipped about it all night. I'm sorry."

"How long would it be for?"

"I don't know, darling. A few months."

"But what about the wedding?"

"Christ, Theo, you'd be back by then. It would just be to help them out, it's not forever!"

But this wasn't just about the wedding, or the books for the troops; his father was in bad shape, and he didn't want to leave him either. In fact, Theo didn't see how his parents would cope without him, especially with his sister so far away too. Even after six months, Howie's death still cast a dark shadow over their family. Theo played with the lighter, flicking the flame on and off, as he thought about what Howie would have said. He'd joined the marines straight out of college, one of the few who was trained and ready for war; as much as anyone could ever be. And he had done his duty. It had come at a price, so the least Theo could do was serve his country with the council.

The band was taking a break, and he was grateful that the noise levels had dropped, changing the atmosphere and making him even more thoughtful. When he looked back at Virginia, her expression was serious too, so he smiled broadly; he reminded himself that it was her birthday, and he looked around again for the waiter.

When Virginia sighed heavily, he slipped his hand around her waist and pulled her close. "We'll work it out, don't worry." He smiled reassuringly.

She looked into his eyes, and he lifted her chin toward him, pressing his mouth over hers in a long, passionate kiss. "I love you," she whispered as he drew away. "You shouldn't go, Theo. Don't let him talk you into it."

Five

BRIGHTON, MARCH 14, 1943

Alice huddled inside the wooden seafront shelter, the pages of her book flapping as the wind howled along the promenade and the discordant notes of the Salvation Army band whined from the nearby bandstand. It was after midday, and the weak sun cast a milky light, creating ghostly images of two young boys as they picked their way through the barbed wire and across the mounds of pebbles. They bent to fill their pockets before racing down to the water's edge and taking it in turns to skim stones across the waves. A woman, presumably their mother, stood behind the fence, hands clenched into tight fists as she yelled for them to come back, her voice lost on the wind.

Seagulls screeched and swooped around Alice, chasing the fish-scented air as she waited for Ruth, who was now officially late. Alice's heart sank as she realized she probably wasn't coming. Ruth had only kept her promise to visit every Sunday for the first month; apart from Christmas, now it was only one weekend in four. Alice had so many questions about motherhood that books alone couldn't answer, and while she understood that her mother had to contend with the demands of her work, the Women's Voluntary Service and the church, Alice was lonely with only Aunt Hope and the other staff at the guesthouse for company.

She glanced at her watch again, then back to her book. This was the third time she'd read *The Age of Innocence*, and she was nearly up to her favorite part: when Newland realizes he has to tell May about the countess. Alice didn't want to stop, but she couldn't concentrate or shake off her unsettled feelings, which had worsened since she'd noticed all the families on the promenade.

Another group arrived and set up outside one of the turquoise wooden beach-huts, the father battling the wind to erect deck chairs in front of the opened doors, the mother brewing tea on a camp stove. The three children ran up and down the grass concourse, then started a game of hide-and-seek between the huts. These simplest of activities were at the root of Alice's sadness, as she would never be able to do them with her own family. Her mother had been right about that: apart from the two of them, there was no one to be family for her baby.

She squinted, scanning the seafront again as she looked for Ruth. It went for miles, the grass-verged road a black ribbon behind her, the gray crisscross of barbed wire along the beach a reminder that their island was under siege. And further ahead still, a veil of blue sky, the aquamarine of a painted handrail, the steel-gray of the ocean—striations of color stretching as far as the eye could see. On clear days like this, she imagined she could see right across the channel, and she searched its choppy surface for any sign of boats as she thought about the young men they'd carried away. It was daft, she knew, but they were out there somewhere, lost to England for now. There was no sign of Ruth either.

Alice had decided to wait another five minutes when she felt a familiar sensation—a frantic flurry—and placed her hand on her belly as a tiny elbow or knee pushed against the skin. She left her hand there, feeling the tiny prods as she tried again to read, but the gulls were getting ever braver, their screeching louder, until they dive-bombed a couple on the bench next to her in an attempt to steal some fish and chips.

Alice hastily gathered her belongings and headed east, back toward Kemp Town and the guesthouse. She walked briskly, inhaling the briny air, taking it down deep into her lungs and measuredly exhaling as she pictured oxygen working its way through her body to the baby's, just like the diagrams had shown in the anatomy book. She felt another kick and had to stop walking as her baby wriggled into a new position, the skin across her belly growing taut again. She carried on, her hand inside her coat supporting the heavy curve as she smiled to herself. In only a matter of weeks she could walk along here with a pram and show her baby off, and she couldn't wait—she'd be glad of any attention or conversation after her forced solitude. There had been the odd letter from her friend Penny that Ruth had forwarded, and some worrying updates from Ursula about how bad things were at Partridge and how they were trying to get on with her book, but Alice hadn't replied to any of them. She wanted to stay in touch with friends and know the news from Partridge, but she didn't trust herself to write back and not to say something that would give her away.

It was a direct walk along the promenade from the Angel, the statue that marked the boundary between Brighton and Hove, where grand Regency buildings gave way to wide Victorian avenues and homes. She ambled slowly, picturing Ruth getting off the train and navigating down Queens Road; Alice imagined bumping into her on the seafront or finding her back at the guesthouse, drinking tea and talking with Hope.

When Alice passed Regency Square, she noticed how some diners talked while others sat and read; everywhere she went now, many more people were reading books—in waiting rooms, at bus stops, and in shelters and cafés, losing themselves to other worlds. It reminded her of how she'd become obsessed with books.

She had been nine years old when she'd come home from school in tears after falling out with Penny, and her father had given her a copy of *Heidi*. Alice read it in one sitting, the candle flickering across the wall as she refused to let bedtime intrude on Heidi's moving friendship with Clara. Her father was right; she and Penny became friends again after she shared the book, and she'd realized there must be a corresponding story for everyone, a book the reader knew had been written just for them. It became a challenge for her to find these stories, leaning against the cold stone wall of their local library, the hardback editions pressed open in her lap, featherlight pages fluttering beneath her fingertips.

Now the sight of people reading was just another source of

frustration to her, because it reminded her of how much she missed her work.

As she passed the security fences of the closed Palace Pier, Alice thought how strange it was that her mother hadn't seemed concerned by her loss of income or the extra expenses of the baby clothes and pram they would have to buy. Ruth's usual parsimony made it even more surprising. Although she didn't show it, perhaps she felt a small amount of pleasure at the prospect of a grandchild.

When Alice arrived back at the guesthouse, Hope was in the hallway, her long gray hair wound into a bun, a patterned apron obscuring her dark clothing. She greeted Alice with a solemn smile. "I'm sorry, pet, but your mother isn't going to make it down today. She says there's disruption on the tracks."

The trains were frequently diverted, the lines commandeered as soldiers took priority, but apparently this was the third time it had happened just when Ruth had planned to visit. Alice found that difficult to believe, and tears pricked her eyes.

To distract herself from her loneliness she'd explored the seafront and hidden parks and squares. When it rained she'd taken refuge at the cinema, and when her feet had grown too sore or her back ached, she'd found a spot, like she had that morning, to sit and read. It had worked for a while, minimizing her anxiety. But now she really needed to see her mother, and she was angry and hurt that Ruth clearly didn't want to see her.

She sighed heavily, and Hope put her bucket down and placed her hands on Alice's shoulders. "How about you come to the sitting room, and I'll make us some lunch?" she said sympathetically.

"Thank you," Alice said, looking into her aunt's pitying gray eyes—eyes that reminded her of her father's—"but I think I'll just go lie down."

Over the past several months she'd felt betrayed, angry, afraid and excited, but no emotion had been as heartfelt as the disappointment that ached inside her now.

"All right, pet, but you let me know if you change your mind. I've got fresh eggs—I could make you an omelet."

"I'm fine, honestly, Hope. Thank you, but you have them." Alice sniffed then tried to smile. "I'll be down later." She climbed the stairs to her room, wondering, as she had the last time Ruth had let her down, whether her mother had become unstable again or if she just couldn't face her anymore—and what that said about the future.

Six

NEW YORK, MARCH 1943

Theo was in the lobby, tapping his feet like Fred Astaire as he waited for the elevator, the burning sensation in his toes barely easing. He'd insisted on walking to work, despite the frost, and a crowd of equally numb-looking workers grew around him, not even their Brooks Brothers coats and hats insulating them against the unseasonably low temperatures. The long winter had brought the worst storm in decades when more than seven feet of snow had fallen in one day, then an onslaught of sleet had brought New York to a standstill. Everyone was looking forward to spring.

When the elevator arrived, Theo stood aside for the other office workers to file in before squeezing in next to the smiling operator, unexpectedly pleased by the proximity of other warm bodies.

"Good morning, Mr. Bloom," said the operator.

"Morning, Kenny. How's the world treating you?"

The Irishman's smile beamed even wider, brightening his already shiny complexion, his pristine gray uniform and its polished buttons. "Couldn't be better, Mr. Bloom. I've got a new grandchild."

"That's wonderful, congratulations. Another boy?"

"No, our first granddaughter. She's a pretty wee thing, but ever so noisy—I thought boys were trouble." He shook his head. "Boys are less demandin' until they get to about ten, and then it switches, you need a good set of lungs for makin' them listen and ears that don't work right so you can ignore the back talk!"

Theo laughed. "I'll remember that."

"Yes, you'd do well to," Kenny said, becoming serious. "How is Miss Virginia?"

"She's very well, thank you, although these temperatures don't agree with her." His fiancée wasn't part of the skiing crowd; she preferred to stay hot and dry, vacationing in Miami and Bermuda, something he would have to get used to after years of family vacations on Long Island.

"Have a good day, Mr. Bloom," said Kenny as they reached the seventeenth floor.

The elevator doors slid open to reveal a bright reception of seamless cream marble, and chrome and leather furniture that appeared to float in midair. The feathers of an oversized partridge were etched into a large glass panel along the facing wall; the words PARTRIDGE PRESS—NEW YORK & LONDON were suspended below in metal letters. On the walls to either side were large framed posters: eye-catching covers of their American bestsellers.

A striking blonde wearing glasses looked up from behind the reception desk as Theo and the other workers stepped out. "Good morning, Mr. Bloom."

"Good morning, Janice." He picked up the latest editions of *Publishers Weekly* and *The New York Times*, then headed to the left of the reception desk and the partition that led through to the offices.

His meeting with Walter wasn't for another fifteen minutes, so he sat behind his desk, elbows on the table and forefingers interlocked as he stroked his mustache and scoured the paper. He didn't want to miss anything before he saw Walter; the publishing veteran was always one step ahead, and he didn't like it if his employees weren't in the know too. When Theo had satisfied himself that he was well versed in the day's news, he strode up the corridor to Walter's office, and the secretary ushered him in.

An expansive window formed one entire wall, framing a panorama of the skyline, from the vast girders of the highways and elevated tracks uptown, all the way down to the Brooklyn dockyards and the semirural suburbs beyond.

Theo accepted the offer of freshly brewed coffee and settled into one of the deep sofas just as Walter appeared in his usual business attire. He had a wardrobe of near-identical clothes—dark brown three-piece suits, pressed white shirts, patterned bow ties and tan brogues—about which Virginia endlessly teased him.

"Theo, how are you?" He walked over briskly, shook Theo's hand and took a seat in the armchair opposite.

Theo found it a bit unnerving to look at the same narrow

face as Virginia's, although thankfully Walter's dark hair had turned gray, and small round spectacles were perched on the ridge of his feline nose, framing dark restless eyes most unlike his daughter's. His uneven frown lines made him look older than his fifty-two years, and he managed to keep his tan all year round.

"I'm well, thank you, Walter. How's everything with you?"

"Good, a busy week. I'm glad we could get together this morning, though. We'll see each other at Virginia's birthday lunch on Saturday, of course, but I wanted to talk to you about something first."

"What's on your mind?" Theo asked. He readied himself; he'd spent most of the night working out the right way to say no, but he knew how convincing Walter could be.

Walter shifted to the edge of his seat, hands clasped together, legs angled outward, tartan socks barely covering his ankles. "You and I know that while the war is taking place thousands of miles away, there's a battle being fought right here—a mental battle." His finger prodded the top of the glazed coffee table, his slow, deliberate enunciation using his Oxford-English diction to its full effect. "It's the ideas we discuss with our friends at the bar, the ones we talk about over the dinner table, that count in that battle."

Theo nodded. People everywhere were talking about the war, not just the conflict but also its political, economic and social effects, and they were forming new ideas. But to Theo, what the troops were talking and thinking about mattered more. What counted to Theo was the reading material soldiers like Howie had to occupy them through the long days and nights, so getting books into their hands was Theo's priority. He couldn't be there fighting alongside them, so he would do everything he could to help, the only way he knew how.

"I agree with you, Walter, and that's why we're carrying on doing what we've always done—publishing the world's best books. There's no denying it's getting harder, but like everyone, we're adapting."

"We wouldn't have to if Roosevelt hadn't gone soft, giving everything away while our own boys go without," Walter said, glowering.

Theo had managed his relationship with Walter by avoiding too much political debate, since he didn't share his future father-in-law's Republican values, or like tempering his own views. Theo agreed wholeheartedly with Roosevelt's Lend-Lease program, which supplied material support and goods to the Allies, and it had been an easy decision for him to help vote the Democrat in for a third term.

"Ten percent of this nation's families can tell you about that support," Theo said, unable to control himself as he thought of Howie and his own family, "and it's not ideals we're trading in—it's their sons."

"So, we give them our money and our future, Theo. What else do you suggest we give away?" Walter frowned at him as he banged down his coffee cup onto the table.

"Let's do something about it, then. Let's give their sons books to distract and motivate them."

"I know you're keen on your council books, but I don't think it's our place to provide propaganda for our troops—and the industry can't afford it."

"I'm not saying we provide propaganda, Walter. The council is publishing fiction too."

Walter went to stand by the window, looking out to the east, eyes scanning the water towers and cranes that punctuated the skyline. Watching him, Theo found it hard to believe he was still so rigidly opposed to supporting their citizens because of his own political prejudices, and that he couldn't see what was happening right under his nose: New York still looked grand, but workers were scraping the metal cornices off its hotels.

"You were at the last board meeting, Theo. You know the cost and what was said."

Theo came to stand next to the older man, observing his profile as he continued to gaze out at the city.

"So, you're not just worried about the profit margin anymore?" he asked.

"That ship sailed a long time ago, Theo." Walter turned to face him. "When they started producing Pocket Books. Besides, we couldn't produce hardbacks now anyway."

The nationwide paper shortage had limited book production, and with the army taking all the cotton for camouflage netting, there wasn't enough left for bookbinding.

"I have something to tell you," Walter said. "I need you to make a trip to our London office. Publishers are facing even more restrictions over there, and the way the British rationing system works means they get paper based on the sales achieved the previous year. It hasn't been good for them." He looked Theo in the eye. "And I do know how you like a challenge."

"Normally, yes, but this isn't a good time, Walter—"

"It's never a good time, Theo, particularly in the middle of a war, but we must all do what we can."

The men surveyed each other. Theo had been willing to make the sacrifice that Howie had, but his government had deemed him more valuable serving the American war economy, and he didn't know how to defend himself to others when he could still taste his own bitter disappointment so strongly.

Theo said, "Hypothetically, what can I do that they can't do themselves?"

"There are some opportunities—paperbacks, access to the new quota systems—but they haven't made the most of them and, as you can imagine, with their lack of resources and skilled labor, it's a precarious situation. Everyone's getting a little nervous. Especially George."

"Is he happy for me to intervene?"

"I'm sure he and his staff would prefer to handle matters themselves, but they've had a rough couple of years. Rupert's departure left a big hole, and I understand there are other staffing issues that haven't been handled well. No matter what George thinks, *I* would rather you went."

Theo knew that Walter's brother was the minority partner in the business, and surely he wouldn't feel great about an American interloper showing up. It would be difficult enough for Theo to abandon his commitments here, let alone offer help that was unsolicited and unwelcome.

"Look," said Walter, "I know it's not ideal, and I know Virginia isn't pleased about it either. But the war isn't as distant as it was, Theo, and with your industry contacts and expertise—well, I need to find out if you can help them . . . or if we might need to close their office."

"It's as bad as that?" Theo asked, struggling to keep the shock from his voice.

Walter nodded gravely. "If they can't meet the demand for books, maybe we can."

This was worse than Virginia had suggested, far worse than he'd contemplated, and he was surprised that Walter expected him to fall into line so easily.

"But you know my work here with the council is important?" Theo said hurriedly.

"Yes, I do, and I know you'll be making a sacrifice by putting it on hold, but we're only talking a couple of months."

Theo had been working with the Council on Books in Wartime ever since he'd attended a meeting at the Times Hall theater last May. It had been filled with writers, journalists, publishers and editors, all eager to explore the power and potential of the written word in wartime. After two nights of discussion, a working committee had been formed of figures from the larger publishing houses and the broader industry, with the motto "Books are weapons in the war of ideas."

Walter added, "You could be one of the few men helping to take more American books to the British market."

Walter was right about increasing the potential to export, and Theo knew the council would be keen on that too, but his employer was wrong in trying to appeal to his ego; he didn't have any when it came to this. It seemed, though, he did need to be Walter's henchman, and he felt uncomfortably hot. *Can I say no? Is that even an option?*

"And the wedding date?"

"That's up to you and Virginia to decide, but from what she's told me you should be back in plenty of time."

When she and Theo had discussed it the night before, they'd decided to keep the original date the following February, whatever happened with this London trip.

He looked out at the smoke trails rising from the dockyards, at the lighters traveling back and forth on the river, and the ribbon of vehicles across the Queensboro Bridge; the sight always filled him with hope for human progress. Hundreds of feet below, thousands of workers made intricate patterns on the frosted sidewalks as they journeyed around the city. He knew he wouldn't be able to stay; he'd contributed as much as he could to the council, and now he would try to make a difference in London.

Seven

BRIGHTON, MARCH 15, 1943

"Your mother is on her way!" Hope said, squeezing Alice's hand. "Just breathe, slowly . . . One, two, three, one, two, three—"

Alice blew out a long forceful breath as another contraction racked her body. Oncc she'd expelled all the air, she collapsed back onto the pillow, hands gripping the bedclothes. After only a few moments, another one began. She groaned louder as she drew another breath, muscles clenching across her belly, gathering their own rhythm as they wrenched at her insides. *"Oh my God!"* she screamed.

The curtains were open, the brightening sunlight sweeping into the corners of the room, throwing a soft haze across her clammy body. Her cotton nightdress clung to her wet skin as she gripped her knees with both hands, neck stretched rigid with exertion.

"I don't care about her," she hissed. "Where's the bloody midwife?"

"The midwife is on her way too," Hope said, peeling moist strands of hair from her niece's face.

Alice slumped back on the bed, waiting for another contraction to arrive, eyes rolled up at the ceiling. Was this her punishment, or was labor always like this? If so, why on earth did women ever endure it again? Other questions flooded her mind as she struggled to remember the small amount of knowledge she'd found in books. How long would it take? How would she know if the baby was all right? How would its head fit through her pelvis? Ruth hadn't been any help; in fact, she'd been very reluctant to discuss her experiences giving birth to William and Alice.

"Sweet Jesus, here comes another one!" Alice dug her nails into Hope's hand and wailed. She desperately wanted to move around, yet she was determined to stay exactly where she was; she wanted her aunt to massage her back, and she didn't want anyone to touch her. She wanted to clamber up onto all fours and bellow at the top of her lungs; she was frantic for some company, and she was impatient to be alone.

She was exhausted after laboring since sundown, and what she wanted most was peace and quiet. But the other residents were waking and moving about the guesthouse: a creak on the stairs, the bathroom door on the floor below sticking as it closed, a murmur of voices through the walls.

"Hope?"

"Yes, love?"

"Have you told them," she panted, "that no one . . . *phew* . . . that no one is being murdered . . . in the attic?"

"Yes, dear. They know. Don't you worry yourself, just concentrate on what you're doing." Hope squeezed her hand again. "You're doing wonderfully . . . you're very clever and very brave."

Alice didn't feel very clever. Labor did feel like a punishment. She'd lost the ability to move, all her strength had gone, her mouth was dry, her eyelids swollen and heavy, and she wanted sleep.

She watched, blearily, as a tall, gray-haired man entered the room, followed by a midwife, grateful that they had sent an Obstetric Flying Squad rather than just a midwife. He looked just as she thought an obstetrician should: a stern, bespectacled elder, the many lines across his face seeming to represent all the babies he'd delivered. She tried to greet him, but each time the pain subsided she barely had the chance to catch her breath before another brutal contraction came.

Her aunt ushered the doctor and midwife to the hand basin in the corner of the room, then listened to his instructions before clearing the top of the dresser with some urgency. He set out his equipment before presenting himself at the foot of the bed, buttoning up his medical coat as he spoke. "Now, you're not to worry, Mrs. Cotton, you're in safe hands now." His deep voice had a reassuring tone that she wanted to believe.

The midwife took her blood pressure as the doctor pulled up her nightdress and examined her without even telling her his name.

Hope looked on anxiously from the side of the room.

"You're already fully dilated, so you need to push when we say," the doctor said. "Do you understand?"

Alice nodded, her eyes involuntarily closing, the warmth draining from her face.

"Come on, dear, you're nearly there," she heard the midwife say.

"I'm so tired."

"You can rest afterward," the doctor said firmly. "First you've got a baby to deliver."

"Can't you give her something for the pain?" Hope asked.

"Not now. It's too late for that." Then he whispered something in the midwife's ear.

"Is everything all right?" Alice said, startled.

"Everything is fine, just take a deep breath and get ready to push."

Another contraction built, more intense than the others, the sheer force making her whole being tremble.

"Where's Mum?" she said, reaching her hand out to Hope, her eyes wide with fear.

"She's on her way. You know she wouldn't miss the birth of her grandchild."

Alice tried to look into her aunt's eyes for reassurance, but Hope glanced toward the window.

Alice's mouth dropped open, ready to wail, when the midwife leaned over and, with a firm voice, ordered her to pant. "Just like this," she said, taking exaggerated breaths.

As Alice panted, she could feel the head crown with a burning sensation, her body stretching. There was a release of pressure and a rush of blood, and as Alice tipped her head backward, releasing an agonized groan, she heard an exquisite cry.

"It's a girl," the doctor announced, lifting up the blood-streaked alabaster body. His hands probed and patted, then he passed the baby to the midwife, who washed and swaddled her, endless minutes passing before she was handed back to Alice.

"Isn't she beautiful?" said the midwife.

Alice took her baby in her arms, breathing her in, mesmerized by the smooth crimson face as she studied every part of it: the perfect lips, the faint arch of the brow, the tiny upturned nose and plume of golden hair. Alice fought off the temptation to judge the resemblance to Rupert; instead, forcing the thought of him from her mind, she examined her daughter's fingers one by one.

"See, you are a clever girl," Hope said, watery-eyed and smiling. She leaned over the bed and brushed her finger ever so gently across her great-niece's cheek. "What are you going to call her, pet?"

Alice looked at her aunt intently. "Eadie, after Granny."

Hope gave her a meaningful smile—it had been her mother's name—then she began to cry, setting Alice off too.

"Your father would have been pleased," Hope said.

Eadie meant "rich in war," and Alice was determined that only good should come from her daughter's arrival in the world.

"Well done, Mrs. Cotton," the doctor said. "You can write to tell the father that she's arrived and that you are both doing well, with nothing at all to worry about."

Alice's lips tightened, but they wouldn't form a smile. She would never share the truth of how Rupert had deceived her with anyone, especially Eadie.

Gently grasping her daughter's tiny curled hand, Alice kissed the crown of her head. Her beautiful dark-eyed girl blinked once or twice before she fell asleep.

Eight

BRIGHTON, MARCH 18, 1943

When Alice woke a few days following the birth, the guest-house was quiet. After a couple of tries she managed to get to her feet and shuffle over to the white wicker crib. With eyes alight in anticipation she leaned forward, ready to see her baby.

But the cot was empty. Her breath caught; she closed her eyes, then opened them, but there was still only the bare wrinkled sheet.

She reached out, expecting warmth but felt only smooth, cold cotton, and she snatched her hand away.

Her eyes darted about the room, searching, as she remembered the birth. How her mother hadn't arrived in time and her aunt had taken charge. Alice smiled in relief as she realized it was clear that Hope had taken Eadie downstairs—then she picked up her daughter's blanket and found the handwritten note.

I'm sorry, Alice, but this really is for the best.

She sat on the edge of the bed, frozen. Obviously her mother had taken Eadie, but her brain kept seeking another explanation. Perhaps Ruth was downstairs, or the note meant something else. Alice kept the blanket pressed to her face as she thought through scenarios, but they all seemed too implausible.

Her memory of the day after the birth was muddled, but she had a vague recollection of voices when the nurse had shown her how to feed Eadie and finally given her something for the pain. It must have worn off a little, and that was when her mother had arrived. Yes, Alice remembered seeing her now, watching Ruth hold Eadie . . . before falling into an exhausted sleep.

The sickening bile of panic rose in Alice's throat. Her mother must have had another breakdown. The birth of an illegitimate grandchild, not long after the losses of her husband and son, had been too much for someone so religious and principled.

Alice reread the note.

But Eadie was Ruth's flesh and blood, her granddaughter.

How could she? And where has she taken her?

It finally sank in: Ruth was going to offer Eadie up for adoption.

As soon as Alice had recovered from the shock, she made her way unsteadily across the small landing to the top of the staircase. She clung to the rail, one hand passing urgently over the other as she made her way to Hope's sitting room, the bloodstained nightgown flapping around her. She turned the handle and pitched through the doorway, nearly toppling over.

"Heavens, Alice, what on earth are you doing?" Hope said, startled.

She was already dressed in a floral housecoat, gray hair pulled neatly back, and she guided Alice over to a small armchair. "What are you thinking? Remember what the doctor said—it's a full week in bed, two if you're not recovered enough."

"Where's . . . where's Eadie gone?"

"I was about to come and see you—"

"Where's Mum taken her?" Alice could barely get the words out, nearly hyperventilating.

"I don't know. She told me she was going for a walk," Hope said uneasily.

"But when did she leave?"

Hope's gaze dropped to the floor and then back at Alice. "I haven't seen her since last night."

"How could you let her go?" Alice said, face crumpling though her eyes were dry.

"I didn't think anything of it at first, not until she didn't come back, but then . . . then it was so late; I didn't know what to do. I'm sorry, Alice," she said, her voice breaking. "I kept looking in on you, but you were so exhausted . . . I couldn't wake you."

"Of course you should have woken me. It's the first thing you should have done. What did she say when she left; can you try to remember? She must have said something."

Alice examined Hope's tear-filled eyes to see if they gave anything away, yet all she could think about was how they mirrored her father's.

"She just said that she was taking her for a walk, to give

you some rest. I was busy with the guests, and . . . I'm so sorry, Alice—" She began to sob.

"Don't cry, just try and think about what she said. Come on, Hope. Did she say she was taking her home? We need to start looking."

"You're in no fit state to go anywhere." Hope sniffed. "You need to go back to bed until the nurse comes back."

"How can I go to bed? I need to find Eadie!" Alice sounded manic as she hauled herself to the edge of the armchair. "You know Mum never wanted me to keep the baby. She's done something with her."

A look of horror passed over Hope's face. "No, Alice, Eadie is her grandchild, for goodness sake." She shook her head in what looked like disbelief.

"I can't get downstairs to the telephone," said Alice. "Can you try to call her at home, just in case she's gone straight back to Dulwich?"

"Yes, of course. That's exactly what I'll do," Hope said, wiping away her tears.

"Thank you, Hope. And tell her . . . tell her that if she brings Eadie back now, I'll forgive her."

"Yes." Hope hurried toward the door, then turned back around. "Everything will be all right, pet. Your mother would never deliberately hurt you."

Alice pressed her lips together; she wanted to believe her aunt, she wanted to think her mother hadn't changed, but she knew that wasn't true.

Ruth didn't come back. Alice waited in bed the whole day, while Hope kept calling Dulwich. Each time she returned upstairs, her expression had grown more grave.

Nine

LONDON, MARCH 18, 1943

Theo bristled at George's welcoming speech. Saying goodbye to Virginia and his family had been difficult enough, and now he was having to listen to a sermon on British book publishing that was as overstuffed with patriotism as the upholstered chair he sat on. George was sitting opposite behind a vast desk, not dissimilar in size to the large black cab Theo had traveled in from his hotel, rhapsodizing about how well things were going, which he knew was far from true.

"Fetch yourself a drink, dear boy," George offered, gesturing toward the well-stocked antique drinks cabinet in the corner of the room, its glass doors finely engraved with the family crest. "There's a bottle of 1921 at the back, saved for special occasions such as this," he said, beaming broadly. He was in a surprisingly good mood, and Walter's description of the state of the company didn't tally with George's account—unless it was an act, bravado in the face of his brother's interference. Or perhaps the decision to send Theo over had been premature.

"Thanks, George, but it's a bit early for me. I'll just stick to coffee." Theo refilled his cup from the silver coffeepot and balanced the saucer on his knee as he took another sip. It was a vile flavored syrup that they passed off as coffee, which they couldn't get hold of, but Theo needed it since he was still suffering the effects of the time difference and travel sickness, as well as his guilt at leaving his parents and Virginia. She'd said she understood when he made it clear to her that Walter had made it impossible for him to say no, but he'd seen the sadness in her eyes. Now he considered what hurt her more: his leaving, or her father's apparent disregard for her wishes.

Bold sunlight streamed through floor-to-ceiling windows, illuminating the heavy furniture, as George kept up his lecture. Theo found his attention drawn to the stone mantelpiece, which housed a collection of carved animals, including ivory elephants, and glass domes that covered stuffed small birds and butterflies: Victorian dioramas, Theo realized, having seen them in photographs. The building and its contents were quite a contrast to the sparse and modern Park Avenue offices, and Theo sensed he would have to get used to many other differences in the weeks ahead.

George leaned across his desk and flipped the lid on an onyx cigarette box. "Help yourself to a Piccadilly—I shouldn't think you get these over there," he said, taking one for himself and leaning over to light Theo's.

"Thanks."

"How did you sleep?" George asked, releasing a ribbon of smoke.

"Like a log," Theo lied. He wasn't about to confess he'd spent the previous night with his head stuck over a bowl and that he still felt like he'd eaten jumping beans and that someone had set off a firecracker in his head. He just hoped he was doing a good job of disguising it.

"That's marvelous. So, how are things on your side of the pond?"

"The rations are making it hard for everyone, but support for the industry has never been better. The New York office is booming, particularly with our crime backlist."

"Surprising, isn't it? You'd think people would want to feel comforted in precarious times with romance and love stories, not give themselves the heebie-jeebies."

"I know, that's what we were trying to figure out. I think it's just another way to escape, pretend the danger is happening to someone someplace else." Theo hadn't verbalized this to anyone before, but he could see from the look in George's eyes that he agreed.

"And what of these special books Walter's been telling me about?"

"We're planning to ship the first Armed Services Editions to the troops in September, and they're going to be as revolutionary for them as paperbacks were to the rest of us," Theo said with pride.

"How so?"

"For starters, the books are small enough to fit in soldiers' pockets and light enough to carry. They're also printed across the two pages so they can be read by more than one reader at a time."

A few days before he'd left, Theo had attended a council meeting in which the details of the project had been unveiled. He'd also told the council about his planned London trip and offered to help them in any way he could. Most of the members had considered it to be fortuitous rather than a disruption, and they'd all agreed it was funny that it had taken war to give the public a greater appetite to read. The council's inspirational books would remind everyone who they were fighting for and against—and why.

"And what propaganda are you feeding these poor impressionable boys?" George asked.

"We're not, most of it's just great fiction. Heroic tales and stories of everyday Americans . . ."

George was nodding, listening with interest.

". . . by authors like Hemingway, Twain, Wharton and Fitzgerald, for starters."

"Goodness, sounds wonderful." George finally looked impressed. "And how's my gorgeous niece?"

Theo recalled Virginia's face as they'd said their good-byes, her lips trembling as she'd struggled to find the words, tears eventually spilling down both cheeks before she'd discreetly wiped them away. Even tearstained she was beautiful, with her luminous skin and mahogany eyes.

"She's really well, George. She's been working at the Red Cross station on the Lower East Side, one of the biggest salvage centers in the city, and she's loving it."

"Good for her!"

Theo's shoulders dropped. "She's disappointed that I've had to go away . . . but she understands."

"Yes, I'm sorry about that. I told Walter that it really wasn't necessary, but you know my brother, he won't listen to anyone. Anyway, am I right in thinking it was Mark Twain who said, 'God created war so that Americans would learn geography'?" George chuckled, and Theo smiled at him ruefully.

George didn't seem so different from Walter as he mentally sparred with Theo while trying to demonstrate his intellect and education. Theo didn't blame George for feeling threatened; after all, he'd started Partridge thirty years ago, with Walter opening the New York office once the British company had been established and made a name for itself. George must have found it galling to have an American sent over to help.

"Yes, that's right," said Theo. "It was Twain."

Despite George's good humor, there was an uneasiness about him, in his nervous fidgeting and the slight downturn of his mouth, that made Theo's task even more difficult. He was about to tell George that what his office was doing wasn't working: they needed to try something new or face losing more money, or even closure. He'd requested the accounts be sent to his hotel, so he could go over them before he came to the office, and they'd made grim reading. Just like at home, the British publishers faced an unusual dilemma: the conditions of war reducing their supply of paper but the demand for books increasing substantially, for the reading public as well as for the troops and for propaganda to send overseas.

They were in a strange predicament, a conundrum that he had no idea yet how to solve.

George stubbed out his cigarette. "You really didn't have to come, Theo. The figures aren't as bad as they look. Things have just slipped a bit, since Rupert left."

"I'm sorry, I forgot to ask, how is he?"

"He's all right, as far as we know. It's hard, though, when you don't hear from one month to the next." George looked pensive. "He's full of bravado, Rupert, but you don't always know what's going on inside. Not like the girls; they never hide anything," he said with a forced laugh. "But he's constantly in our thoughts. And our other brave chaps."

"Yes, of course, always." Theo hoped that George wasn't taking a subtle swipe at him; it was easy to become paranoid when you weren't in a uniform.

"The RAF must have been pretty desperate by the time they got to the second round, if they took him with his injury." George raised his eyebrows. "His knee's shattered from his rugby days, but if you're only getting in and out of the cockpit, it doesn't really matter, does it? Anyway," he said, livening up again, "this afternoon I want you to sit down with Tommy. He's taken over most of Rupert's responsibilities . . . until he comes back."

Theo knew they needed to replace Rupert but couldn't afford to—that, if anything, they needed to cut more of the already small staff. Meanwhile, Partridge Press US was housed in a space ten times larger than this, and they would soon need to expand further. Their operation had grown since Walter had married an heiress who'd supported his foray into publishing and then bankrolled the expansion. Pocket Books and its imitators had changed the way Americans read; for a quarter, they could pick up a book from a drugstore, a magazine rack or a gas station. Surely the British book revolution wasn't far behind with Penguin Books now publishing paperbacks for the Canadian armed forces, in addition to the Forces Book Club in Britain.

George bent to stroke his Labrador, Nelson, who gave an appreciative whimper. When he straightened, he said, "Tell me more about this council you're involved with. It sounds a lot like our Forces Book Club."

"Maybe," Theo replied. "We've got thirty titles planned for the first series. One and a half million in total, but as well as books for troops we want to promote books that help people think; ones that will inform and inspire them. The public are hungry for information—they know their news is censored, and they want to know what's going on."

George raised his eyebrows. "That sounds very ambitious."

"Wasn't it Chesterton who said, 'The true soldier fights not because he hates what is in front of him, but because he loves what is behind him'?"

George gave a thin smile. "Indeed. And so now you're here to advise us and share your ideals. Aren't we the lucky ones?" He sounded sincere enough, but Theo still detected more than a note of cynicism.

"I feel lucky too, George. I believe there's a lot we can achieve together, and a lot that we can learn from each other."

George nodded, his smile warming. "Let's leave it there for now. We can reconvene after lunch, talk to Tommy and bring the editors in too." George placed a hand on Theo's forearm. "I'm sorry you'll be missing Virginia, but the good news is that the pheasant season has run late this year. We'll head up to Norfolk soon for the weekend."

"That's very kind of you, George, but I think I'll stay in the city, catch up on things—"

"Nonsense. I won't have you staying in London on your own. Walter would never forgive me. Besides, Clare would love to meet you. And so would my girls."

Theo smiled. "Thank you, that's very kind of you, but—"

"Splendid. We'll leave around three, miss the traffic heading out of town."

Theo smiled his acceptance, realizing that he couldn't refuse.

"The bad news is there are decidedly fewer people on the estate now," George told him, "but the good news is there are more pheasant for us."

"So, is this going to be our last print run?" Emily asked, eyes darting between George and Theo.

It was after lunch, and Theo was revived, the nausea subsiding for the time being. They were seated at the boardroom table with Ursula and Tommy, a pot of tea steaming in front of them and Nelson snoring at George's feet as the wind lashed the trees outside.

"No," George replied, "Theo is merely saying that we need to find somewhere more competitive to print our books."

"That's right," Theo agreed. "There's not too much we can do about our fixed costs, but if we found a cheaper printer . . . maybe one that's not so local, well, I think it's worth looking at."

"I don't see why; everyone knows the printers have been taken over by our government," Tommy said, pointedly looking at Theo.

"Look," George said, "Theo isn't here to frighten us or threaten your jobs—the simple fact is that we need to adapt like other publishers."

"It's not just about the war," Theo put in, "it's these new forms of paperbacks too, and the emergence of companies like Penguin, both here and in the States." He glanced around the table. They all looked tired: Emily had dark shadows under her eyes, Tommy had the kind of stubble Theo hadn't seen since his last visit to Little Italy, and Ursula looked distracted. Morale was certainly low. "Penguin might have only been around for a few years—"

"Eight," Ursula said, with a decisive look on her face.

"Thanks," Theo replied, "but they're already taking a large share of the market."

"The team is aware of that," George said impatiently.

"Sure, I'm getting up to speed." He didn't want to worry them, and he certainly didn't want to patronize them, but he also needed to get the job done so he could return to Virginia and his parents, and that involved laying down the cold hard facts.

"I don't know how you do it over there, but we'll only be able to be competitive if we get enough paper ration, and to get that we have to sell more books," Ursula said in near-perfect English—was that an eastern European accent? "Our quota is based on what we sold last year."

"Yes, I understand that," Theo said, nodding. He didn't add that it had already been explained to him several times.

"Perhaps if we take you through the planned list of titles?" Emily suggested.

"Well, it's not complete, as we probably have to replace the title that Alice was working on," Tommy said. "It was going to be the next big thing."

"I know," George said, frowning thoughtfully. "You still haven't managed to find her, then?" He was looking at Ursula.

"She's still helping her cousin with the baby, as far as we know. I tried contacting her and her mother, but they haven't replied. So, no news, I'm afraid."

"Strange—let's hope she's okay," Tommy said, exchanging a look with Ursula.

"Who's this?" Theo asked.

"Our assistant editor, Alice Cotton," George replied. "She was developing a title with the potential to be the first in a popular series, something that might rival the Ministry of Information books—nonfiction titles about real people in wartime, remarkable true stories, that sort of thing."

"Until she disappeared," Emily said.

"Where did she go?" Theo asked, interest piqued. He knew how popular the MOI books were; how they had sold over twenty million copies already in Britain and overseas.

"No one knows—that's generally what happens when people disappear," Tommy replied without any hint of sarcasm.

"She took leave to look after a family member, but no one's heard from her," Emily said, and shrugged. "You should ask Ursula. Alice is her protégée."

Theo glanced at Ursula, but she looked the other way, her mind clearly elsewhere, and he wondered if there was something more to it.

"Does Alice have an employment contract with Partridge?" he asked.

"Yes, she does, as a matter of fact, but it's irrelevant if we can't find her," Tommy replied.

Theo narrowed his eyes at George, wondering why he hadn't told him about this woman and her book idea before. Then Theo glanced back at Ursula. "What if Alice has gone to one of the other publishing houses? If it's as good an idea as you say it is—"

"There's no way she'd do that," said Ursula. "Alice is far too loyal."

"It's been a difficult time for everyone. Perhaps someone offered her more money?"

"No, not Alice," Tommy said emphatically.

"Well, then, can't someone else work on them?" Theo asked.

Tommy shook his head. "We've got a freelance writer on it, but she can't seem to drum up the right stories. It would be good to get Alice back on it—if we can find her."

"Can I take a look?" Theo said. He was surprised they'd given up so easily; where was the British fighting spirit he'd heard so much about?

Tommy turned to Emily. "Where are the mock-ups?"

"In my office—the production office," Ursula said, ignoring Emily's glare. "I wanted to review them again, see what the freelancer had missed, but I can find them after this meeting if you like."

"Thanks, that would be great."

Theo was curious about this woman who was held in such high esteem but who had mysteriously disappeared, and it seemed Ursula was the key to finding out more.

At five o'clock Ursula was in the production office when Theo tapped on the doorway. This was obviously her domain; she'd personalized it with crimson velvet curtains that divided the room in half, and a bench seat that looked as if it belonged in a cinema. Old typesetting trays were propped on top of bookcases with large fragments of text and letters still visible between the lead lines, along with other printing paraphernalia.

"I'm trying to find the mock-ups, I just got caught up in something else," she said, looking flustered. "I'll bring them down to you."

"That's okay, whenever you're ready. I was just headin' out for something to eat. It's still lunchtime in New York, and to be honest with you, the journey knocked me about more than I thought it would."

"Yes, I've heard it can be quite exhausting; like a seasickness too."

His head wasn't spinning anymore, but he was having trouble fending off the current wave of sleepiness.

"That sounds about right. My fiancée said I should eat when I'm tired, so I was gonna have an early dinner. Do you want to join me?"

"Thank you, but I've got a lot to get through." She glanced at the stacks of documents and manuscripts on her desk, completely concealing the wooden surface alongside pots of pens, stock images and paper samples. She gave him a thin smile before turning her attention back to what she'd been working on.

"What are you doing?" he asked casually.

"Just another rejection letter," she said without looking up.

"Tough, although I can imagine that you let them down gently."

"Is there ever a way of being let down gently?" she said without a hint of innuendo as she glanced up at him.

He smiled. "I don't know, why don't you try me?"

She hesitated, then she put on a clipped upper-class British accent and read the letter aloud. "'Dear Miss Carmichael, I am sorry that we are not able to publish your collected poems. As delightful as these volumes of verse about woodland creatures are, they don't hold much relevance for our readers under the current conditions of war. In addition, wartime exigencies leave us very little opportunity to publish new authors.'"

"That's very gentle, and I can see why you don't have any time to come out," he said, still leaning against the doorframe.

Ursula shrugged. "Another time, perhaps."

"Of course. Care to point me in the right direction?"

The office had large sash windows, the astragal bars dividing up a sky of low gray clouds that momentarily threw the room into darkness.

"All right, I'll show you," she said, relenting. "It's probably time I called it a day anyway."

He helped her on with her coat, a brown trench that could have come straight off the front line its edges were so grimy and frayed, the hem spattered with mud. It seemed British women were quite a contrast to those of New York, and Ursula was no exception, her thick tweed trousers unlike anything he'd seen in Virginia's wardrobe.

"Thanks," he said, "I appreciate it. I've heard your London

cafés can be kinda hit-or-miss." He followed her down the staircase and through the lobby.

"I'm sure you'll find something to your satisfaction," she said, her voice warming. "You'll get a decent soup or sandwich at any of the places around here, but if you're looking for a hot meal I'd head to one of the pubs. Friend at Hand is probably the best. Or you could try one of the Ministry of Food's British Restaurants—they're rather good."

It had stopped raining, but it was still windy, and the morning's chill had lingered. Theo puffed on an imaginary cigarette, blowing condensation through pursed lips, which made her smile seemingly against her will. "Which way is it?" he asked, buttoning up his expensive navy coat and adjusting his fedora.

"This way," she said, and started to walk.

As they fell into step beside each other, he decided it was time to draw a line under this missing woman, forget about her or replace her, so they could all move on to more important issues. "I know you're busy, so I'm just going to ask you outright. What's she like, this Alice? I mean . . . what kind of person is she?"

"What kind of person is she?" Ursula repeated, sounding surprised. "Well, she's kind and caring, and she's not the sort of person who would run off with trade secrets, if that's what you're thinking." Ursula cast him a sharp glance and scowled, and he tried not to smile. "She's as passionate about books and about Partridge as the rest of us are, and there's no way she'd do anything to jeopardize the company."

They reached the busy main road and crossed over to where two cafés stood next to each other in a parade of shops. As they stopped outside, he turned to face her. "So, why hasn't Alice been in touch with anyone?"

"I really don't know. She was a little preoccupied the last time I saw her." Ursula frowned. "She was worried about her cousin, who was expecting a baby and had just lost her husband."

"You said earlier that she went to look after them—"

"Yes, but that was only supposed to be temporary. We thought she was coming back, but it's been five months now."

"And you really have no idea where she could be?"

"No, I'm afraid not. She's certainly not back in Dulwich with her mother, but I do know for sure that she would be here, unless something more important was keeping her away."

"Why can't she be replaced? There must be hundreds of girls suitable for her job."

"Actually, there's not. There's a shortage of workers, in case you hadn't noticed, and our freelancer had to leave us because war work takes precedence over books." Ursula rolled her eyes. "Anyway, Alice hasn't had as much training as the rest of us, she just seems to know what readers want. She has this special sense for understanding people, an intuition for what they want to read."

"Go on."

"It's because she's one of them, a real reader. Not like you lot in your waistcoats and Savile Row suits—she lives where ordinary people live, talks to the people who actually buy and read the books."

"And what about you, are you ordinary?"

Ursula smiled coyly. "No, I'm not very ordinary either."

"What would you say about Emily and Tommy?" He fixed her with a stare. "Does she know better than them?"

"No, of course not." Ursula pushed her hands deep inside her coat pockets. "Alice just has an instinct for it, I suppose."

"Is there anything else?"

"Yes, the authors like her."

"Well, that's certainly something."

Her lips curved into another smile, and this time he smiled back.

It was obvious that Ursula and the others were suspicious of him, unhappy about his involvement with their work. If he could help bring Alice back to the fold, that might be a way of showing them he was on their side.

Ten

BRIGHTON, MARCH 19, 1943

Alice winced with each movement as she crept down the stairs, eyes darting back and forth along the empty landings as she feared running into Hope, who was certain to try to stop her for the sake of her health. Breakfast wasn't served until seven, another hour yet, so she had little chance of meeting any guests, who must have grown suspicious of the woman in the attic after her shrieking and her visitors' comings and goings.

She carried on, lightly down the last flight, through the hallway and out the front door, closing it softly behind her.

It was still dark, and a thick fog was coming off the channel, threading spectral tentacles along the promenade and through the deserted streets. Alice shivered and clasped her coat tighter as she set off in the opposite direction, away from the seafront. She held one of the guest maps from her room that showed points of interest in the town: the Duke of York's Cinema, the piers and arcades, the dance hall and restaurants—and the hospital and police station.

Alice had barely slept at all. Hope had carried on calling Dulwich the whole of the previous day with no answer. Where had Ruth gone, and what exactly was she planning? Alice hadn't believed her mother capable of harm before, but now she wondered what else Ruth might do.

She followed the road north, her hand tucked inside her bag, fingers curled around the crocheted blanket. It should have been a ten-minute walk from the guesthouse on Atlingworth Street to John Street Police Station, but she could only walk slowly, one foot carefully in front of the other, measured breaths with each sharp stab of pain. Of course, Hope was right about her need for bed rest; her breasts were sore and she'd padded herself with rags, but every step was accompanied by a burning sensation and a fresh flow of blood.

And a rising panic that she would never see her daughter again.

She tried to imagine what the police would say when she told them what had happened, and what they would do to help.

There weren't many people around, yet the streets seemed overly loud, every sound magnified: two pedestrians talked noisily as they strode by, a truck engine groaned angrily as the driver shifted gears, and a bus strained up the hill—it was as if she was seeing and hearing everything for the first time, as a baby might.

A homeless man was slumped in a doorway, and she crossed the street to avoid him, then felt a rush of pity before thinking again of her mother and the look of genuine affection on her face when she'd held Eadie for the first time.

Is this really happening to me, or is it a terrible dream?

The fog was giving way to a wind that blew with fury along the road, pulling her toward the corner of John Street. There the larger buildings provided shelter from the wind, and she sighed with relief when the blue lamp of the police station came into view.

Time's ticking by; they could be anywhere by now. I have to hurry.

This was going to be the hardest thing she'd ever done: report her own mother, putting her at risk of being arrested and imprisoned. When Alice walked through these doors, it would change everything.

She cautiously mounted the steps, trying not to flinch at each movement. Her stomach was empty, and in her dizzy, weakened state she reacted too late as the double doors flew open and two policemen burst out, a man arm-locked between them; they nearly knocked her over. "Sorry, miss," one of the policemen said, steadying her with his free hand. "You all right?"

"Yes, yes, I'm fine," she said, forcing a smile.

"Are you sure?"

"Yes, I'm certain. Thank you."

The smell of alcohol was pungent, and they both watched as the other policeman steered the drunk down toward a waiting police car. The man was getting more agitated, his language becoming even more obscene.

Alice said, "It looks like you're needed . . ."

"I know . . . and, again, I'm sorry."

Inside the station, a frosted ceiling lantern cast an insipid light over the worn wooden counter, the smell of disinfectant doing little to mask the odor of acrid smoke. Alice rang the brass bell and glanced around as she waited. There was a glass partition to one side and a large noticeboard on the other covered in lost and founds: pictures of pets and missing people vying for attention. The rest of the décor and furniture seemed unwelcoming: two wooden benches against anemic walls, and closed doors either side.

A young policeman appeared behind the counter. "Good morning, miss. How can I help you?" He looked her up and down disdainfully, and she registered how creased and filthy her clothes were, but it was too late to disguise them.

"I need to report a crime," she said, pressing her hands onto the counter for support.

"What sort, miss?"

"I don't know—kidnapping, child abduction . . . I don't know what you call it. My baby's been taken."

"Someone's stolen your baby, miss?" he said, sounding puzzled.

"Yes, my mother."

He frowned momentarily before breaking into a smile. "Well, I'm sure she'll bring her back. Probably just lost track of time."

"No, you don't understand. She's taken her without my permission. She's not allowed to do that, is she?" Alice asked, the words tumbling out as she grabbed hold of his sleeves. "She's not allowed to take my baby."

"Madam," the policeman said, as he pulled his arms away and straightened out his cuffs.

"I'm sorry." Alice's breath caught in her throat, threatening to suffocate her.

"No, your mum can't, miss—I mean, madam. But are you sure about this . . . ? I mean, what about the father, is there a chance he's got the baby?"

"None," Alice said, eyes welling with tears. "He's no longer with us. It's my mother. . . . You have to help me. . . . I don't know where they've gone."

"You'll have to wait for the station sergeant to come back, but I can take a statement. Why don't you come through and have a seat? I'll get you a nice cup of tea and take down some details," he added, at last showing some concern.

"But why can't *you* do something?" she said, staring at his dark navy tunic and the helmet with POLICE written on it. "We have to hurry," she pleaded. "You need to start looking. They could be anywhere by now."

"I'm sorry, madam. I can take a statement, but the rest will take time. There's far too much crime for the regular police to investigate, let alone us special constables. But let's start with your name."

Of course, she needed to keep herself in check and act reasonably, so they would take her seriously and not question her story. She thought for a moment: was it better to give her real name or a false one?

"Cotton, my name is Alice Cotton."

"And your mother's name?" The constable glanced at her again, eyes lingering on her messy clothes as she took too long thinking what to say. She couldn't say Ruth Cotton because then he'd realize she wasn't married, but she couldn't lie about that and the father too.

"Ruth Cotton."

He frowned, then put the pen down and leaned closer. "So, what makes you think your mother would take your baby?"

"Because she . . . *we* no longer have anyone to support us. She's scared. But it's illegal, isn't it? I mean, she can't do it?"

"I don't know about illegal, though it's certainly unusual. I haven't had to deal with anything like this before."

"You can help me, then?"

"How old is the baby, madam?"

"Four days," Alice replied, tears leaking from the corners of her eyes.

Just the thought of her newborn made her breasts tingle as the let-down reflex released some milk, and she glanced down to check her coat still covered her.

"Any distinguishing features?" he asked as he started to make notes.

She'd barely had the chance to look at Eadie's tiny body; all she could think of was a small birthmark on her left shoulder.

He looked up. "Any distinguishing features?" he repeated, still sounding patient.

"A small birthmark on her shoulder. Barely the size of a pea."

"And the father's name?"

"I told you, he's no longer with us," Alice said sharply.

"But I still need to know his name. Presumably you have the birth certificate?"

It was no good, she couldn't give Rupert's name; if they

contacted his family, she stood to lose Eadie anyway. And if she gave a false name, there was a good chance the police would find out she'd lied, and then they might refuse to help her.

"No. No, I don't."

"I see," he said as he stopped writing and looked up at her again. His brow furrowed. "Are you sure about any of this, Mrs. Cotton? Are you unwell, or perhaps you're just confused? Or maybe you've done something with your baby—left her somewhere, or done something you regret, and now you're trying to blame somebody else?"

"No, that's not true. I told you, my mother's taken her. Here . . . I've got a note." She pulled the crumpled paper from her bag and handed it over to the sergeant.

"Look, I'm sorry, but you could have written this yourself. Can anyone corroborate your story?"

"Yes, the doctor . . . he can, and my aunt, Hope. She'll tell you what happened."

"What's this doctor's name?"

Alice wanted to scream his name as loud as she could to make the policeman listen, but she had no idea what it was.

"His name, Mrs. Cotton?"

"I don't know," she replied, lips quivering.

"So, let me get this right. You don't know the name of the doctor who delivered your baby, you don't know where your mother is, you don't know where your baby is, and you haven't got a husband. Are you really a new mother?" He gave her a slow once-over, and she saw herself through his eyes; she looked and felt every bit as powerless as the homeless man she'd passed on the street.

She could barely speak, the tears were falling so fast, but

she finally managed to say, "My aunt, she can tell you what happened—"

"Look, luv, my advice to you is to go home and stop wasting police time. I told you, we've more than enough to deal with without loonies."

He lifted the wooden hatch and came around to her side of the counter, standing too close with his arms folded across his chest.

"Off you go, then," he said sharply.

Alice backed away, silenced by her disbelief, and stumbled through the doors and out into the bitter morning air.

Ruth's wet umbrella stood in the corner of the porch, raindrops spilling down the dark fabric, water pooling at its base. Alice's breath rasped as she closed her eyes and turned the key, pushing the front door wide open while she listened for the cry of a newborn.

She'd left the police station and hurried west past the incongruous turrets and domes of the Royal Pavilion, barely silhouettes in the burgeoning daylight. Alice's legs had been weak and trembling, her mind still reeling from her ordeal at the police station, so she'd hailed a passing taxi to take her to Brighton station where she'd stopped to look back down over the rooftops at the skyline she was leaving behind. From this station, there were trains bound for London, as well as other destinations to which her mother could easily have traveled—north to the Midlands or even Scotland, or the West Country. So many infants and children had been evacuated, no one would notice one more baby without its mother. *Where are you, and why have you taken Eadie? Why did you come up with our plan, go along with it for months, and then take her now? It doesn't make sense.*

It had taken all her strength to force herself through the station entrance. Platforms and trains had been visible through the large archways, the immense glass-and-iron roof cantilevered overhead. Vehicles had been making deliveries and collections from the forecourt, milk pails rolled down the concourse onto a waiting train, and her eyes had darted everywhere, searching for her mother and her newborn.

Thankfully the ticket office and café had already been open, a window sign announcing, OPEN AS USUAL, MR. HITLER. She couldn't remember the last time she'd eaten, and she had realized she was hungry. It was then that her mind had gone blank, unable to remember exactly where she needed to go—Victoria station, or Clapham Junction and a change for Dulwich? She had hidden her distress as she bought a ticket and some breakfast, and then saw to her padding again before boarding what she'd decided was the right train. As it had pulled out of the station she had watched, with bittersweet emotion, the shadows of terraces and open green squares recede; she had been sorry to be leaving Eadie's birthplace, yet hopeful that she was traveling closer to her.

Now in Dulwich, outwardly she felt calm, strangely disconnected, as she stepped through the doorway and hurriedly explored the downstairs rooms. She used the handrail to help her climb the stairs, already sensing the search was pointless. The rapid thud of her heartbeat echoed a mounting panic that she wasn't going to find Eadie here.

Alice's bedroom was empty, and when she rushed into her mother's room she found immaculately made beds and an icy coldness. Even before she opened the door to her brother's old room, now Eadie's nursery in her mind, at least, she knew what she would find: empty cupboards where she'd stored baby clothes.

She buried her head in her hands as frustration, anger and fear rose up inside her, but she couldn't cry.

Where would Ruth go with Eadie? All Saints in West Dulwich was the most likely answer: the church she'd attended, rarely missing a service, since their move. It was only a ten-minute walk through Dulwich Village, but Alice didn't have the strength. All she could do was wait for her mother to return

Her thoughts had taken her on a disturbing journey as she'd imagined all the places Ruth might be and what she might have done with Eadie, but Alice kept coming back to the same notion: in spite of Ruth's disapproval and deteriorating mind, surely her religious faith would stop her doing anything too bad. She'd been an active church member even through the Blitz, attending services in a blacked-out crypt. It had always made Alice smile to think of the non-worshipping locals' displeasure at sharing their air-raid shelter with a full choir and congregation, but today all she could think about was how her mother had such kindness for strangers but had shown such cruelty to her.

Then she remembered the dressing table where Ruth kept their important documents and hurried back to her mother's room. The drawer was locked, but the key wasn't hard to find.

She soon pried it open and tipped the contents out: a few pieces of jewelry and a ten-pound note. The birth and marriage certificates were gone.

Alice sank down on the edge of the bed as her breasts released another sharp wave of heat and pain. She was clutching Eadie's blanket, staring at the empty drawer, when the framed family photographs distracted her. Except for the photo of her father in his zookeeper uniform, all the pictures morphed into people she barely recognized; once important family occasions took on a somber meaning.

Alice stared at the image of her and her mother on her twelfth birthday—a party at the zoo—their faces pressed together as they beamed at the camera. They had been close before grief had distorted Ruth's emotions and religion had made a fossil of her heart. After learning of her pregnancy Alice had managed her heartbreak and humiliation, quarantining her feelings of shame and disgrace for the more important ideal and role of motherhood. Was it too much to ask for her mother to do the same?

Finally there was the sound she'd been waiting for: a door opening and footsteps in the hallway below. The light outside had faded, and Alice rose quickly and hurried downstairs, glancing into the empty living room as she walked past.

A loud male voice echoed from the kitchen, making her hesitate before she threw open the door. Ruth turned abruptly, and Alice realized the voice was coming from the wireless.

"Where is she? Where's Eadie?"

Ruth was at the sink and froze as her daughter advanced on her. "I'm sorry, Alice . . . I can't tell you."

"Why? What have you done with her?"

"You won't make me change my mind." Ruth glanced at the blanket then back at Alice, her lips tightening.

"How could you?" Alice shouted, moving closer, eyes wide with fury. "Where is she?"

Ruth backed away, gripping hold of the countertop behind her with both hands. "I can't tell you. It's best for everyone. Are you all right? Did the nurse take care of you?"

"You lied to me. You were supposed to help me . . . help us." Alice clutched the blanket to her chest.

"You shouldn't have come, Alice, you really shouldn't have. You should still be in bed." Ruth snapped off the wireless broadcaster mid-sentence. "I'm helping you. Can't you see that? This way you'll have the chance of a future—"

"A future . . . without my baby."

"But you can have a husband now—a husband and a family you can call your own," Ruth said, stretching out a hand.

"Don't touch me!" Alice screamed, backing away. "I don't care about that. I don't want another family."

"Maybe not now, but you will."

A tremor of pain passed through Alice's abdomen, and she put out a hand to steady herself. She was too weak to maintain her anger and needed to try something else; it was only Ruth who stood between her and Eadie. "Mum, it's me, Alice," she pleaded, looking into her eyes, searching for the woman who had nurtured and raised her, the woman who was supposed to know what it meant to be maternal.

"I know you can't see it now, Alice, but one day . . . one day you will thank me." Ruth seemed so calm, so composed, and then it dawned on Alice: her mother *actually* believed what she said, that she was helping her.

Alice stepped forward, inches from her mother's face. "I don't care about the future. All I care about is Eadie. Now, where is she?"

"This really is best for both of you."

It seemed hopeless; her mother was unreachable, and Alice slumped back, propping herself up with one hand on the table as the tears began to fall. "How could you possibly know what's best for us? It might be best for you, but it's not best for me, and it's certainly not best for Eadie."

"It might not seem that way now, but I sought guidance and the Lord answered."

"You have to tell me where she is," Alice pleaded.

"Hebrews, Alice. 'Marriage *is* honorable in all, and the bed undefiled: but whoremongers and adulterers God will judge.'"

Alice could feel hysteria overtaking her, and she took a deep breath as she tried to stop shaking. She'd once been grateful for her mother's faith, as it had helped Ruth grieve when her father died, but this was beyond pious; it was irrational.

"Haven't I always taken care of you? Aren't I doing that right now? Just let me take care of things—"

"For God's sake, who's feeding her? You have to tell me where she is, or I'll go to the police and tell them what you've done."

"No, you won't, or you would have already done it." Ruth stood stiffly while Alice was cowed and trembling, her body failing her, and she tried to summon more strength.

She leaned closer to Ruth. "Yes, I will," she said slowly, enunciating each word.

"And what do you think they'll do? There are thousands of

missing children, and the police certainly won't care about the illegitimate ones."

Something inside Alice snapped. She had never so much as raised a hand to her mother before, but now she grabbed her by her wrists, fingernails digging into her skin. "Tell me where she is!" she screamed into her face. "Tell me!"

"Get off. You're hurting me!"

Ruth tried to break free, but it only made Alice tighten her grip and dig her fingernails in more. "You can't do this, you're my mother. How *could* you?"

"You brought this upon yourself. I am saving you, Alice." Ruth was still struggling. "You will thank me for it in the end."

"No, I won't. Now tell me where she is."

"I will not."

Alice released her grip, body weakening, barely able to stand. She locked eyes with her mother, their familiar gray flecks now stony and cold, and Alice fought the urge to strike her, knowing it would only make her feel better for an instant. "Why are you doing this to me?" she said, leaning into the table again. "Just tell me why."

Ruth swallowed and looked at the floor before gazing back at Alice. "The day your father died, I promised myself I would always protect you, I would always put you first . . . and that's exactly what I'm doing now."

"But don't you think I know what's best for me?"

"You aren't thinking clearly, Alice." Ruth's expression hardened.

"Whose idea was it . . . Father Mitchell's? Did he put you up to this?"

Ruth cast her eyes down as her fingers played with the tea towel in her hands. "It's got nothing to do with him."

"I bet it's got everything to do with him."

"You know that God will make his own judgment. It's not ours to make."

As repugnant as she found it, Alice believed her mother might be telling the truth. She glanced around, realizing how the kitchen had become even colder and how the smell of her mother's cooking was repellent where once it had been comforting.

Alice gathered her thoughts. "I'll leave here, no one will know. You can come and visit us if you want to. The shame will only be mine."

It looked as though Ruth might be relenting, her eyes becoming glassy. "I never wanted to hurt you, Alice. I know what you've been through."

"Then don't do this," she pleaded. "It doesn't matter what anyone else says or thinks. I'll take Eadie far away. No one will ever know."

"How? Where would you go . . . how would you manage?"

"I don't know yet, but I'll find a way," Alice said, beginning to sob again, tears streaming down her face. "She needs me . . ."

Ruth remained mute, and they stood in silence, listening as a train rumbled along its tracks in the distance and birdsong sounded from the garden. The longer their silence stretched, the more Alice hoped her mother would change her mind.

Then she noticed the table was set for two. "Who are you expecting?"

"This is your home, Alice. There will always be a place for you here."

It was unfathomable that her mother could believe she would want to be in the same room as her, let alone at the same table, and Alice shook her head in disbelief.

"You might not understand now, Alice, but you will, in time."

Alice's gaze fell to a stain on the linoleum, and she felt herself go limp. All she could think of was how Eadie had felt the last time she'd held her: her warmth, the scent of her crown, her weightlessness. And of how quickly their fragile bond would be broken.

"Just tell me she's all right. If you're not going to tell me where she is, at least tell me who she's with."

Ruth glanced up at the ceiling and clenched her jaw, the muscles in her neck tightening. "There are people who are experienced at this, Alice. People who do this all the time and know how to take care of things."

Alice stopped crying and held her breath.

"Eadie has a wet nurse. That's all I can say."

Alice gave her an icy stare, unable to speak.

"There won't be so many choices once this war is over. It will take all our young men. You should know; war took your brother—"

Something in Alice cracked at the way Ruth was using William to justify herself. "What makes you think I would want a husband more than my own child?"

Ruth folded her hands in front of her. "It's too late," she said matter-of-factly. "I don't know where the baby is."

"You must have a number, an address—"

"No, nothing."

"But how did you contact them?" she asked as a numbness crept through her.

"It was an advert in the newspaper. They had a postal box number—they wrote back to me and arranged the place and time. Then I met them at a hotel in the city."

"What newspaper? Who are they?"

"It was the *Daily Mail*, and I told you, I don't know who they are. Just a couple who look after babies and find them good homes. They thought it was best if I didn't know too much, and I agreed. I only saw them twice before . . . before they took her."

The bile Alice had been fighting back finally rose in her throat, and she tried to swallow. This was far worse than she could ever have imagined.

"What kind of woman gives her grandchild to strangers?" she spat.

Ruth pressed her lips together. "There are couples who can't have babies, who are grateful of the chance to raise a child together. Married couples."

Alice was moments away from vomiting, but she had to concentrate: perhaps Ruth was on the verge of giving away important information. Then something occurred to her. "Did they come with you, when you stole her?"

"No, they were supposed to," Ruth said, sounding more uncertain. "They wanted to take the baby as soon as they could."

"You mean as soon as I gave birth."

There were tears in Ruth's eyes, and she raised a hand as if she wanted to offer comfort. "I am sorry for that, Alice. It would have been better for everyone if they had taken her straightaway, but you went into labor early. You wouldn't have formed such an attachment—"

"Do I know them?" Her voice came out as a whisper.

"No, they only visited Brighton once," Ruth said earnestly, as though she had been doing Alice a service. "They wanted to be certain."

Alice recoiled, rushing over to the sink and reaching it just in time.

Eleven

LONDON, MARCH 19, 1943

"You'll have to sit and wait," the old officer behind the desk said gruffly. "There's no telling how long it could take."

"I understand," said Alice. "I'll be right here." She sat gently on the closest bench, feeling uncomfortably hot, with cramps in her abdomen.

She had been heading to her old friend Penny's house when she'd had a change of heart and decided she had to try the police again, so she'd stopped off at Marylebone Lane Police Station on the way. In light of what her mother had said, she couldn't afford to wait or to worry about revealing Rupert's identity. And she'd realized that she didn't need to; she would simply claim she didn't know who the father was.

Around her were benches packed with members of the public in varying states of disgruntlement, victims of London's crime epidemic. The newspapers were filled with stories of how the city was rife with lootings, murders and gang activities, which added to the wartime atmosphere of fear and uncertainty. The police would see Alice as one of many victims, but she was determined not to put up with the same treatment as before. *It's the best thing for you to go home and get some sleep, indeed!* This time they had to believe her.

Half an hour passed before a middle-aged officer, his uniform too small and his thinning salt-and-pepper hair too long, showed her into a small interview room. Under different circumstances she would have been disturbed to be enclosed in the white-tiled room, with its dreary concrete floors and barred window, but as she sat on the opposite side of the desk Alice wheeled between impatience and relief.

In the waiting room the officer had introduced himself as Special Constable Bobby Relf, and she'd given him her name, but now he didn't remember. "Is it Miss or Mrs. Cotton?" he asked, pencil balanced between his fingers.

"Miss."

"And can you tell me why you're here, Miss Cotton?"

She bit her lip to stop it from quivering, and her eyes flicked up at the ceiling as she tried to keep them dry while she spoke, managing to stay composed as she gave a censored version of the preceding months and he scribbled in his notebook. Finally, she told him about the advert in the *Daily Mail* and the couple who now had Eadie, downplaying her mother's involvement because she still couldn't comprehend her actions or know whether they could place her behind bars. "So," she said, "you can help me . . . can't you?"

"I'm going to ask one of our women officers to come talk to

you, Miss Cotton. A4 usually deals with the juvenile cases, and I'm sure you'll feel more comfortable going through the details with her. Just wait here, if you don't mind."

After he left the room she watched and listened to the hands of the clock tick noisily for fifteen minutes. Her breasts grew more painful and she became increasingly uneasy, close to despair at the thought of another woman feeding her newborn.

Constable Relf returned accompanied by a young woman in a dark skirt and belted tunic, whose unruly red hair sprung from beneath a police hat. "Hello, Miss Cotton, I'm Sergeant Mildred Burns from the Women's Branch. We deal with all juvenile cases and crimes relating to children, and first, let me say how very sorry I am." She sat down next to Constable Relf, then leaned forward so Alice could see the freckles that mapped her pale face. "I can assure you that it's a priority to prevent crimes against children, and in particular to stop these unlawful adoptions."

Alice sighed, relieved that someone finally wanted to help.

"That said, I have to ask you not to set your expectations too high."

"But you just said you can help me."

"We can look at the Juvenile Index to see if there's any record of your daughter," she said, exchanging a look with Constable Relf, "although I think it's unlikely that she will be on it. We will certainly investigate further, but I want to make sure you know that before we can make any arrests we need to have enough evidence. It's then up to the courts to decide whether to prosecute—it's not up to us. I just want you to know that, Alice. We will try to get justice for you, but it's not entirely in our hands."

"I don't care about that. . . . What I mean to say is that it's not about getting justice. I just need to find my daughter—quickly."

Constable Relf and Sergeant Burns exchanged another look, then the policewoman glanced down at the papers in front of her. "I suggest that I take your statement and then you contact the National Council for the Unmarried Mother and Her Child. They may have resources and ways to help that I'm afraid we don't."

"So, what are you actually going to do?" Alice asked, growing frantic.

"As I said, I'll take a statement and we'll investigate."

"But how long do you think it will be until—"

"Look, Alice, it's frustrating for us too, but we're having to enforce the blackout, help with evacuations and restore communications, all things we didn't have to do before the war, and many of our staff are police pensioners and War Reserve officers."

Alice could see what she said was true, and that she was genuinely trying to help, but it wasn't enough.

"What about the father, is he going to help?" Constable Relf asked.

She'd decided not to name him, but her disappointment now threatened her resolve. Could he be any help? She reminded herself of how little he'd cared about her. "Come on, Alice, don't be a bore," he'd said, temper flaring when she'd refused to go out with him the last time he'd asked. "I don't want to force you to . . ." His eyes had blazed with desire, a look that she'd once been attracted to. That day she'd felt scared and had stood her ground, and he'd eventually left her alone.

"Fine, there are plenty more fish in the sea," he'd said, and laughed.

"I . . . don't know. He's not in the country anymore . . ."

"Is he serving?" Sergeant Burns asked.

"Yes."

"I see," she said, looking searchingly at Alice.

Alice thought of Rupert's reputation, of his society links and his large group of friends, and then she thought of her own and how her situation would look to an outsider. She didn't name him.

It was lunchtime when Alice left the station and made her way to Primrose Hill. As she traversed the wasteland between Oppidans Road and King Henry's Road, staircases disappeared into open ground, doors lay horizontal, shattered walls exposed musty cellars, and she realized this was a real battlefront. There was a lingering metallic smell in the air, but in among the chaos a group of children played on precarious-looking rubble, making a game of throwing rocks into the ornamental pond of a former grand garden. Alice thought about warning them off, shouting to them to be careful, but she knew it wasn't her place. *Can't they see how dangerous it is, how fragile everything has become?*

Penny's café had always been tucked between a grocery shop and a hardware store, yet Alice searched the streets for several minutes trying to get her bearings and calm her nerves. It was hardly surprising that the area was unrecognizable; with its anti-aircraft guns on one side and the main railway line from Euston on the other, it had never stood much of a chance.

Even the silver-tailed barrage balloons at the nearby Lord's Cricket Ground couldn't have done anything to deter the Luftwaffe. What surprised Alice was that Penny's family had stayed instead of going to the countryside, but Penny had insisted she couldn't leave the community and that Chalk Farm Underground station was as good a place as any to take shelter.

It took Alice a while before she realized she was going in the wrong direction, and she had to retrace her way to the junction of Regent's Park Road and its familiar row of white houses. She recognized the parade of shops instantly, except enormous chips of granite had been gouged from the curbside, the iron lampposts were dented and most shopfronts were boarded up, the rough edges of hastily sawn planks still visible.

Just across the street, kids played hopscotch outside Penny's café, socks around their ankles, their noisy shrieks of laughter incongruous with their game. Before Alice had started working at Partridge, she had been a regular visitor here since it was so close to the zoo. But time had slipped away, and she hadn't seen Penny for a year; she wasn't even sure which kids were Penny's.

She crossed the road without looking and peered through the café window; she couldn't see Penny behind the grime-coated glass. Perhaps she'd been wrong to come, she thought, although she had nowhere else to go, and her friend had been so insistent when she'd telephoned to ask if she could visit, perhaps even stay for a few days.

The café was crammed into the downstairs of a Georgian terraced house, a low set of stairs leading off to another salon at the back while a steeper staircase led to Penny's family home on the two floors above. There were more tables and chairs than Alice remembered, and the once-full bookshelf across the back wall was now populated with mismatched cups and saucers, china ornaments and jars of dried flowers. Framed photographs of popular actors and sweethearts decorated the walls, some bearing autographs.

Penny stood behind a brass counter, squawking orders at a waitress, her light-brown hair twisted into a loose bun with a pencil sticking through it. "Alice!" she shrieked when she noticed her. "How long have you been here?"

Remembering her new shape, Alice quickly clasped her hands in front of her and attempted to smile. "Long enough to see you haven't changed—still just as bossy."

Penny raced across the room and hugged her so tightly that Alice thought she'd have to ask her to stop. "It's so good to see you," Penny said as she released her.

Alice felt the same way—in fact, she wished she could keep hugging her friend, but she wasn't sure she could do it without breaking down. "I'm sorry it's been so long . . ."

"It doesn't matter, you're here now. Anyway, I've been just as bad. I could have called you." Penny took hold of her small suitcase and placed it on a chair. "Come sit down, we'll have a proper catch-up once the lunchtime rush is over."

"Thank you so much for letting me stay, you've no idea how much it means to me—" The words stuck in her throat, but she caught herself and managed not to cry.

Penny was beaming at her. "It's fine. More than fine, it's wonderful. Say, are you hungry? You do look a bit peaky," she said, her smile fading.

Alice had barely eaten in the last few days, and she did

feel rather unsteady on her feet. "A little something would be nice."

"Right, I'll be back in a tick. I'll just fetch some tea."

Penny's family came from Yorkshire, and Alice never tired of the soft landing her friend's words made on her ears—or her northern hospitality.

"Sure, take your time," Alice said, forcing a smile. "I don't want to interrupt." But she was desperate to talk to her old friend. Something about seeing her had unlocked all the emotion she'd been struggling to contain, and she would have to try hard not to cave in and tell Penny everything. Some time ago Alice had confided in her that something was going on with someone at work, and Penny had told her to be careful.

Alice watched as she organized her staff and chatted with the customers. *Should I tell Penny the truth about everything?* She and her husband, Michael, had been childhood sweethearts, and Alice didn't want to bring her sordid drama into their home. There was a part of her that wanted to keep their friendship pure and untainted, honest and safe like it had always been.

Somehow she needed to get through the next few days—the next few hours, even—but the café was uncomfortably noisy: ragtime played loudly on the radio, and voices crowded her in. Then came the rising panic, an unfamiliar sensation that threatened to overwhelm her, making her feel the need to escape. She moved to a more secluded seat nearer the bookcase and tried to focus on the few books while she waited. It was an eclectic selection of old fiction and classics, shabby editions of highbrow literature and poetry muddled in with the distinct golden spines of *Reader's Digest* books. A noticeboard advertised local community events along with a regular book group held at the café that Penny had invited her to on more than one occasion.

A young serviceman at the nearest table caught her eye and smiled, so she averted her gaze, quickly turning back to the shelf. She pulled out a random book, its withered spine nearly disintegrating as she opened it and very carefully turned the pages. If she concentrated hard enough on the story, she was sure it would stop her from crying—but her vision misted, and the words blurred into each other.

"Which one would you recommend?" the serviceman asked.

It would be rude to ignore him, but she didn't want a conversation either, so she replied without looking up. "I'm not sure I could recommend any of them."

"Seen better days, haven't they?"

"I'm afraid so," she said, trying to hide her distress as she traced a finger along the barely readable spines. She came to a copy of *To Have and Have Not* in passable condition. "I'd probably try this. Have you read any Hemingway?"

"I'm more of a Dickens man—*The Pickwick Papers . . . Bleak House*. I like reading about home rather than foreign places."

His Cockney accent was clearer now, and she passed him the book. He looked barely twenty with his baby face and slicked, parted hair.

"Yes, I know what you mean," she said, and smiled.

"I tried *A Farewell to Arms*, but I couldn't get into it," he said. "I just wish there was a bit more choice."

"You know, there are book clubs you can join."

"Yes, but they run out of books too quickly."

Alice thought of her brother and was about to remind the young man of the subscription libraries when she realized that servicemen weren't around long enough to benefit. It was all right for the public to rely on book lending by the local and circulating libraries, and the big four—W.H. Smith & Son, Boots Book-Lovers' Library, Harrods and the *Times* Book Club—but if he was only home for short periods he wouldn't be able to make the most of them.

"I wouldn't have survived my first tour if I hadn't had a book," he said solemnly. "Lots of the chaps are the same. It's the only way to lose yourself . . . to forget what's really happening."

This was what William had always said, and why she had sent books to him whenever she could. In fact, this man reminded her of Will, only he was even younger.

"So," she said, "what do you like to read so you can forget?"

"It depends. I don't always like a book when I first start it. Sometimes it takes me a while to get into it."

She knew what he meant; it was something she'd given a lot of thought to over the past couple of years. A novel didn't really begin until the reader was engaged enough to want to accompany the characters on their journey. Ursula told her that her instincts for such things would help make her a good editor. Of course she'd appreciated Ursula's faith in her, but she knew that would never happen now. Anyway, those roles were usually reserved for the Oxbridge candidates, of whom there were already plenty behind the desks of London's publishing houses.

Penny reappeared with a tea set and a plate with nearly a whole Victoria sponge cake.

The serviceman smiled shyly at Alice. "It was nice talking to you."

"You too," she replied.

Penny glanced back and forth between them. "Sorry, I'm not interrupting anything?"

"No, it's fine."

Penny sat down noisily and dragged her chair toward the table, then cut off a large chunk of cake and nudged it toward Alice. "So, how are you?"

"I'm fine, really fine . . ."

"Suits you, by the way," Penny said, looking her up and down. "I always said you were too skinny."

Alice opened her mouth but wasn't sure what to say, so instead she took a bite of the cake. She pretended to enjoy it, but the whole process felt like a betrayal. How could she possibly enjoy dessert when another woman was breastfeeding her baby? It just wasn't right or natural.

"And how's your mum?" Penny said, leaning her elbows onto the table and resting her chin on her hands.

Alice struggled not to choke and keep the food in her mouth.

"Sorry, take your time." Penny wiped the crumbs from the side of the plate then licked them off her fingers.

Penny had spent a lot of time at Alice's house when they were children, and she knew Ruth well—so well that Alice was tempted again to tell her what had happened. But would she even believe it? Alice barely could herself. She took another mouthful and eyed her friend thoughtfully, considering what a relief it would be to share her burden. Together they could try to fathom what her mother had done. And, most important, they could search for Eadie.

"Mum's still the same," Alice said at last, mustering a smile. "Still praying for Will's return."

"But I thought—"

"No, he won't be coming home, but she still refuses to believe it," Alice said firmly. Then her lips began to quiver and she pressed them together, biting back tears.

Penny placed a hand on hers. "I'm sorry, Alice. I didn't mean to upset you."

"It's fine. It's not your fault. I just miss him."

A look of concern passed over Penny's face, then she suddenly became animated again. "Vicky and Peter should be home soon. You won't recognize them."

"I think I might have seen them playing outside."

"Probably, they're not allowed to go far," Penny said, rolling her eyes.

"Oh, really?"

"Yes, one of their friends was killed at the wasteland. A phosphorous bomb went off as they were collecting shrapnel for a game."

"Oh God, that's awful!" It must have been in the ruins she'd walked past.

"There are signs with warnings all over the place, but I suppose they're just kids, aren't they?" Penny sighed. "You can only tell them so many times." She looked tired now, fine lines around her eyes and mouth showing the strain of the past few years.

"Yes, I thought it might be them. They've changed so much."

"It's been nearly a year, Alice."

"I know . . . I'm sorry."

"It's okay, I don't mean anything by it."

Alice forced another smile.

"Are you sure you're okay?" Penny asked, squeezing her hand.

"Yes, really, I'm fine." She searched Penny's pretty green eyes, trying to decide whether she should confide in her.

"You seem . . . I don't know . . . sad, I suppose. You would tell me if there was anything wrong?"

"Yes, of course." Alice placed her other hand over Penny's. "Of course I would." She attempted another mouthful of cake, chewing slowly, but she started to cry and couldn't seem to stop.

"Alice, what is it?"

She took a deep breath and sniffed, then looked Penny in the eye again. "Well, there is actually something that I have to tell you . . ." And then she told Penny about the events of the past year: the seduction, without identifying Rupert, then the pregnancy and being banished to the seaside, and, finally, her mother taking the baby. Penny's eyes grew wider, her jaw dropping open.

"So, you see," Alice sniveled, "that's why I need to keep looking."

Penny didn't say anything, she just lunged forward to wrap her arms around Alice, holding her close for what seemed like hours but must have only been minutes. Alice let her friend's love flow through her. *Definitely a radiator*, she thought as she allowed herself a half smile, remembering Ursula's comparison of her mother to a drain.

As Penny pulled away, she looked Alice directly in the eyes and clasped her hands. "We're going to look after you. Have you seen a doctor?"

Alice shook her head.

"Right, that's first, then I want to know about the father and what he's going to do to help."

In her mind's eye Alice saw fragments of Rupert's face, his mouth flashing in front of her, his eyes wild as he straddled her, laughing as if it were a joke. She felt so ashamed, and she didn't know what was worse: that she'd let it happen, or that she'd believed his lies and thought she was the only one.

Penny said, "Ah, was he someone at work . . . the one you told me about?"

Alice nodded and kept on nodding; she couldn't stop.

"It's okay, Alice, it's okay." Penny moved a comforting hand to Alice's shoulder until she grew still again.

From the corner of her eye, Alice noticed the young serviceman stand up to leave, the other diners glancing in their direction. Penny followed her gaze and then turned back to Alice. "Don't you worry about them—they've seen everything there is to see. And they're friends." She smiled. "I'm taking you upstairs for a bath and some rest, and I bet you need a cold compress and some cabbage leaves. *Then* we're going to talk about what we're going to do."

"So, it's still all right for me to stay, then?"

"Of course it is. Why wouldn't it be?"

"It's just . . ." Alice dropped her head. "It doesn't matter." Her humiliation felt as visible as her grubby clothes, and she worried Penny could see it too—and that Michael wouldn't approve when he found out why she was there.

"No one should have been through what you have, Alice, *no one*. You can stay here as long as you want. And you must say if there's anything you need, anything at all we can do to help."

"I will . . . and thank you." It was as if a weight had lifted, and Alice knew it had been the right thing to come here.

Penny was still shaking her head. "It's horrific. Truly horrific. I can't believe your mother could be so cruel. Are you sure the police can't do anything more?"

"They said it will take time—there are so many missing people. They told me to be patient and not try to do anything myself."

"And of course you're going to ignore them," Penny said with a small smile. "So, where are you going to start?"

"Well, where would you go if you desperately wanted a baby?"

Penny looked aghast. "The adoption agency—I think they're called the National Children Adoption Association."

"Yes." They would have records, and perhaps she could learn the names of couples the agency had rejected, those who might have turned to another source to find a baby.

"You can borrow Michael if you need to pretend to be married," Penny said earnestly, "don't worry about that."

That hadn't crossed Alice's mind, but it was something to remember if doing things this way didn't work, and Penny's gentle giant of a husband would agree to be involved.

"Thanks very much," said Alice. "For now, I just need to find their address."

"That's easy, it's in the newspaper. They often have adverts in the classifieds section. And they always break my heart."

"I don't suppose you've got any papers, have you?" If Alice

had a copy of the *Daily Mail*, she might be able to find the advert her mother had described.

"Sure, over there." She pointed to a wooden rack near the window. "You take a look while I get the kids in, then we're taking you upstairs."

"That sounds good." Alice squeezed Penny's hand. "And thank you."

Alice examined the papers from cover to cover but couldn't find an advertisement for the National Children Adoption Association or a notice for private adoption. She was ready to give up when she found a group of adverts in the classified section.

> **Wanted**—a baby-lover to adopt a baby girl;
> love only. Slough.
>
> **Offered for Adoption**—month-old baby girl.
> All rights forfeited. Contact PO Box 575,
> Guardian Office.
>
> **His Job Is to Find a Baby Girl**
> WANTED—a baby girl for adoption by English
> people in Ecuador, South American Republic of
> the Pacific, over 5,000 miles away. The baby must
> be typically English, must be a girl, and must be
> strong enough to withstand the journey.

She clamped her hand across her mouth as she fought to stay calm. The adverts made her even more certain that she needed to ignore the police and act quickly.

Twelve

LONDON, MARCH 22, 1943

Wanted—a baby girl for adoption by English people in Ecuador . . . must be strong enough to withstand the journey. The words still echoed in Alice's mind as she made her way down Sloane Street early on Monday morning, looking for the National Children Adoption Association. She'd struggled to sleep in the attic room as she thought about unmarried mothers, babies and childless couples, and the people who benefited from all their misfortunes. She had finally drifted off just before dawn, and Penny's kids had woken her soon afterward, so her feet were clumsy and her eyes gritty as she searched for the address.

Most of the local buildings were given over to support St. George's Hospital—various departments and training centers housed in Edwardian apartment blocks, specialist offices in white stucco terraces, their names and specialties inscribed on bold brass plaques—and there squeezed among them was number nineteen, the only house between the hospital and the Old Barrack Yard. Behind its glossy black door, a vast white hallway was lit by gold filigree wall-lamps, and a luxurious red carpet covered the expansive curve of the staircase. Alice climbed it steadily, her pain dulled for the moment by drugs, her mood optimistic at the prospect of making progress.

An engraved wall plate on the first floor announced the association, and she knocked and entered, tentatively looking around. The large room could easily have been mistaken for a theater lounge: brocade curtains encased the floor-to-ceiling windows, and rosewood side tables sat next to two green velvet chesterfields on thick oriental rugs. It struck her that this environment couldn't be further from the kind of place the infants the association sought to help usually came from. Then she saw the certificates on the wall and understood the extravagant furnishings: HRH Princess Alice, Princess Victor Napoléon and Reginald Nicholson MP were among its patrons, as well as the founder and executive director, Miss Clara Andrew.

Then Alice noticed the two anxious-looking couples eyeing her from the sofas, and she quickly approached the reception and introduced herself as Mrs. Cotton.

"I'm afraid you need an appointment to see Miss Swift," the plain-faced receptionist explained.

"I'm happy to sit and wait."

"I'm sorry, but that's not permitted."

"I really don't mind how long it takes."

"We work on an appointment system, and there are no

appointments available for the next two weeks," the receptionist said, sounding exasperated.

"But what if Miss Swift finishes early. Can't she squeeze me in?"

"Look, I'm sorry, but we can't help you"—the volume and pitch of the receptionist's voice rose—"I really don't know how many times I have to explain!"

Alice tried to reassure her that she *really* didn't mind waiting, when an interior door opened and a young couple filed out, followed by a well-dressed older woman, presumably Miss Swift. She said good-bye to the couple before turning her attention to the flustered receptionist. "Whatever is the matter, Julia?"

"This lady . . . Mrs. Cotton—she won't take no for an answer."

"I'm Miss Swift," she said matter-of-factly to Alice. "How can I help you?"

Alice had worn the only other of her dresses that fit her and swept her hair into a respectable chignon, yet she knew she didn't look anywhere near as suitable as the other women in the room. "I need to speak with you, but your receptionist says there are no appointments for two weeks."

"Exactly. As you can see, we are very busy," she said brightly. "You will have to come back then."

"But I can't wait that long." Alice was trying to stay calm, keep her voice even.

"That's what they all say, but believe me, my dear, two weeks won't seem that long at all." Miss Swift laid a dainty hand on Alice's arm. "Once you've registered for a child, it could take months or even years to find one, so you will need plenty of patience."

"But I don't want someone else's baby," Alice said loudly, her voice fracturing. "I want mine . . . and she's been stolen."

Miss Swift glanced at the horrified couples on the chesterfields. "Excuse me," she said to them, "we shan't be a minute," and she ushered Alice into her office. She closed the door behind them and stood in front of Alice, her arms folded, manner still composed. "I don't want a scene in the middle of my waiting room. These people are very vulnerable and have been through years of anxiety in their quest to become parents. Now, I don't know exactly what you think we can do to help you, but if your baby is missing then surely it's a matter for the police."

"They don't know anything, but perhaps you do. Where do you get your children from?" Her voice broke. "And the couples you reject; do you know who they turn to for help after they leave here?"

"No. Mrs. . . ."

"Cotton. My name is Alice Cotton."

Miss Swift scrutinized Alice. "Look, Mrs. Cotton, the children we place with adoptive parents come to us from all sorts of places, but I guarantee that none of them are stolen. Most unmarried mothers willingly give up their babies to us. Of course, some have second thoughts, but I'm afraid to say that in most cases it's too late."

Alice shook her head disbelievingly: the one place she thought she might receive help, and she wasn't even being listened to.

"It's perfectly understandable if you've changed your mind.

Parting with your baby is difficult under any circumstances, but you have to think about what's best for the child. Consider why you made the decision to give it up." Miss Swift enunciated her words so carefully that Alice was almost convinced they were true—until she came to her senses.

"But I didn't give her up. My mother took her." She articulated carefully too, so there could be no misunderstanding. "And she's given her to a couple—paid them to take Eadie, in fact. I need to find them. Will you help me?"

If Miss Swift was shocked, she didn't show it. Her expression changed, sharp features softening, then she unfolded her arms and stepped closer. "I'm sorry to hear that, Alice. Why do you think your mother would do such a thing?"

Alice's gaze dropped to the woman's navy tweed suit and the Union Jack brooch fixed to its lapel near the collar of her lilac blouse. Her graying hair curled at the front and fell longer at the back. There was an idiosyncrasy to her manner, and Alice knew that anyone who did what she did must have remarkable inner strength to deal with many unconventional people and might not judge her harshly.

A lump had lodged in her throat, and she struggled to reply. "I'm not entirely sure why." She hesitated, her mind going to an uncomfortable place. "I think she loves her God more than me . . . more than us."

It looked as if Miss Swift was about to say something, but she must have changed her mind since she simply pressed her lips together and blinked slowly.

"We'd agreed to pretend it was my cousin's baby and raise it together." Alice swallowed. "She made the arrangements, but she didn't follow through with them."

"And when did all this happen?"

"Eadie was born a week ago, and taken six days ago."

The older woman looked at her worriedly. "Have you seen a doctor?"

"I'm fine, Miss Swift. I just need to find Eadie." Alice wasn't fine; her tear was bleeding badly, despite the baths Penny had insisted she take. Her breasts were engorged and she had a mild fever, and while she knew her despair and sleeplessness were partly caused by anxiety, her friend had told her it was the baby blues and perfectly normal to be tearful and overemotional after giving birth. She'd been learning all the things she had expected her mother to share.

Miss Swift regarded her carefully, then took her by the hand. "Come and sit down. And call me Joanna, please." She led Alice to a small sofa in the center of the modest office, the furniture far less ornate here and altogether more functional. Alice bit her lip, trying not to cry, and concentrated on the reading material that lay on the coffee table in front of her. There was a pile of academic texts and a large encyclopedia, and there were also popular magazines and journals with editions of *Illustrated London* and *The Spectator* recognizable by their spines. Alice considered how well versed Joanna Swift must be in understanding human nature—and what atrocities and acts of kindness she must have seen.

"I wish I could help you, Alice, but I have no idea what happens to the couples we don't accept as adoptive parents, although I can assure you that we *do* know the origin of every baby that comes to us. However, the Adopted Children's Register might help. The entry won't contain any information about the birth, though, only about the adoption."

"How can I find it?"

"It's held by the General Register Office, not by local Register Offices."

"That's okay. It's a start." Alice attempted to smile. It sounded more promising than the Juvenile Index that the police kept for "stray or missing" children, which Eadie hadn't been on. Although if she was on this one that Miss Swift spoke of, it would mean that she might already be too late.

Joanna smiled back. "It's difficult for everyone, I know." She sighed. "Formal adoption didn't even exist in the United Kingdom until nineteen twenty-seven, and there's rarely any documentation. The Adopted Children's Register is really all there is."

"But how can there have been so little progress in sixteen years?" Alice said, wiping her eyes and fueled by a newfound anger. "There must be something else I can do."

"Eadie is only a week old?"

"Yes."

"Have you tried the foundling hospitals? There's the Thomas Coram register, which lists children given to those hospitals. That's probably your best chance, although they do baptize them with new names." Joanna looked thoughtful and pursed her lips.

"But Eadie was only a day old when she was taken—she hadn't even been baptized," Alice said, as she dabbed at her eyes.

"You could try the Dr. Barnardo's Homes too, where apparently quite a few children are claimed."

Alice's optimism was evaporating, a cold nausea taking hold. "There was an advert in the newspaper . . . that's what my mother responded to. Maybe you've seen it, or something similar."

"Oh dear. If that's the case, then I'm afraid I really can't offer you any help. I'm afraid we are all at the mercy of the government in that respect."

"What do you mean?"

Joanna sighed and then spoke in the slow sympathetic tone she'd used earlier. "I can't advise you, I can only tell you that we exist to protect infants and children, not exploit them. If there is any way I could help you, Alice, I would. And if you had come to me in a few months' time . . ." She paused and sighed. "I might have been able to help you then, but I'm afraid you're too early."

That didn't seem to make sense. "What do you mean 'too early'?"

"You've heard of baby farmers?"

Alice nodded; she hadn't heard the term for some time but knew it was associated with child trafficking that had existed in the early part of the century. It brought to mind images of alleyways engulfed in fog and grim reapers trading babies, and these thoughts chilled her to the core.

"In the two decades after World War I, the buying and selling of children became such a big problem that an act was proposed in nineteen thirty-nine that should have put an end to it." Joanna's gaze was intense, her words full of fervor. "But when World War II broke out, the act was shelved, and so the abuse continues." She walked over to her desk and picked up a newspaper. "Sadly, the conditions of war—more vulnerable women, more illegitimate babies—have provided the perfect environment for the baby farmers to thrive more than ever."

Alice shuddered. "I really had no idea."

"Yes, it's quite scandalous that it's been allowed to carry on this long. And so blatantly too—newspapers carrying adverts for babies before they've even taken their first breath. It makes my blood run cold."

Alice was aghast; she had never contemplated this.

Joanna must have seen the horror on her face, because she continued in a more measured tone. "Fortunately, at last the government seems to be listening." She handed her the newspaper. "This explains it all far better than I can."

The paper was dated March 20, only a couple of days earlier, and the headline read: *Law Will Put Baby Farmers Out of Business on June 1.* The article described how the Adoption of Children Act was supposed to come into effect before the war but had been "put on the shelf." Recently Mr. Herbert Morrison, the home secretary, had brought it in under growing pressure from welfare societies over the growth in child trafficking. It was just as Joanna had described; Alice read how the act forbade anyone other than a local authority or registered adoption society from making any arrangements for the adoption of a child. The article set out how the act would also ban payments and adverts for adoption, and how it would include restrictions on sending children abroad.

Alice looked searchingly at Joanna. "So, this is good news?"

"Yes, for some. But I'm afraid not in time to help you."

Alice rose shakily to her feet. She handed Joanna back the paper, unable to fully grasp the situation, only knowing she needed to get out into the open air; her wound burned, her breasts were leaking and her head spun. "Thank you. I'm very grateful for your time."

Joanna put her hand on Alice's arm again and gazed at her with concern. "Please, do me a favor and go see a doctor. You do look awfully pale."

Alice nodded, but she didn't care. All she could think about was that baby farmers might have Eadie, and if she was taken overseas there would be no chance of getting her back.

Thirteen

LONDON, MARCH 25, 1943

Late at night Alice's eyes flashed open. She was lying on her back, something misshapen and lumpy pressed against her side. She rolled over and reached down to lift the bedclothes, uncovering the tiny form of her newborn. But Eadie's eyes were closed and she wasn't moving, and Alice screamed and screamed.

She woke with a start and sat bolt upright, heart pounding as she panted into the darkness, her nightdress clinging to her damp skin. She gradually took in the unfamiliar surroundings, her breathing ragged as she struggled to work out where she was. Tears sprang from her eyes as she realized. She was at Penny's house in Primrose Hill, and it was over a week since Eadie had been taken.

Alice wiped her eyes on the bedsheet as she tried to recover—to separate the real from the imagined, what she knew had happened and what was part of the nightmare.

Loud shrieks pierced the stillness, followed by a chorus of otherworldly cries. Then it registered: the cacophony was from the nearby London Zoo. Many of the creatures woke around dawn, and for the briefest moment Alice was drawn into a happy memory of zoo visits with her father.

She groped around on the bedside table until she found the lamp and switched it on, a small halo falling across the iron bed and the carved wooden cabinet. The rest of the room was still in shadow, except for the oak chest containing her few possessions that stood underneath the casement window. Her journal lay open on the bed, and she leafed through the pages of scribbled notes: not quite stories but memories her father had shared and which she'd recorded for Eadie. She reached the gray pencil-shaded face of the elephant, a child riding high on its back; she'd left the image in monotone but colored in the elephant's vivid headdress. It was supposed to be Elor, who had been at the zoo since 1918, a favorite among the keepers and visitors. While the experts had said an elephant would never breed in captivity, Elor defied them by having two calves.

See, miracles do happen, Alice thought as she studied the picture.

She would find her daughter, and she would read her father's stories to her.

Alice went to the window where she'd sat up late looking out across the rooftops, the panorama of London a checkerboard of dark and light because some buildings had been razed.

The small attic window opened out onto a ledge that she'd climbed onto. From there she'd watched the sun set and wondered if Eadie was in any of the houses spread out before her.

Now she brought Eadie's blanket up to her face and inhaled. It was losing its scent, and she worried that the image of her baby's face was also fading, slowly slipping away—just like the chance of ever finding her. She needed to try something else, and quickly, putting all physical discomfort aside. She'd had no success with any of Joanna's suggestions, and there was no news from the police. Of course she would keep visiting the foundling hospitals and child welfare organizations whenever she could, just in case.

Penny's children woke up, squealing and chatting in the room beneath hers.

A gold light flowed through the half-closed curtains to the chest beneath the window, highlighting the stack of newspapers on top. She'd checked through all the local and national newspapers, and there were so many adverts for babies that she'd become totally overwhelmed. The *Sunday Dispatch* Wartime Aunts Scheme promised to organize at least two adoptions a week, and other regional newspapers carried adverts for organizations offering to do the same.

One name had kept coming up: that of a journalist, Olive Melville Brown, who had written the piece in the *Daily Mail* that Joanna Swift had shown her. That article appeared to be part of a bigger story that the journalist was following. As she stared at the papers, Alice realized that Olive probably knew plenty more, perhaps even the names of well-known baby farmers. And that the newspaper's library would be a good resource for her too, if they would only allow her to look.

Alice couldn't believe she hadn't thought of it sooner. She dressed as quickly as she could; she would tell Penny where she was going, then she'd visit the newspaper's offices to see if she could find Olive.

Fourteen

"That's Alice," Ursula whispered, nudging Theo with her elbow.

He was as taken aback by her action as he was by the young woman who stood talking with another woman behind the counter of the small café. Alice was surprisingly tall and strong-looking, with a mass of wavy blond hair. Her attractive face was devoid of makeup; in fact, she appeared in every way the opposite of his petite and elegant fiancée.

"Alice!" Ursula called, her voice brimming with relief. "Finally, we've found you!"

As Alice looked up and saw them, her mouth fell open. "Ursula . . . what on earth are you doing here?"

"What are *you* doing here is more to the point!" Ursula said, as she embraced her.

When Alice moved away, she gave her a weak smile. "It's a long story."

"Well, make it a short one."

Alice glanced at Theo.

"Alice, let me introduce you to Theo Bloom—"

He smiled and offered her his hand.

"He's visiting from our New York office."

Alice looked startled and hesitated, then she shook his hand. "Pleased to meet you, Mr. Bloom."

"And you, Alice. I've heard a lot about you." He had, but those descriptions didn't seem to fit the young woman standing in front of him. Her hair wasn't styled, just pinned casually back, and her clothes were loose-fitting and unflattering. She had lovely features—a heart-shaped face and unusually deep blue eyes—but her style didn't match those of the rising stars he knew in the New York publishing world.

"So, what are you doing here?" she asked Ursula.

"I remembered you talking about Penny and visiting her. We have been trying to find you, Alice. You did just vanish!"

"I'm sorry. Things have been . . . well, difficult."

"Is your cousin's baby all right?"

"The baby is fine." Her gaze darted to the floor. "Thank you."

"I'm sorry to just turn up like this, but Theo wanted to meet you, and—"

"I can't really talk now. I'm just on my way out."

"You must have a few minutes, surely. We've come all this way."

Alice gave Ursula an unfathomable look, then glanced at Theo. "All right, a few minutes. Do you want some tea?"

"It's fine. We don't want to hold you up, do we, Theo?"

"No, of course not," he said, and smiled again, hoping it wasn't going to be a wasted journey.

They found a table by the window, and Ursula launched

into conversation, not leaving it to him to do the talking as they'd agreed beforehand. He waited, controlling his instinct to interrupt and hurry them along, while he smoked a cigarette. His mind turned to the difficult phone call he'd had the day before with Walter, which the switchboard operator had abruptly ended at the predetermined five minutes. Walter had wanted an update on George's office, but Theo had barely had time to formulate an opinion, let alone one he was prepared to share. Walter's impatience had already forced Theo to take a meeting at the Ministry of Supply, where Sir Duncan Castles had told him that the Board of Trade's priority was supplying books to the Commonwealth to keep up the flow of knowledge and ideas, but that they faced obstacles like lack of shipping space. Theo had listened even more intently as he spoke of the opportunity for American publishers to satisfy the hunger for books in countries that Britain no longer could because they were under-resourced, and an island under siege. There wasn't time to relay the information before the operator cut them off, but he recalled Walter's earlier words fading in and out as the line crackled. *You need to consider yourself part of the family already, Theo. That way I know you'll make the right decisions when you're there.* Theo pictured Virginia sitting beside her father, head tilted up and smiling at Walter's sentiment.

"I thought you must have fallen out with your mother, Alice—she really was most unhelpful when I said I wanted to find you," Ursula said, which caught Theo's attention because it sounded so strange.

"It's a long story," said Alice. "I can't really go into it now, but I'm sorry that she wasn't very welcoming."

"Oh, well, we know your mother is a drain and not a radiator!" Ursula said, but Alice didn't smile. "Well, will you at least tell me why you're here and why you haven't been in touch?"

"Penny's an old friend," Alice said, lowering her voice. "And I needed somewhere to stay."

"Why? What's happened?"

Alice glanced again at Theo. "I'd rather not talk about it now." She looked very uncomfortable, and for a moment he felt they'd been wrong to chase her down. Sounding apprehensive, she asked, "Why exactly are you here?"

"Theo wants to talk to you about your book, Alice."

Alice turned to him, eyes searching.

"Theo?" Ursula prompted.

"I understand that you had reasons for leaving Partridge . . . family commitments," he said, and cleared his throat. "If you've carried them out, then we'd like you to come back. I've seen the mock-ups of *Women and Children First*. It has a lot of promise, Alice. We've allocated the paper and the print run; the schedule works. It's all possible. All we need is for you to help find the stories and edit the book. Ursula says you can do it."

Ursula smiled at her encouragingly.

"That's very kind of you," said Alice, "but I don't know if I can. My cousin still needs me . . . and, well, I don't want to let her down."

"Oh dear, poor thing." Ursula sounded disappointed. "I thought it was only meant to be for a little while?"

"It was . . . I mean, is—"

"Well, I'm sure it's easier to replace a babysitter than a book editor," Theo said with a small laugh. He couldn't believe she would pass up this opportunity; from what Ursula had told him, it was all she'd ever wanted.

Alice frowned, her gaze settling on the tabletop. "Look, I'm really flattered, and in one way I'd love to come back, but I think it's too late."

Theo glanced across at Ursula, meeting her puzzled eyes with his own. Then she shrugged at him and turned to Alice. "Partridge wants to go ahead with your book, Alice. Don't you remember the ideas we talked about? Everyone can see how emotive it could be, how successful. And we've all missed you."

Alice smiled softly.

"We did some testing with the mock-ups," Ursula told her. "The readers loved them. George has agreed to dedicate more of the paper ration for it."

"Really?" Alice said, brightening further.

Ursula nodded. "Even Emily was enthusiastic—imagine that!"

Alice's smile widened, but then it faded and she grew serious. "Is Rupert back?"

"No, he's still in Asia. I don't think he'll be back for some time. Don't you listen to the news? The Japs have more firepower than us and the Yanks combined."

Theo saw something resembling relief flicker across Alice's face before her gaze returned to the middle of the table. Ursula chattered on about what had been happening at the office, while Alice appeared lost in thought. She seemed far too timid to be responsible for this big book idea. How had she become such a valued part of the team? It struck Theo that she lacked pretension, just like the girls in his neighborhood growing up, and so he decided to keep an open mind although his first impressions hadn't filled him with confidence. He was even more worried by George's unwise decision to allocate a lot—too much, in fact—of their precious resources to her first book.

So, it was up to Theo and Ursula to convince this nervy young woman to return to Russell Square, and to ensure the success of her series, or it could be the end of the London operation. Working in business affairs and on Book Row, he'd learned enough about human nature to know that people weren't always what they seemed. *Never judge a book by its cover*, he thought, smiling inwardly at the cliché. Although he had the feeling that Alice Cotton wouldn't surprise them in the least.

Fifteen

As Alice walked to the Underground later that morning, off on her search for Olive Melville Brown, she thought about Theo's offer and the book Partridge wanted to publish. If the past few days had taught her anything, it was that there were hundreds, perhaps thousands of missing or stolen children whom the public needed to know about, infants taken from their mothers and traded like food or fuel. For the briefest moment she'd been tempted to say yes, before deciding there was no way she could work and keep looking for Eadie.

She'd realized she had another problem to contend with: she was finding it difficult to go into confined areas. Ever since she'd woken to find Eadie gone, she'd felt increasingly uncomfortable in cramped spaces. She'd never experienced claustrophobia before—had even doubted its existence—but now she had a fear of being trapped whenever she was hemmed in. It was primal, and she had no idea what to do about avoiding small places when there were so many designed for Londoners' survival.

She took a deep breath as she made her way down the charcoal-colored steps and through the painted barriers, following the crowd as they entered Chalk Farm station. When she reached the top of the steep escalator, she grasped the handrail and peered down, but she couldn't see the bottom, as if the whole mechanism plunged into the center of the Earth.

Her breathing quickened, and she took off her coat as the heat of panic rose.

Then she squeezed the handrail, gritted her teeth and kept her eyes fixed on the steps as the escalator began its long journey down.

The platform was busy and the first train overcrowded, so she waited for it to pass through and for the platform to clear. She focused on taking measured breaths as the platform started to fill again, nearly as populated as before. As soon as the next train came she settled into a carriage, pulled out the copy of *To Have and Have Not* that she'd plucked off Penny's bookshelf, and tried to concentrate on reading, but a woman with a baby girl got on at Angel and sat opposite. The baby looked about six months old with soft brown locks curling from beneath a knitted yellow bonnet, and her arms and legs pumped the air on either side of her mother's embrace. The mother smiled, and Alice tried even harder to focus on the pages of her book but couldn't look away as the baby drooled, her big blue eyes flashing around the carriage. Then she fixed her gaze on Alice, staring expressionlessly through long spider-leg lashes as if waiting for something, and Alice found she couldn't help staring back. There seemed to be so much locked behind those eyes; the girl hadn't existed long enough to have the knowledge she appeared to possess, and it confounded Alice.

"She's a terrible distraction," the mother said.

"She's beautiful," Alice said, smiling. "What's her name?"

"Jessica."

Hearing her mother call her name, the baby abruptly turned toward her, neck and head wobbling unsteadily, and she bumped her nose against her mother and cried out.

"Come on, you're all right," the mother said, jiggling her up and down. "That was such a tiny bump."

"I'm sorry," said Alice.

"Goodness, wasn't your fault, you know what they're like at this age. Do you have children?"

"Soon." Alice's smile tightened, and she turned her attention back to her book. Yes, she had a daughter, and she needed to focus her mind and decide what she was going to do next to find her. Miss Swift had already shown her that there were other avenues to pursue; the National Adoption Society, Dr. Barnardo's Homes and the foundling hospitals, but they would all take time—time she didn't have. The National Adoption Society was known for sending children overseas; Dr. Barnardo's Homes were also committed to fostering older children, so it would seem obvious that she should keep looking at the foundling hospitals. But Alice sensed the exercise was pointless; Eadie was in the hands of baby farmers, and trying to track her down through other avenues was just a waste of time. She'd lain awake most of the night growing more upset and frustrated at why her mother hadn't given Eadie to one of these more trusted institutions—at why she'd given her to the least legitimate of them all. And placed her in unnecessary danger. That was why she needed to talk to Olive Melville Brown: the most obvious place to try to find out about the baby farmers was with the journalist who was following their story.

As the train hurtled through the tunnel, wheels scraping along the track, Alice kept rereading a sentence before she finally gave up. The light spluttered as the train slowed on its approach to the next station, and the mother stood, steadying herself on the handrail as she waited by the doors. Alice watched as she stroked her daughter's back, whispering soothingly into the blanket. When the doors slid open, the woman glanced up at Alice and smiled. Alice smiled back, then watched her progress along the platform until she disappeared through the white tiled archway, feeling the simultaneous ache of longing and relief that they had gone.

The unmistakable gray-white dome of St. Paul's floated on the horizon, merging with the pale gray sky, as Alice hurried east along Fleet Street, looking for the *Daily Mail*. Buildings on both sides of the road dwarfed her—vast neoclassical stone structures and Art Deco blocks, and smaller offices with Tudor or Gothic frontages, all with one thing in common: a guard at their entrance. She'd never had reason to visit this part of the city before, and the atmosphere was markedly different from Bloomsbury and Fitzrovia; there was an air of quiet authority, a seriousness with which those who brought the nation their news took their wartime role. And as Carmelite House came into view and she climbed the steps to the entrance, she considered that since the newspaper had been reduced to only four pages, the office staff would likely have been cut too. The author Evelyn Waugh was also a regular contributor to the paper, but since reporters were rarely at their desks, there was little chance of seeing him either.

Her footsteps rang hollow across the dark marble foyer, causing the dark-haired receptionist to stop her conversation with the security guard and smile as she looked up. "Good afternoon, how can I help you?"

"I'm Miss Alice Cotton, here to see Miss Olive Melville Brown."

"I'm afraid you just missed her."

"If it's all right, I can wait."

"She might be some time. Do you have an appointment?"

Alice had intended to call ahead, but the surprise of seeing Ursula, and meeting Theo, had distracted her, and she grew deflated as she realized that she might not meet Olive today.

"Can I leave a message?" Alice asked, barely recognizing her own meek voice as she waited for the receptionist to hand her a pencil and paper. "Thank you," she said, then hesitated, "but perhaps I could use your phone and call up now?"

"There's really no point—everyone's at lunch."

It was only just midday, but why would the receptionist lie to her? Perhaps because of how she looked; she'd worn the cleanest of her two dresses but certainly not the smartest.

"I understand that your library is on-site," she said. "Could I talk to your librarian?"

"It's not open to the public."

Alice didn't identify with the timid creature she'd become; if she was to get what she wanted, she would certainly need to be a lot more cunning. "I'm not the public," she said, stepping closer. "I work for Partridge Press. You probably know of Patricia Reece—"

"Why didn't you say so before? I love her novels!"

Alice smiled. "Next time I visit, I'll try to remember to bring you a signed copy of her latest book. Today I just need to confirm some information for a special project I'm working on."

The slender receptionist stood up and then pushed the visitor book toward her. "Just sign in here." She watched as Alice wrote her name, then beamed at her. "The library is on the lower ground floor. The stairs are on the left of the lift. And I'll phone Elizabeth now and tell her you're on your way down."

"Thank you so much."

"Not at all, Miss Cotton."

It grew colder as she descended into the basement, smooth stone steps giving way to the black-and-white tiles of a wide empty corridor. There were multiple doorways; the closest one was fully open, light pooling on the floor, and Alice walked tentatively through into a narrower passageway. Here another entrance gave way to a deceptively large room that smelled of dust and paper, and had a long wooden counter at the front. There were bare brickwork walls with mosaics of rudimentary plaster, and a ceiling covered in a skeleton of pipework. Rack upon rack of metal shelving and closed cabinets ran parallel from the counter all the way to the far wall. The air was thicker here, an almost tomblike stillness with no sign of life apart from the shadows that flickered across the room as pedestrians passed on the glass bricks of the pavement overhead.

A woman appeared dressed in a WAAF uniform, her dark hair curling around her collar. "Miss Cotton?"

"Yes. Are you Elizabeth?"

The woman nodded, and Alice couldn't help but stare; her eyes were so pale they were almost translucent. "I didn't get time to change after my shift this morning," she said in a south London accent as she glanced down shyly at her uniform.

"Oh, I see," Alice replied. "Well, thank you for seeing me at such short notice."

"That's quite all right. It's lucky you caught me, actually. I was just going on my lunch break." She glanced at the large wall clock.

"I'm sorry, I don't want to hold you up."

"It's quite all right. How can I help?"

"I'm interested in the baby farmer articles by Olive Melville Brown."

"Ah, yes." The woman's eyes widened. "Unbelievable, isn't it, what some people will do? Taking advantage of the vulnerable in these precarious times."

It seemed she was waiting for Alice to reply, but she could only nod and ask, "Do you have her stories on hand?"

"I do, actually. I file the articles under reporters' names and in chronological order, so it should be easy enough to find what you're looking for. Is that all you want?"

"I think so," Alice said, encouraged. "For the time being, at least."

She listened to the vibrations of traffic and indecipherable conversations from passersby as Elizabeth wrestled with the metal drawers, returning with a tray of newspapers. "Now, you take these through to the reading room next door, and I'll come and see how you're getting on when I return."

Alice had never felt as vulnerable and alone as she did now, not in all the days since Eadie had gone, as she grasped the immense task ahead of her, and Elizabeth's kindness made her suddenly teary. "Thank you," she said, turning quickly before the woman noticed.

Alice settled under the glare of an overhead light and picked up the first newspaper, recognizing the article as the one she'd seen at the adoption office. She felt a flicker of hope at the first few lines: *Britain is ending the baby farming scandal. An act that comes into force on June 1 will prevent this and other forms of traffic in children.* She reread the article because she couldn't remember all the details. Only local authorities or a registered society would be able to make arrangements for child adoption and, most important, there could be no payment for a child without permission of a court.

She leaned back in her chair, gazing at the blank wall as she thought it through. Even though the act wouldn't come into force for a few months, perhaps it could help her by scaring the traffickers. They had to know they couldn't get away with it for much longer.

Encouraged, she turned to the next article, dated more than a month earlier, on February 2. The headline was even more explicit: *Law Will End Baby Farming Evil.* But as she continued reading, the blood drained from her face.

The byline announced: *Jail for Women Who Sell Children*, and the article reported that mothers who gave their babies up for illegal adoption would face either a fine of two hundred pounds or six months' imprisonment. It added that these children had no name or identification, and therefore no citizenship or rights. Alice couldn't draw her eyes away from the last sentence: *By law they have no status.* It was sickening, and far worse than Joanna had let on: Eadie didn't even count as a person under the law, and Alice could be fined or sent to prison after June 1 if anyone thought she had given her daughter up voluntarily. And presumably the same law would apply to her mother since she had done exactly that.

She struggled to breathe as the low ceiling seemed to press down on her. Now she would have to be even more careful with the truth, and she urgently needed to speak with Olive Melville Brown: the journalist was the expert on this world and the people in it—and probably Alice's only chance of finding Eadie.

Sixteen

The entrance to Ye Olde Cheshire Cheese was tucked in an alleyway off Fleet Street, its dark nondescript exterior making it so difficult to recognize that Alice passed it by a few times before finding the doorway. Once inside the narrow flag-stoned entrance, her eyes took a moment to adjust to the dingy light before noticing the cozy bar of dark-paneled wood, the dramatic portraits and the sparkling etched-glass windows.

Alice smoothed down her skirt and coat, then stepped toward the bar. The place was no bigger than a modest living room, with a fireplace on the wall opposite and a few low barrel-end tables and chairs scattered around, but it was obvious from the creases of the well-worn seat cushions and the patina of the tabletops that history was made here; this was the kind of place that writers and journalists liked to visit. At five o'clock it wasn't busy, with a group of men drinking at the bar, and no one who fitted the description Elizabeth had provided when Alice had asked where she might find Olive.

Then, through the thick smoke, she glimpsed a woman sitting alone on a stool halfway along the bar, her neck craned down as she read. Noting the dark hair and small frame, Alice squeezed her way through the men to approach her. "Miss Melville Brown?"

The woman swung around. "Yes?"

Alice felt a wave of relief; Olive appeared much younger and friendlier than she'd imagined her to be. "I hope you don't mind . . . Elizabeth mentioned you might be here, and I wondered if I could have a moment of your time."

"Well, that depends."

"On what?"

"On who you are, of course, and what it's about."

"I'm Alice Cotton, and I've been following your stories on the baby farmers—"

"Well, I've got half an hour before my train if you don't mind the location," Olive said, glancing at the rowdy group next to them. "I find it's the perfect transition from the busy day to the quiet of home."

"It's perfect," Alice agreed, feigning enthusiasm. "Very lively."

Olive studied her for a moment before returning her smile. "Do you want to go somewhere we can talk?" she asked in an even tone.

"Is there somewhere a little quieter?"

"Yes, of course. We can go through to the restaurant. There's usually more room anyway."

"Thank you," Alice said appreciatively.

"Let's get you a drink before we go. What would you like?"

"What are you having?"

"Stone's ginger wine, not everyone's pick."

Alice hadn't contemplated having a drink, as she'd gone without for so long, but maybe it would be an idea to have one now, steady her nerves. "I'll have the same, but let me—"

"Not at all. As I said, I've only got half an hour, so let me. Besides, the job does still have a few perks."

Alice felt awkward as she waited for Olive. Glancing around self-consciously, she thought about the journalist's measured way of talking; she gave equal emphasis to each word so that everything she said sounded important.

During the few hours between the library and now, Alice had decided that it would be too confounding to tell a stranger the truth, no matter how sympathetic they might be to the provenance of illegitimate children, so she'd had the idea to try another approach. Once they'd settled into a quiet nook in the restaurant, Alice carried out a plan she'd come up with in the library. She told Olive about the book she'd been working on for Partridge Press, *Women and Children First.* She explained that as Olive was an expert in the field, Alice would like to interview her for the project. It would reflect the experiences of women and children on the home front, and at the same time could help the cause that seemed so close to Olive's heart.

"I'm afraid my work is copyright of the paper—I'm a staff reporter, you see," Olive said, with a kind expression. "There's not much I can tell you outside of what you've read in my articles."

"But you must know quite a bit more about these baby farmers. Things you haven't included in the paper."

"Well, yes, that's true."

"Like who they are?"

Olive narrowed her eyes.

"And where they might be? I get the sense, reading between the lines, that you might have spoken to some of them."

"I'm sorry, your book does sound interesting, but I'm afraid I don't think I can help you," Olive said, straightening. "You're asking me to share confidential information."

Alice worried that she'd pushed too hard. She really didn't know where else to turn, so she took a calculated risk. "Are you a mother?"

"Married to the job, isn't it obvious?" Olive said, sipping her drink.

"No, not at all. . . . The thing is"—Alice took a deep breath, noticing the journalist glance at her watch—"this isn't strictly a work matter."

"How so?"

Alice's feet fidgeted under the table and her fingernails dug into her palms. "I have a friend who's fallen victim to one of the baby farmers, and she needs help."

"She should go to the police."

"That's the thing, she did but their investigations have led nowhere—"

Olive stopped stirring her drink and looked Alice in the eye. "So, you want me to help, is that what you're saying?"

"Yes, I suppose I am."

Olive gave her an unfathomable glance before she took another sip of her drink and rested the tumbler on a coaster, gazing thoughtfully into it. Then she looked back up.

"Have you ever heard of Clara Andrew?"

Alice shook her head.

"She helped find homes for more than six thousand children in the last war, and she founded the National Children Adoption Association—"

"That's right," Alice said, remembering the certificates in Joanna Swift's office. "I saw her name recently. Something to do with the Adoption Act."

"It was another of her achievements—getting the Adoption Act passed in nineteen twenty-six—and lobbying the home secretary to set up a department on child services. If it wasn't for Miss Andrew, there would be far more baby farmers than there are now."

"And there's been no one like her since?"

"Not just that; as you know from my stories, the nineteen thirty-nine Adoption of Children Act she fought so hard to get through was never passed. When war broke out, the bill was set aside, until now. Too late for your friend."

"I know, but you've done such a good job of drawing people's attention to it."

Olive gave a small smile. "I appreciate your confidence, Alice, but have you seen the news lately? Even though we like to believe it's women and children first, the money is being spent on munitions and transport; it's going to the weapons that everyone hopes are going to win the war for us, not the innocents."

Alice recognized the determination in Olive's voice. "Why do you care so much?" she asked.

Olive's mouth twitched; the beginnings of a smile. "Let's

say I know what happens when there aren't any formal adoptions in place."

She gave Alice a meaningful look, and Alice was about to ask her what she meant when Olive said, "What information can you give me about the mother . . . or the child?"

"She's a baby, a newborn," Alice said, a lump forming in her throat. "I have the date and place of birth, and the date of the handover. Is that enough?"

"It's a start."

"She was given to a couple from London."

"That makes sense, they usually work in pairs."

"Are they real couples?"

"Sometimes, sometimes not. They might just pretend to be doting parents."

Alice's mind wandered, goose bumps tingling up her spine. "Will you help me, then?"

"All I can do is see if my contacts might know of anyone operating in the area. They do tend to work regionally, so that could be useful. And I'd like to help with your book, so I'll have a chat with my editor to see what information I can give you—on the record. The more people who know about these monsters, the better."

"Of course."

"Can I reach you at the Partridge office?"

Alice had been relaxing into her chair, smiling with relief, until with Olive's words she realized she would have to take Theo up on his offer if she was to engage Olive's help. But how would she have time while she was looking for Eadie?

"Well, Alice?"

There really wasn't an alternative. "Yes, here . . . I'll write it down." She handed Olive the slip of paper, and the two women smiled at each other.

Alice felt a stirring deep inside, not unlike the quickening she'd felt with Eadie, infused with nervousness. She had achieved what she came for: Olive's promise of help. Now she had to hope that it would be enough.

Seventeen

LONDON, MARCH 29, 1943

As Theo raced up the stairs to the boardroom, a spring in his step, he thought about the telephone call he'd just had with Virginia and her excitement when he'd recounted the events of the weekend.

He hadn't been able to refuse George's offer to be his guest in Norfolk, but it had been a resounding success; while there had been disappointingly few grouse, George's family had been faultless in their hospitality. As well as his wife and two daughters, there had been a horde of neighbors and other London visitors. Friday supper had grown into a rowdy affair that lasted until well after midnight so that their dawn hunting departure came far too soon, then luncheon rolled into another long supper. He'd captivated Virginia with his descriptions of the estate: the handsome seventeenth-century house, sandstone walls covered with ivy and wisteria; a formal garden with fragrant verbena, lavender and rose; and the kitchen garden of equal size featuring herbs he hadn't tried before, including borage, lovage and lemon thyme. Not even Walter owned such a prepossessing home.

On Sunday, Theo had been driven back to London feeling a little shabbier than on the drive up, relieved he'd accepted the Alka-Seltzer and packed breakfast offered by the butler on departure. He'd wanted to go through everything before the Monday morning meeting, and he was glad he'd spent Sunday afternoon doing just that; there were still areas he didn't understand and British terms he couldn't fathom.

George had stayed in Norfolk, but the others were in the boardroom when Theo arrived: Tommy, Emily and Ursula. And, to his surprise, Alice Cotton sat at the far side of the table. Ursula had been right about her after all, although he wondered what had changed her mind. "Good morning," he said. "And welcome back, Alice."

"Thank you, Mr. Bloom."

"Theo, please."

A cold spring air blew through the open windows, the fresh sunlight whitewashing the room, and Theo took the seat opposite Alice. It was only a few feet away yet close enough to see how her appearance had improved: blond victory rolls framed her made-up face, and she wore a smart blouse and jacket. She still looked rather pale, her features altogether more fragile than they'd appeared in the café, but perhaps that was just the contrast of her navy eyes against her delicate English skin.

Ursula brandished a large cardboard poster. "Ta-da!" she

announced, holding it upright on the table. It featured an assortment of images of children: innocence caught in some expressions, others with beaming smiles, and emotive photographs in front of ruined homes.

"So, what do we have here?" Tommy asked.

"It's the new mock-up of the cover for *Women and Children First*," she said with a smile. "Now that Alice has agreed to come back part-time, the content will be ready by the start of June—won't it, Alice?"

"Um, yes . . . that's right," she replied, sounding less than confident.

"But I've got the print run booked for early July, so that's cutting it a bit fine, isn't it?" said a worried-looking Tommy.

"I think that should work," Alice said, exchanging a look with Ursula. "The typesetting is being outsourced, but everything else is in-house. The schedule is under our control."

Theo hoped she was right.

"And what is the content, exactly?" Emily asked, arms folded across her chest.

"Well," Alice said, "as you know, it was going to be about ordinary women and children in extraordinary situations on the home front."

"We're all in extraordinary situations, surely?" Emily said.

"Yes, although some of us are more ordinary than others," Ursula said with a straight face.

"Alice, perhaps you can elaborate for us," Theo said, smiling at the banter.

"We already have interviews with families, accounts of children thought missing who have been miraculously found, and stories of children placed with new families"—Alice hesitated and caught Ursula's eye—"and then there are the stories about children who have been stolen and sold."

"What?" Emily said with a look of horror. "You're including those in the book?"

Alice nodded. "We're planning to."

"That's different than what you told us before you left, and I for one think it's rather bad form. I mean, who wants to read about that? It's frightful!"

"Lots of people do," Alice snapped back, "because it's been happening all over the country, and the government is soon to pass an act in an effort to stop it."

Emily looked around at the others. "I'd have thought we wanted good news stories, uplifting ones that make people want to pick up the book, not throw it in the bin!"

"There will be lots of those too," Alice said, "but we can't ignore what's going on right under our noses. We need to draw people's attention to it, and—"

"Thank you, Alice," Theo said, concerned about her growing agitation. "I'm sure they would all be very worthy stories, and perhaps they can be included."

"Are you sure about your sources?" Tommy asked. "After all, we do seem to be spending a disproportionate amount of time and money on this book. We need to know it's real, and worth it." His eyes darted from Alice to Theo.

"Yes, Tommy, I understand," she said, straightening in her chair. "We're working with a good journalist—an exceptional one, in fact—who is bringing us valuable material and has spent her career fighting for the rights of these children."

"So, she's got an ax to grind," Emily murmured, "or papers to sell."

"On the contrary," Alice said, "Olive is just a damn fine journalist!"

Theo finally understood what Ursula and George had meant about her; she was so passionate that he could tell how much she loved her work. And she clearly knew what she was talking about: she gave them an impressive rundown of the information she'd gathered. By the time she'd finished, they were all soberly staring at her.

Theo cleared his throat. "These stories have a huge emotional impact, and you've done terrific research, but why include them in this book?"

"Isn't it obvious?" Ursula said, looking perplexed.

"Children are the innocent victims of this war," said Alice, "and they have no voice, these stolen kids in particular. Why not incorporate inspiring stories of them being reunited with their families? The book will be optimistic, full of happy endings. A way of giving children their voices back."

"I see," Theo said thoughtfully. They all knew what a gamble they were taking on this new book, and he still wasn't convinced. In spite of Alice's passion, he wasn't persuaded that she could pull it off. He picked up the mock cover, studying the faces of the children: a curly-haired infant; two school-aged children, a boy and girl of about seven or eight; and a boy of sixteen or so in a zookeeper's outfit.

Alice pointed to the two school-aged children. "They're Martha and Duncan—their friend was killed by an unexploded bomb while they were playing. They've founded their own junior wardens group, patrolling playgrounds to make sure kids know where it's safe to play."

Theo was starting to see what Alice was aiming for—but would it work?

"And that's Christopher," she said, pointing to the teenager, "one of the lads from Eton who works as a boy-keeper at the London Zoo. He's got some wonderful stories to share, about the animals and the other boy-keepers."

Theo nodded. Yes, he could see it now: extraordinary stories of ordinary families. It wasn't likely to rival *Bomber Command*, but it might do well enough. He tried to use his imagination as Alice continued to describe the stories—until a heavy logbook in the center of the table caught his eye. It was their record of all the papermaking stocks they had to list; materials that had become scarce because wood pulp could no longer be sourced from Norway and esparto grass came from North Africa, which was now controlled by France.

"Let's think about it," he said, studiously avoiding Alice's gaze. "Let me talk to George, and we'll make a decision for when we next come together."

"I'll support whatever decision you make," Tommy said.

"Me too," said Emily.

Alice and Ursula exchanged a puzzled look, then they both reluctantly nodded their agreement.

"Thanks," Theo said, "I appreciate it." He summoned a smile as he turned to meet Alice's curious expression, but it felt hollow. The hurt was clearly visible to him in the depths of her beautiful blue eyes, but he knew that whatever he and George decided, he needed to think of the New York office first and foremost—and getting home to his fiancée and parents.

Eighteen

LONDON, MARCH 31, 1943

When Alice arrived back at Penny's after work, she heard her friend's laughter and followed it through the hallway into what Penny called her "second salon," where the community book group was under way.

Penny had given Alice a rundown on the personalities involved: a warden, a serviceman, a retired major, a librarian and a civil servant, all of whom were mothers or fathers, or brothers or sisters, or uncles or aunts. Penny was convinced they might be able to furnish Alice with more stories for the book. Alice was grateful to her friend, even though she was still anxiously waiting to hear if Theo and George would go ahead with the new version.

She didn't know what she would do if they rejected it. She had no other leads on Eadie, and she'd almost forgotten her daughter's face. She could still feel the barely there weight of her in her arms, the shape of her imprinted on her skin, yet she didn't know how long it would last. Even her body was losing signs of her daughter: her stomach flattening, stretched skin resuming its elasticity, and her milk reabsorbed. The bleeding was reduced to spotting, but still the baby blues and the sleeplessness were reminders that she was a mother now.

Although Alice expected the book group to be there, the sight of the darkened room, the shadowy bookshelves and the unknown faces distorted by the trembling candlelight took her by surprise. They were assembled in a horseshoe of chairs, the remnants of an afternoon tea on two of the café tables. Alongside the assorted crockery and crumbs were their copies of *How Green Was My Valley*.

Trusting in her friend and her friend's husband, Michael, had been good for many reasons, not least of which was Penny's idea about the book group. Another was because of how supported and grateful she felt by Michael's calm acceptance of her and for putting a roof over her head.

Penny was still in her work clothes—a dirty gray smock—and frizzy haired as she stood up, eagerly gesturing to Alice in the doorway. "So, everyone! This is Alice."

Alice tried to look as open and friendly as she could as she smiled at each of them, trying to distinguish who was who based on Penny's earlier descriptions. The young woman with milky white skin and auburn hair must surely be Helena, the librarian. Then Rex, the friendly warden with a shiny red scar across the left side of his face. Beside him was a nervous ball of energy, Marjorie, the civil servant who volunteered to repair books for the services. Then Terrance, the youngest member,

Oxford-educated and on sick leave from the Royal Air Force. And, of course, the bespectacled Henry, dark-haired and intense, just as she'd imagined the retired major to be.

"Alice is a good friend of mine," said Penny. "She works at a publishing house and has offered to get us books for our group." There was a murmur of appreciation before Penny carried on. "Alice is working on a new book, a very important book," she said, growing serious, "and she'd like to ask for our help. I thought it was the least we could do to show our gratitude."

Penny sat down, leaving Alice standing by herself, nervously rubbing her hands together. "Hello, and it's nice to meet you all. I've heard a lot about you."

"Some good, I hope," Rex said, and chuckled.

"Shush," Marjorie said with a frown. "Let her finish. Go on, dear."

"Fire away!" Henry added.

Alice cleared her throat and looked at Penny. Then she bent down to retrieve the newspaper articles from their folder and place them on the table. She had spent hours poring over these cuttings. Several of the accused baby farmers' names appeared more than once, and although she'd tracked most of them down and ruled them out as the people responsible for taking Eadie, there was one couple Olive had warned against trying to trace in one of their off-the-record conversations: "The Pritchards are not only evil but very dangerous." The journalist had promised to help, but she wanted to run it by legal affairs at the paper first. There was no telling how long that might take—it could be any number of days or weeks.

"First of all, thank you for letting me join your group."

Alice paused. "I'm working on a book called *Women and Children First*—and, well, it's about just that really. We're collecting stories of remarkable relationships, bravery, family reunions, you know the kind I mean . . . to do with women and children, the uplifting ones. Stories of battling the odds and winning." She hoped that even if George and Theo turned down her initial proposal, she would be able to convince them if she just gathered enough good material. She'd pinned clippings to a board that dominated her office, a decoupage of children's faces. But Theo was right, there had to be an overwhelming optimism to the book, the triumph of human nature, and she wasn't sure they had that yet—and she was running out of time.

"So how can we help you?" Helena asked.

"Well, first, by putting me in touch with anyone you know who would be willing to share their experiences."

Rex and Helena nodded, but Marjorie just listened.

"Can you give us an example?" Rex asked.

"All right . . . well, did any of you hear about the boy who was saved from a burning restaurant just before Christmas? A daring rescue by a Polish refugee. It would be that kind of heroic act—a real story, not fiction. One where we would include pictures of him and his family being reunited, and the rescuer, of course."

Helena tilted her head as if she was giving it some consideration.

"Other stories we're looking for are those that might not have such happy endings, ones about children who have been taken by baby farmers—"

"By whom?" Henry asked.

"Baby farmers," Alice said louder, "like the ones in these articles." She passed the clippings around—stories about children being shipped overseas without any checks or safeguards, photographs of railway stations where infants were swapped, and of notorious maternity homes selling babies to adoptive parents and earning fees from both the parents and the birth mothers—and her heart beat a little faster as she watched their expressions change. Helena shifted uncomfortably in her seat, while Marjorie chewed her lip as she read. Terrance's feet tapped nervously on the floor. Rex leaned closer, straining to read the print. Their involvement made her feel that it wasn't just about Eadie anymore, that they were investing their support to help all the poor helpless children who were being traded like the Lend-Lease food.

When they had all finished, Alice said, "I wonder if in your neighborhoods, or among your families and friends, you might know of anyone this has happened to."

"I say," Rex said, "I've an idea."

"What?" Marjorie said, head bobbing up.

"Well," he said, shifting to the edge of his seat, hands clasped together, elbows on his legs as he leaned further in, "it seems us wardens know our neighborhoods better than most . . . and who and what goes on there." He widened his eyes at Alice.

"And?" Helena said.

"I'm just saying, there's a lot that goes unsaid but not unnoticed, if you know what I mean." He tapped the side of his nose with his forefinger, then gave them each a purposeful stare.

"Can you elaborate for us, Rex?" Penny asked.

"Of course. I know most of the streets and what goes on,

and it strikes me that most of the other wardens would be the same. It would only take me having a word with some of them to see if anyone knows of anything untoward in their area."

Alice caught Penny's eye and smiled, feeling hopeful at this new avenue to explore. "Thank you, Rex," she said. "That's a marvelous idea. You've been most helpful."

"It doesn't seem right to me," Terrance said with a sniff.

"What do you mean?" Helena asked.

"Isn't there some code of conduct, something wardens have to sign to protect our privacy? I mean, what goes on in our homes should stay in our homes, shouldn't it?"

"What have you got to hide, then?" Rex asked crossly.

"I don't have anything to hide, but I also value my privacy," Terrance said, looking affronted.

"I understand what you mean," Alice said. "Remember the posters: CARELESS TALK COSTS LIVES? But we also have a moral obligation, don't you think? It's our duty to be vigilant."

"Exactly," said Penny. "It's our duty to look out for spies. And baby farmers."

"So, you'll talk to the other wardens from the different areas?" Alice asked Rex.

"I'll certainly talk to the ones I know."

"And how can the rest of us help?" Helena asked.

"By talking to your friends and family," said Alice. "Ask if there's anything unusual happening in your area—couples with babies or children they didn't have before." Her energy was ebbing away, and she sat down. "Thanks, all of you."

"Can we get on and talk about the book now?" Marjorie said with a sigh. She picked up her edition of *How Green Was My Valley*, the cover image bearing the stoic faces of miners.

"In a moment," Penny said. "Alice?"

The room suddenly felt quite stuffy; the windows were closed, the blackout blinds drawn, and steam from the kettle had heated the limited air. Alice undid her top button and wiped the hair from her face, then took a large gulp of water. She felt faint and couldn't keep track of what they were all saying.

"Are you all right, love?" Rex's voice echoed distantly.

Penny's face loomed in front of her before it began to spin, and everything went black.

When Alice came to, she was lying on the sofa in Penny's empty living room and straining to hear whispers in the hallway outside. After a while the door opened, and Penny and Michael came in.

"Saint-John's-wort tea," her friend said as she handed Alice a mug and sat in the chair opposite, Michael perching on the armrest. "It should help relax you."

The steam rose quickly and filled her nostrils with a bittersweet smell, and Alice placed the mug down on the carpet. "I'm so sorry."

"Don't be silly. You've nothing to apologize for. But, Alice, we've been talking, and we think you need to see a doctor first thing in the morning, then go back to the police."

Alice pulled herself up to sit. "There's no point—"

"Yes, there is. I'm not going to take no for an answer," Penny said sternly. "Can't you see? You're not well enough for all this. You've done great work looking for Eadie, and now you have to let the authorities handle it."

"I told you, they'll never find her, that's why I have to keep looking. And thanks to you, we might have found another way, through the warden network."

Penny and Michael exchanged a look before she turned back to Alice. "Is that the real reason?"

"What do you mean?"

"Well, I have to ask . . . have you told the police who the father is?"

Alice looked away. "I don't see that it matters to anyone else," she said sharply. "And there's a chance his family might want to keep Eadie . . . then I'd be certain to lose her."

"Surely it's worth taking a chance," Michael suggested gently. "Better to risk finding and losing her again—at least you'd know she was safe."

"It really makes no difference to the police."

"But it *might* help if they knew," said Penny.

Alice grew quiet. How could she explain to her friends how women like her were treated? It was all right for Penny—Michael was a loving husband and father, she was respectable—but there was little time or pity extended for women like Alice. Giving Rupert's identity to the police wouldn't help them find Eadie; it would just mean that there was a chance that he and his family could make a claim on her.

Penny glanced at Michael, who shrugged, and she pressed her lips together. "Well, thanks to your performance the book group left very motivated, so hopefully they'll come back with some stories."

Alice looked at her friend and smiled weakly. "Yes, I hope so."

Nineteen

LONDON, APRIL 5, 1943

When Alice arrived in the boardroom, she smiled briefly at Theo before taking a seat next to Ursula. The women glanced at each other, Alice clearly as anxious as a cat in an air raid with her desire to know about the fate of her book project, but George unhurriedly took a piece of paper from his pocket and cleared his throat.

"I've had a letter from Rupert."

"What does he say?" Tommy asked.

"How is he, George?" Emily interrupted.

"As you know we haven't heard from him in quite some time—" George broke off, his voice hoarse.

"Can you tell how he's coping?" Emily said insistently.

George unfolded the thin sheet of paper and pushed his spectacles up the bridge of his nose as he looked down.

"He's all right as far as I can tell. He asks after all of you," he said, looking around the table, gaze lingering for a fraction on Alice. "And he says he's looking forward to reading our new titles when he comes back. He mentions the possibility of some leave in coming months—"

There was a murmur of excitement and George's broad smile was replicated around the table, except for Alice, who listened benignly as George recounted the remaining contents of the brief letter.

"So there you have it. And with Mussolini's weakening position, and the Allies' advance into Tunisia, let's hope that the tide is turning and that he will soon be home."

George turned to Theo and caught him off guard since Theo shared the widely held belief that anticipated the war continuing, and a 1944 campaign.

"Yes, George. Let's hope so," he said, hesitating. "In which case, hadn't we better get on with publishing some of those books for him to read?"

It had the desired effect, and George laughed.

"Then we're all agreed; time spent waiting on a rooftop or in a shelter, or an aircraft hangar, could be better spent with a book," George said cheerfully. "The question is, which one?" He looked at Theo.

"We'll get to that in a moment," Theo said, avoiding Alice's stare, "but first of all, Tommy has an update for us."

The production controller nodded. "Our biggest worry has been about the board and paper, but with the success of salvage and pulping this has temporarily abated. However"—Tommy paused to look around—"the type metal for printers is growing ever more scarce—even the standard type usually kept for reprints is being taken down and melted. We've had to do this ourselves on a few of our titles."

"How scarce?" Ursula asked.

"Like the dodo—zinc, copper, brass, all the materials used for block-making and cover-stamping are virtually extinct."

"What does that mean?" Alice asked worriedly.

"It means there's little chance of us, or many publishers, for that matter, printing illustrated books until the war ends. Especially ones like *Women and Children First* with screened half-tone photographs."

"We can use line blocks," Ursula said.

"Or we could just have a cover," Alice suggested, looking more animated. "We don't need pictures inside, we could make do."

"We can afford a four-page spread inside," said Tommy, "but it would only be for this title. It's all a trade-off. Is it a sacrifice we're prepared to make?"

"It's one book," Ursula said, holding his gaze.

Theo was watching them thoughtfully, keeping his opinion to himself.

"She's right," George said, "it's one book. But each book deprives the war effort of metal. We have to decide if that one book is really worth it." He turned to Alice. "I've looked through your proposal and given it a great deal of thought. And we've talked about it," he added, glancing at Theo. "We think it's worth it. Don't we, Theo?"

"Indeed, we do, George. It's going to be the major release in the new season titles—if we can get it ready by then."

He'd expected Alice to be more excited by the news, but her smile was fleeting before she grew thoughtful again.

"So, Alice, will it be written in time?" Theo asked as he leaned back in his chair, cradling a cup of coffee between his palms.

"Yes," she said firmly, "but are *you* going to be able to pull everything else together in time?"

"You couldn't be in better hands, Alice," George said. "Theo has learned a great deal from the Armed Services Editions. They're in production now."

"That's right," Theo said, "they'll be shipped to the troops in September. And it hasn't been easy. Our skeptics said the paper was such poor quality it would fall apart, and that the glue would never hold when it got to the tropics, but we adjusted the prototypes."

"What did you do?" Ursula asked.

"We've used staples, and the paper is twice the quality of that used for newspapers. Everything is designed to make them withstand the harshest conditions, so they can be read and shared by the men again and again." Theo leaned in, resting his arms on the table. "If we want this series to become collectible, the paperbacks need to be able to withstand the same handling and conditions as hardbacks. Right, George?"

George nodded, giving a faint smile. He appeared to be following their conversation, but Theo noticed the drumbeat of his fingers on the table and his frown lines deepening. The months of concern over Rupert and the business had clearly taken their toll, and Theo felt a wave of concern for the older man. Unlike Walter, George shared Theo's view that books should be used as weapons in the war of ideas—Theo just needed to help him find a way to carry on doing that.

Twenty

LONDON, APRIL 8, 1943

Every desk in the production office had been taken over as work began in earnest on the book: interviews were being scheduled and stories written up, and a photographer had been booked for the four-page spread. But Alice was immune to the excitement that surrounded her; she found herself staring into space, unable to concentrate.

"The War Economy Agreement is on the poster over there," Ursula said, pointing at the back wall. "Alice, are you all right? Have you been listening to a word I've said?"

"Yes, of course," she replied, with a cursory glance at the poster. "The poster is over there, and I'm fine, thank you."

The truth was that she was far from it. On the one hand, working on the book was the best way she could gather information on baby farmers; on the other, she was working so hard that she couldn't follow up on any leads. She'd been forced to take things slowly in recent days, partly by Penny and Michael—no more visits to the foundling hospitals or any child welfare organizations—and she knew that any information from the book group would take a while to trickle in. She'd had a medical checkup and been told she was physically recovering as well as could be expected under the circumstances, but it was her feelings at being back in the office that she hadn't counted on—being faced with George's likeness to Rupert and all the memories of the past couple of years. Now she was torn between the desire to repay the trust that George and Theo had placed in her, and her certainty of the need to leave Partridge as soon as she could. The American had won them over, and she could see why: it wasn't just his support and hard work, it was his integrity. And that was yet another reason she wanted to remove herself—she'd found herself distractedly thinking about him, and she couldn't afford to let that happen.

She tried to focus on the galleys in front of her, pen poised as she read through the Patricia Reece novel. Light pooled around the document as her hand moved down the page, stopping at each line as she methodically checked the punctuation and grammar.

"How are you getting on?" Ursula asked.

"Only another couple of hours, if all goes well."

"Have you got the right measurements for the margins? And remember the new obligations for typography and binding."

"Yes, I know."

"What are they, then?" Ursula said half-seriously.

"Type area not less than fifty-five percent of the printed

page, no more than four introductory pages." Alice squinted again at the poster on the back wall. The print was barely legible from where she sat, but she knew it listed all the wartime requirements.

When she looked back at her work, the proofreader symbols appeared as unfamiliar as Arabic script, and she realized she had mistaken colons for semicolons and inserted hyphens instead of transposing words.

How can I be here when I still have no idea where my daughter is?

Ursula leaned forward, touching her forearm lightly. "Alice, are you really all right?"

"Yes, of course I am. Why shouldn't I be?"

"You're crying."

Alice brushed her fingers across her cheeks, wiping away the tears. "Oh."

"What's the matter?"

"Nothing. I'm fine."

"Oh, really? You don't look fine."

"I am," Alice said, more tears springing from her eyes.

"What is it, Alice? I know there's something wrong. You haven't been the same since . . . well, since you came back. I don't understand—I thought you'd be so pleased that the book's going ahead."

"It's nothing."

"Doesn't look like nothing to me," Ursula said, keeping her hand lightly on her arm. "Let me help. At least let me try."

Alice's fingers played with the edge of her sleeve, running back and forth across the seams, but she stopped as soon as Ursula noticed.

A moment passed before Alice said, "I really admire your strength, your courage."

"What makes you say that?"

"It just seems as if nothing bad has ever happened to you, like you've never been touched by sadness."

Ursula laughed. "Well, you know that's not true."

"I'm sorry," she said immediately. How stupid of her. She knew all about Ursula's estrangement from her family and her frequent spells of loneliness and depression. "You're right, there is something," Alice said, and sniffed, her eyes stinging. "I haven't been entirely honest with you."

"What is it?"

"I've not told you the truth . . . about the baby."

"Yes?"

"It's just that . . ." Alice hesitated. She was on the verge of telling Ursula about Eadie when a memory emerged of a conversation in which Ursula had claimed she would never have a child. At the time Alice had brushed the comment away, but Ursula had been adamant, and now Alice didn't want to be insensitive a second time. She also cautioned herself against sharing the truth unnecessarily. "My cousin's baby hasn't been well, and it's not been easy with Mum since we fell out. I think it's all just got to me."

Ursula's face softened. "I'm not surprised. I think you've done marvelously. Living with all that chaos at Penny's too. Are you sure you won't come and stay with me?"

Alice loved Ursula's home, with its salvaged furniture and bohemian décor. It was a perfect reflection of her personality and Hungarian heritage, richly decorated and full of warmth. But of course Alice needed to stay with Penny and Michael, as they knew the truth. "I'm happy where I am, but thank you," she said, tears falling freely now. "You're a good friend."

That was still true, but a gulf had opened between them because of her secret, and soon she would let Ursula down by abandoning Partridge again. She felt trapped.

"What are we going to do with you?" Ursula said as she rested her chin on her upturned palm. "I know," she said abruptly, "you should go to the Foyle luncheon next week in my place. It will do you good."

The luncheons were a monthly highlight, and tickets were hard to come by. As a junior staff member, Alice had never been given the opportunity to attend until now. She appreciated the thought, and Ursula's enthusiasm, but it was totally out of the question. "Getting our book finished, that will do me good," she said, wiping her eyes on her sleeve. "No, you must go."

"Absolutely not, I've already made up my mind. And it will give you an opportunity to talk to Theo about the book—see if you can talk him into a few more photos."

An afternoon away from searching for Eadie, in the company of Theo, was the last thing Alice wanted, but she didn't know how to say no to her friend.

Twenty-one

LONDON, APRIL 15, 1943

"Are you hungry?" Theo asked Alice, as the gray cornices and turrets of Piccadilly flashed past. The rain grew heavier, bouncing noisily off the roof and hood of their black cab.

"A little," she said, "although I've heard the speaker outshines the food at these luncheons."

Theo smiled, feeling his mustache curve up against his cheeks. Over the past week he'd been spending more time with Alice, and she kept managing to surprise him with her perception and knowledge. Her quirky way of looking at the world was so different from that of anyone else he knew, especially Virginia. Even her clothes were original, her tight-fitting emerald green jacket and flared navy skirt unlike anything he'd seen other British women wear. Virginia would probably have thought her unsophisticated, but he saw her as inventive.

Today her classic pearl earrings were her nod to conventionality, and the only similarity he'd noticed so far between her and his fiancée.

He said, still smiling, "There's likely to be several courses, you know."

"I'm not sure I'll be able to make it through them all," she said, head turned away as she gazed out the window.

Theo had been delighted when Ursula suggested Alice accompany him, but she didn't seem quite as enthusiastic. Either that or she was nervous about the event, since she hadn't stopped fidgeting in her seat, folding one leg over the other and then uncrossing them again. Not that he minded admiring her long legs; it was difficult not to stare, especially when she was gazing off in the other direction.

"The speaker can go on for hours," he said, forcing himself to look away.

"You sound like you've been to one of these before," she said, finally turning toward him.

"They hold similar events in New York. That's where I met Christina."

"Is she as eccentric as people say she is?"

Christina Foyle was the daughter of William Foyle, co-founder of Foyles bookshops, and she'd started holding the luncheons more than a decade earlier to bring together readers, writers and thinkers. It was well known that she'd written to Hitler to offer to buy books written by Jewish authors after the Nazis burned thousands, and apparently she'd received a reply.

"She brings together remarkable and unusual people. I think that speaks for itself." He smiled warmly, very much doubting that Alice had met anyone like Christina; or that Christina had met anyone quite like Alice.

As they neared Park Lane, the Dorchester came into view, its pale stone exterior transformed into an unexpected waterfall of flowers, wrought-iron balconies cascading with red and white. The entrance was a crescent of verdant shrubs, the drive lined with topiary, and urns of ivy sat on either side of the lobby doors. Only the sandbags stacked against the windows gave an indication that the times were anything but ordinary.

"Impressive, isn't it?" Theo said, noticing her stare.

"Yes . . . and somewhat of a surprise."

"Why's that?"

"Well, most Londoners are getting rid of their flowers in favor of edibles, but this place looks like it's growing enough for everyone!"

Theo laughed. "It's magnificent, though. And a lot like the architecture in Manhattan. These great concrete monoliths are everywhere you look now."

"George told me it's hard to impress an American, so I'm glad we've managed to do that," she said with a straight face. "You know Eisenhower stayed here last year. Tommy said they're considering naming a suite after him."

"Gee, that's really something. I read that almost half the hotel is underground, the perfect shelter." His gaze locked on the building. "Must be one of the safest places in London," he said, remembering the reason he was there—to meet important figures in the trade and the government; to work out how to improve Partridge's position and supplies.

"Who did you say today's guest speaker is again?" she asked, glancing at her watch.

"Graham Greene."

"Oh yes, that's right. I met him once—he works in Fitzroy as an air raid warden."

"You don't say."

"Yes, that's why his prose is so rich and detailed, and why he's so popular with the soldiers."

When the cab stopped, a doorman in a brown-and-gold suit and top hat opened their door and sheltered them from the rain with an oversized umbrella, escorting them up the stairs into the sleek marble lobby. Theo led the way toward the back of the hotel, passing through the Promenade, a spectacular room transformed into an intimate dining space by decorative columns, gilt filigree and ornate moldings. Guests sat on high-backed upholstered chairs and chintz banquettes, while a professional musician played Schubert on a grand piano. Oversized lamps, floor-to-ceiling mirrors and sweeping velvet curtains added to the magnificence of a room equal to any he'd seen in New York. They passed white linen tables with cake stands five levels high, full of pastries so petite they looked too dainty to eat. All the way down the room, lacquered consoles held gigantic vases of flowers from where waiters balanced trays of silverware.

When they reached the doors to the ballroom, Alice stopped to stare; they were decorated with sculpted pewter flowers, delicate pearl embellishments in the center of the petals unlike anything Theo had ever seen. Then he opened one of the doors, and the ornate mirrored entrance of the ballroom came into view—and, with it, a dazzling blast of sunlight and a torrent of conversation. He held the door wide, smiling discreetly as Alice gaped at the Corinthian columns with their regal marble and gold leaf, and the painted walls. He had to admit to being impressed too; everywhere they looked, plinths held oriental vases overflowing with fresh blooms, and Venetian-style mirrors adorned elegant ivory walls. "Shall we?" he asked Alice.

She gave him a dazed smile and walked in.

He soon found the board that displayed a seating plan in exquisite calligraphy, and he spent a few moments running through the names to see if the people he had hoped would attend were present. He wouldn't recognize them by sight, but if he knew their tables he could go around making introductions as soon as the speeches were over.

They were the first guests at their table. He pulled out Alice's chair and she sat down, smoothing her skirt and placing her bag and gas mask over the seat back. He still had trouble remembering to carry one everywhere, but Londoners were all used to it.

After he sat next to Alice, he glanced around the half-full ballroom, nodding discreetly to a woman standing in a group a short distance away. "That's Christina Foyle," he said in a hushed tone. She was of average height and build with light-brown hair that had been teased into a shape both higher and fuller than seemed necessary for a lunchtime function. Even from where they sat, he could see her ears and neck glistening with diamonds—too many, in fact, and he could tell that Alice didn't approve either.

She looked at her watch again, gripping her wrist as though there was somewhere else she needed to be.

"Mixed crowd," he said, leaning closer and catching the light floral scent of her perfume.

"Yes, I suppose it is," she said, glancing around. "Who do you think they are—politicians, industry leaders, literary aficionados?"

"All of the above," he replied, gazing more intently at the assembled men and women, the servicemen and civilians.

The next time he looked at Alice, her chin was tilted up at him, an expression of curiosity on her face. "I've always wondered what it's really like, New York. Not the version they show off for visitors, but the real one that you live in."

"There are writers who could do it justice far better than me."

"You could try."

"Wine?" he asked, as a waiter appeared at their side. She shook her head, and Theo nodded toward his glass, which the waiter filled as he talked. "It's an incredible city—I mean, London is beautiful, but New York, well, there's an energy to it. Even walking the few blocks to work is invigorating. And visiting the dockyards when one of the ships is coming in—that's positively euphoric." He smiled. "Really, though, it's spectacular, especially when the dockworkers and their families are all lined up on the quay, waving flags and streamers. It's the gateway to America, but it feels like the center of the world."

"It looks that way in photos too."

"Maybe you'll visit one day."

"I don't think that's very likely," she said dismissively. "Tell me about where you live."

"It's all right if you don't mind traffic jams. It's on the west side. Manhattan is made up of hundreds of neighborhoods, so you don't need to go far to find a grocery store or a restaurant."

"Sounds convenient."

"It's more than that. They're like villages—you find your tribe, and you stick to it."

"I like the sound of that," she said, playing with the stem of her empty glass.

"There's an area known as Book Row, where all the bookstores are, dozens of them. It's like Charing Cross Road, but much, much bigger. It would take you a week to work your way around them. It's an enclave for booksellers and book lovers."

"Maybe I should come, then. Where is it?"

"Fourth Avenue, between Union Square and Astor Place."

"I've never heard of those places."

"Well, it's crazy. There are seven blocks of bookstores."

"That does sound crazy."

"There're a lot of books in the world!"

"I don't even think a lifetime of reading would be enough to get through just one shop."

"I guess not." Theo took another sip of wine. "There's one store that sells only cookbooks—that's on the corner of Astor. Then there's At the Sign of the Sparrow, which sells just theater books."

"That's marvelous!"

Alice seemed much less anxious now, delighted by his descriptions of Book Row. He could see she immediately understood that it was unlike anywhere else in the world: store upon dusty store with stands spilling onto the street—Lowenstein's, Mosk's, the Strand—all peopled with fascinating, eccentric intellectuals and bibliophiles, students and writers. She laughed when he told her that Friendlies had the unfriendliest owners.

"Charing Cross Road just isn't going to seem the same

now," Alice said with a rare genuine smile. But then she stole another look at her watch, and he wondered again where she really wanted to be. She caught his eye, and her face flushed. "You haven't told me how you got involved with publishing," she said quickly, before he had the chance to ask what was going on.

"I was a student in thirty-three when Hitler burned the books. 'Literary holocaust,' the press called it. We were all horrified." Tens of thousands of books had been destroyed at the Bebelplatz in Berlin, setting off a chain of similar events around Germany. Millions of books were annihilated, and it had caused outrage around the world. "I'd always loved books, but that was when I understood the power they held to alter lives, and history."

"I remember . . ." Alice murmured, deep sorrow in her eyes.

"I don't know what happened here, but Americans reacted by donating millions of books to the armed services. I remember standing on the steps of the New York Public Library and watching as all these famous New Yorkers and celebrities turned up to make donations. It was really something." He broke into a smile, the memory rekindling the passion he'd felt. "Some wars can be won in the mind as well as on the battlefield."

Most of the tables were full now. Christina Foyle stood up, the crowd grew quiet, and the opening address began, then a discreet army of waitstaff filed in with the first course of fresh English asparagus and hollandaise. He couldn't ignore how Alice kept glancing at her watch and fidgeting. She ate quickly and was sociable enough with the other guests, but he found he couldn't sustain a conversation with her. Then, halfway through Graham Greene's speech, she stared at the door and shifted in her seat.

He leaned close. "Is everything all right?"

"I'm sorry, Theo, but I'm afraid I'm going to have to go." She slid to the edge of her seat, grabbing her gas mask and bag. "I just remembered something terribly important that I need to do."

"Surely it can wait?"

"I'm afraid not—it's something I should have paid more attention to before. Entirely my fault."

"Do you want me to come with you?"

"No, thank you. It's something I have to do on my own."

And then she was gone.

It was still raining when the luncheon finished, but Theo decided to walk back to the office. He wanted some fresh air as he reflected on the valuable introductions he'd made and conversations he'd had. His pocket was full of business cards, and he'd seen Sir Duncan, so the luncheon had been a success from a business point of view. But for some reason, he felt deflated.

He sidestepped another puddle, his hat pulled on tightly and his collar upturned as he kept his head down, thinking about his conversation with Alice. Her interest in his life had surprised him, yet she'd been so unwilling to talk about her own. She'd only become animated when they spoke about the local publishing industry, telling him how it had started alongside St. Paul's and Paternoster Row way back in the sixteenth century, until one night in 1940 when seventeen publishing offices were destroyed. She spoke with sadness as she told him how it had changed the landscape of the British book trade forever. Duncan Sutherland's painting *Twisted Girders* had become synonymous with that tragic night and was circulated widely in newspapers and magazines; Theo was familiar with the image.

The only time Alice spoke about herself was when she talked about her favorite parts of London, and he realized he was walking one of them now, tracing her recommended route through Mayfair back to Russell Square. The journey stretched to places he'd not yet visited; it took him through the streets and alleyways of Soho, past fabric shops and department stores, picture-book houses and street traders, and he felt the pulse of the London she'd described.

Theo's footsteps quickened the closer he got to the office, as he kept returning to the same question: where had she gone so urgently, and had she returned to work?

He left the taller commercial buildings and shops of the main road behind, making his way along the adjacent streets, and his thoughts turned to home and the difficult conversation he'd had with Virginia the night before. It was hard enough to make an international call, let alone limit their conversation to five minutes, and six days had gone by without any contact. Last night she'd told him how much she missed him, but when he'd echoed the words they hadn't rung true. Why hadn't they felt sincere? He reached for a recent memory of being with Virginia: at the waterfront, where they often stood hand in hand as they watched trading ships and passenger boats weave across the harbor.

By the time he reached Russell Square, the rain had

stopped, the sun leapfrogging through the clouds. His imaginary walk with Virginia had taken them along the wooden boardwalk as fishing boats unloaded their hauls and transatlantic planes skimmed the surface of the Hudson as they landed. He could see the sunlight dance across the rippling water, the ships and lighters crisscrossing on their inter-harbor runs, but to his surprise he wasn't hand in hand with Virginia anymore—it was Alice by his side.

Theo stopped walking and ran a hand across his face, the roughness of one day's stubble already coming through. What was he thinking? He told himself he had briefly mistaken his professional admiration for something more. He now understood why the team had fought to get Alice back: her clear-eyed honesty was helping them to create finely nuanced books that made a positive difference in these turbulent times.

As he looked at the brass plaque bearing the Partridge name, something caught in his throat. He was finding it increasingly difficult to contemplate Walter's threat to shut the office down when it really felt as if they were close to turning things around. Hopefully they would soon accomplish that, and then he would return to New York and put Alice out of his mind.

Twenty-two

Olive had left the *Daily Mail* office by the time Alice arrived, so she hurried straight down to the basement, nearly tripping on the stairs in her rush. The luncheon had dragged on far too long, and even with Graham Greene as speaker Alice would have gladly passed it up. A note had been delivered to her office from Olive just before she'd left, saying the journalist had news but not giving any other details. There had been no progress for nearly a week, and no communication from the wardens either, and now this. Olive had asked her to come in after the luncheon, but it seemed she might be too late.

The underground library was darker than usual, the overcast skies creating deeper shadows in the sparse rooms, and the desk was unattended. Alice waited anxiously for Elizabeth to appear, desperately hoping Olive had good news.

Footsteps approached. "Alice, I'm so sorry," said Elizabeth, walking out of the gloom. "I hope you haven't been waiting long?"

"Not at all, it's fine. I got a note from Olive . . . You have something for me?"

"Ah, yes. Here it is." The librarian reached for a pile of manila folders and handed the top one to Alice with a smile. "How's the book coming along?"

"Very well, thank you. I—"

The lights flickered, and a rumbling grew louder as the sound of an Underground train closed in around them, transforming the space into an eerie cavern. They looked at each other, and Alice shuddered as they waited motionless for the noise to fade and the light to be restored, Elizabeth's pale eyes still visible through the near darkness. "You always wonder, don't you," she whispered, "if they're coming back."

Alice knew she was referring to the Luftwaffe and the raids that were still so fresh in their minds.

"I know . . . but we're okay." Alice squeezed Elizabeth's arm reassuringly. "And thank you. I really appreciate this."

She left quickly, before the librarian had the chance to reply, and settled at a table in the adjoining room. A handwritten note from Olive was clipped inside the folder: *I thought this might be of interest for the book. P.S. It's been cleared for use.*

Alice felt completely deflated and then a flash of anger; all this time she'd believed Olive could give her leads, but these were just articles she'd already seen.

Only when she calmed down did she realize the misunderstanding was entirely hers: these were clippings she hadn't seen before. She scanned them, desperately searching for a new clue, the musty newspaper reminding her of the time and distance that separated her from Eadie.

What had Olive noticed that she'd missed? She'd spent days down here researching all she could about baby farmers.

Another slip of paper was tucked behind the note: a list from Olive with names and districts, some of which Alice recognized from other articles. She spread the clippings out across the desk and saw that the same three names kept appearing. She glanced over the articles again, noticing that the offenders were all suspected baby farmers because their charges were in relation to children, for cruelty and manslaughter by willfully withholding food.

It was wrong for her to have doubted Olive—this was just what she'd been waiting for, some names and places to start looking. But she had expected more. Three seemed such a small number compared to what she'd learned of how widespread the practice had become, and these were just the ones who had been caught.

Alice's gaze focused on the dark stone walls as she thought how unwelcoming it was below ground. At least it was safe here. She shuddered at the thought of approaching these criminals in their homes, but there wasn't any other way; these were the people she should be going after, the ones who had been investigated before—the ones who could be out there, still operating.

She made her way through to the other room, where Elizabeth was filing. "Did Olive leave me anything else . . . another folder of clippings, perhaps?"

"I don't think so. There were plenty that she requested, but she told me to put them back." Elizabeth glanced at the stack of documents on the counter, the same pile from which she had retrieved Alice's folder.

"Do you mind if I take a look?" Alice asked.

"I suppose not. I was just about to put them back, but it can wait."

"Are you sure?"

"Yes, yes, of course, knock yourself out," Elizabeth said with a smile. "Anything that helps put these bastards behind bars."

Back at the desk, Alice spent the next hour working her way through the folders. The articles made bleak reading, all ending in the conviction of the suspected baby farmer for the death of a child. The headline of an article in the *Cheltenham Chronicle* read: *Baby Farmer Sentenced to Ten Years' Penal Servitude.* The brief article recorded that Jessie Byers, forty-three, had been found guilty of the manslaughter of Reginald Turnbull, aged five months; after the prisoner adopted the baby, he was given laudanum and abandoned.

Alice's eyes were dewy, and she strained to read the small print in the gloomy light, while her body grew rigid, stiffening in protest at the awful stories. It was almost too much to bear, the thought of these poor mites suffering so horrifically—and she struggled not to think that anything like this might happen to Eadie.

The next article was an older piece about a conviction some years earlier and she instantly recognized the name as the couple Olive had warned her against.

> At Woodford Police Court yesterday, Frank Richard Pritchard, 50, clerk, and Beatrice Pritchard, 46, his wife, of London Road, Woodford, were charged on remand with being concerned together in the manslaughter of Sally Merriweather, aged seven months,

> by willfully withholding food from her. The child was found dead in a carriage at the prisoners' home.

Alice took a deep breath, understanding why Olive might have kept this from her, then forced herself to keep reading, knowing that no matter how disturbing the material was, she needed to collect as much information as she could.

> Sub-Divisional Inspector Robert Warner stated that on June 14, with Inspector Nixon, of the NSPCC, he visited the house at London Road, Woodford. Receiving no answer to his knock, he climbed the wall and entered by the back door. In the front room on the ground floor he saw a woman named McIntyre and three girls, Yvonne Ellis, Betty Pritchard and Annie Pritchard. On a broken couch he found the boy Norman Rogers, aged 11 months, lying on some newspapers and covered with a piece of filthy canvas. The child had on two wet garments which were black and filthy. He was emaciated and covered in sores. The girl, Ellis, was sitting in a broken armchair nursing a boy of about 11 months. The boy appeared to be fairly well nourished but was very dirty. Ellis was unwashed and badly clothed. In the back room was a child named Malcolm Strong, aged about 16 months, sitting on a chair-bedstead. There was another child, Hannah Rogers, about 1 month old, lying in filth and covered with vermin bites. The mattress on which the child was lying was filthy and covered with vermin. In an upstairs room a girl, aged 18 months, was lying motionless on a

> mattress on the floor, and appeared too weak to move. In another room were three infants covered with a quilt. They were dirty and when looked at by the doctor they uttered feeble cries. He visited a back room and there found a girl of 11 months lying in a crib covered with maggots; she was apparently too weak to move.

Alice pressed her lips together, placing her hand over her mouth as she forced herself to carry on. She glanced quickly through to where Elizabeth worked as she considered what her mother would say if she read about these monsters; maybe then Ruth might reconsider giving her more of the facts.

> In a carriage in the same room he found the dead body of the child, Sally Merriweather, covered with an old frock and swarming with maggots. The children were removed to the infirmary. The house was in a filthy condition. The beds were broke. And the mattresses verminous. There was hardly any food in the house. Mrs. Pritchard returned at 3:15 p.m. and asked, "Where are my children?" She said that she had been up all night and had been out to try and find the dead child's father. The child, she said, died at five o'clock in the morning. Detective-Sergeant Ryder said that he arrested the man Pritchard at an office in the City. Pritchard stated that he had been trying for a long while to get his wife to return the babies to their mothers.

Alice just managed to place the article out of sight in her bag before she retched into her handkerchief.

Twenty-three

Alice's legs were still shaking as she made her way up the path to the Dulwich house, suddenly aware she didn't know what to say, and had no idea what state of mind her mother would be in. It was unlike the last time she'd seen Ruth, when she'd spent the whole train journey in disbelief and with only one question on her mind: where was Eadie? This time she had dozens of questions, as well as the mental image of the Pritchards' filthy home and the poor children they'd kept prisoner. She had the article in her bag along with others; if her mother wouldn't believe her, perhaps she'd trust the black-and-white print.

Their family home was even less inviting than it had been the last time she'd visited, the windows dark shallow craters, muted light bleeding from the corners of the blackout curtains. She knocked and waited, listening as a door opened inside. The light came on, and her pulse grew faster as footsteps came toward her.

"Who is it?"

"It's Alice."

There was a rattle as the lock was unfastened, and the clink of a chain being lifted from its hook. Then the door swung open. Ruth stood alone, a silhouette in the dark hallway. "Alice . . . how are you?"

"Can I come in?"

"Yes, yes, of course."

Alice suddenly felt calmer—much calmer, in fact, than she had on leaving the library, as if somehow being in possession of this knowledge gave her power. But as she walked past her mother into the kitchen, a knot tightened in her stomach as she looked around her former home and breathed in the familiar smells of beeswax polish, soap and tea.

Ruth followed her in and leaned back against the counter, arms crossed in front of her. Under the harsh white glare of the kitchen light, Alice noticed that the lines around her eyes had deepened, and how the slackness of her jaw dragged down the corners of her mouth. It unbalanced Alice, seeing her mother look so old—so vulnerable—and then she remembered why she was there.

"Sit down. I've got something to show you." Ruth did as she was told, and Alice spread the articles out on the table in front of her. "You want to know about the kind of people you've paid to take care of your granddaughter? Read these."

As she stood watching her mother, Alice wondered how many other parents had lost their children in this way, their lives cracking apart with the tectonic force of this grief. She wondered, as she had so many times since she'd lost Eadie, whether she would ever see her again or if she would have to accept a life without her. Her life was divided into two parts: before and after Eadie.

It was also divided into life before and after her mother's betrayal.

Ruth's eyes stayed fixed on the newspaper articles, and Alice saw her swallow hard as she tried to conceal a sob, then her shoulders shook and her body released a shudder as she placed her hand across her mouth.

These were the arms that had once held and comforted Alice, hands that had fed and cared for her. Parents were supposed to nurture and love their children. But the natural order of things had changed for Alice, starting from when her father and then William died, then Ruth had become mentally unstable and begun trusting too much in her faith. Now Alice didn't understand her mother at all.

Ruth looked up from the articles, her eyes reflecting her horror. "I'm so sorry."

Alice was still standing, arms crossed, looking down at her. "Are you going to tell me the truth now?" she asked in a level voice.

Ruth sniffled. "There's nothing left to tell. I answered all the questions the policewoman asked."

Sergeant Burns had contacted Alice after the interview as she'd promised she would, but told her she'd learned nothing from Ruth that would help with their inquiry.

"There *has* to be more," she pleaded. "What did the couple look like? You've never told me that."

Ruth's neck snapped back as she gazed upward and Alice wasn't sure if she was looking to her God for inspiration, or just staring at the ceiling.

"Come on, Mum. If you met them twice you must have some recollection?"

"They were different. The man I met the first time had dark hair that was combed back behind his ears, and he wore a suit. The man who collected Eadie was in a uniform. I remember him now," Ruth said, frowning in concentration. "He had terrible skin, but I thought he must be respectable because he was a member of the Home Guard."

"Did you tell the policewoman that?"

"Yes, I think so."

Alice wanted to take her mother by the arms and shake her; ask her how she could forget something so important, but her mouth wouldn't form the words.

"That's why I trusted them, Alice," Ruth said with a tentative smile. "And the woman was tiny, and so overjoyed to hold a baby in her arms."

She must have realized how insensitive she'd been because her smile quickly faded. "I'm so sorry. I didn't know about any of this. . . ." She pushed the clippings away, suddenly looking as revolted as Alice felt. "I know what you've been through, and what I've done must seem cruel, but I had my reasons."

"What reason could there possibly be for farming out your own grandchild?" Alice spat the words, and Ruth recoiled in her chair.

Then Alice took her journal out of her bag and placed it on the table in front of her mother.

Ruth sat motionless, her knuckles white, lips pressed together.

"Go on," said Alice. "Look inside."

Ruth opened the cover to reveal the handwritten title of

The Zoo Chronicles: Tales from London Zoo. The first page had a clipping from the newspaper about Mr. Vinall, the penguin keeper, alongside Alice's illustrations of the penguins jumping off the rock. Ruth took time to read it before turning the page and reading the article about Churchill's gift of a lion, placed beside more of Alice's illustrations. Then Ruth read the next page and the next, while Alice stood and watched, remembering the times she had worked on it, looking forward to the day she could read it to her daughter. Alice wondered what her mother thought of the animal stories her father had told her, and the tales she'd created since. Eventually Ruth reached the last page, which featured a photograph of Alice's father in his zookeeper's suit with the inscription: *For my father, Frederick (Freddie) Charles Cotton, and his granddaughter, Eadie.*

When Ruth looked up, her eyes were swimming with tears.

Alice waited, letting the moment linger as she savored the comforting memory of her father and the warmth of his love, allowing it to suffocate Ruth's betrayal. "What would he say now?" Alice said coldly.

There was a silence, then Ruth cleared her throat. "I would never expect you to understand, that's why I've never told you."

"Well, why don't you try now?"

Ruth rose to her feet and disappeared into the living room, returning with some papers that she handed to Alice: the birth certificates she'd been unable to find in the usual hiding place. The first was hers: *Alice Elizabeth Cotton, born April 20, 1920. Father: Frederick Charles Cotton, Agriculturalist. Mother: Ruth Cotton, domestic servant.*

She glanced up; there were no revelations here.

Ruth sat back down and nodded for her to carry on.

Alice unfolded the second piece of paper, expecting to see a similar birth certificate for her brother, but it was a form with only his name and date of birth: *William Frederick Cotton, born May 22, 1918.*

"What's this?"

"I wanted a child so badly, Alice. Your father and I, we tried for so long." Ruth wouldn't look Alice in the eye, her gaze locking onto a place somewhere out of sight. "It was during the Great War, there was so much sadness and loss . . . so many unmarried mothers. So many babies without homes. This is what childless couples did then, what they're still doing now."

"What are you saying?"

"William—"

"He wasn't yours?"

"He's always been ours, Alice. Always wanted, loved, cherished."

"And what about me . . . am I yours?"

"It was a miracle when you came along. We were so shocked, but it was obviously God's will. He decided to bless us after all." Ruth leaned back in her chair and let out a guttural groan. "I made a promise, Alice. When we were given William, I knew it was wrong in God's eyes. Then we were blessed with you . . . I knew we would have to pay for it, one day."

"So, when Eadie was born you decided she would be the sacrifice for the choice that *you* made."

Ruth shook her head. "No, it was never like that. I never wanted you to pay for my mistake, or your own; we've paid enough with your father's and William's lives. No, I thought it would be better for her, and that you could recover from being a fallen woman, and even have a real family of your own one day."

Alice's whole being ignited with rage. She held her fists at her sides, suddenly aware of what she was capable of. "I had a real family," she said. "Eadie and I were family—and now look what you've done."

Twenty-four

LONDON, APRIL 17, 1943

"I want to see the lions," the boy shouted as he skipped along the path.

"We will . . . just slow down!" his mother cried as she chased along behind him.

The walkways and gardens were crowded with families, children pulling parents from one enclosure to the next, as well as lots of servicemen—American, British and Royal Indian Army—all of whom Alice knew gained entry for half price. In fact, it was as if the two thousand daily visitors had descended at that very moment to invade her solitude. She sat on a bench, watching numbly as the boughs of a tree danced in the wind, white blossoms leaping like kids on a trampoline, the sunlight behind them crafting lacework from the leaves. Children's squeals and laughter looped and fell, as though distant and then close again. It had seemed like a good idea for a Saturday outing: get the trolley bus to the zoo, stop at the corner store where her father had always bought sweets for her and her brother, re-create their childhood ritual. She had so desperately wanted to build the safe world for Eadie that her father had for her and William, but look how badly she'd failed. And she didn't even know her family anymore; it was like seasickness, everything she knew kept shifting and changing. She really had no idea what to do next, so she just sat with the half-eaten bag of boiled sweets in her lap, feeling hopeless.

A mother and her young daughter sat at the other end of the bench, the girl's gray wool coat buttoned up to her chin, faux fur around her collar and cuffs, her feet encased in a pair of navy Mary Janes. The mother smiled at Alice, and she was forced to get up and walk away, the thought of the simple act of choosing clothes for Eadie, and the likelihood she never would, setting her off crying again.

She took a familiar path, one that in summer was lined with colorful shrubs: hydrangeas with their emerald-green leaves and scented flowers, and cotoneaster, with its herringbone branches, providing a home for the bees and a forest for the insects to dance through. Today thick stalks and branches were exposed like skeletons.

Alice dried her eyes and headed toward the Penguin Pool, where she watched their show blankly, as the keepers rewarded them with fish and spectators arrived and left. Still she couldn't feel anything, just a gnawing emptiness.

She carried on toward Three Island Pond, always one of her favorite places, yet when she reached the metal railings she noticed how much smaller it seemed now than when she was a girl, and how much slighter the grasses and rushes were that grew on the banks of the moat opposite.

"Look, Mummy, look. There's our flamingo!" The boy held his mother with one hand and pointed with the other.

"Yes, darling, isn't he delightful?" she exclaimed.

"They're not going to play croquet with him, are they?" he asked worriedly.

"No, darling. Of course not."

Alice's thoughts turned to the times her father read her Lewis Carroll stories. Then she remembered one of their other favorites: Rikki-Tikki-Tavi, who'd been Rudyard Kipling's and her father's hero mongoose. Rikki had protected a family that wasn't even his, so surely Alice should be able to protect hers.

On the fence in front of her was an engraved wooden plaque: TRINK THE RATEL (HONEY BADGER) PROUDLY SPONSORED BY MR. AND MRS. ATKINS, FROM HARROW. She knew that the zoo's adoption scheme was a success since *The Sketch* and *Evening Standard* often featured the zoo news, with articles by the eponymously named Craven Hill. But while she'd always been glad that the adoption scheme had worked, right at that moment she felt as if it existed merely to taunt her—that Alice Cotton couldn't even look after her own child, let alone anyone else's.

As she stood watching, the helplessness was replaced by a nagging sensation, like a sinew being pulled. She realized nostalgia had driven her to come here. What was it that she could learn from the animal kingdom about how they cared for their offspring? They all looked after their children first and foremost, not their parents. Perhaps it was that simple, the message she needed: it was time to stop protecting her mother.

Ruth had committed a crime, and she would have to face the consequences, because her daughter couldn't wait for her any longer.

When Alice passed under the blue lantern above the door of Marylebone Lane Police Station, she felt a fleeting sense of déjà vu. Her stomach gurgled yet outwardly she was calm, glad she looked more respectable this time. After all she'd been through, she now knew for certain that she would only get what she wanted by persistence and cunning, not by being compliant.

Although reception was busy again, the duty officer showed her straight to an interview room once she'd provided Sergeant Mildred Burns's case number. Alice felt encouraged when the young policewoman appeared a few minutes later in her dark Women's Branch uniform. "Miss Cotton, how are you?" she asked as she closed the door behind her.

On the way to the police station Alice had decided to reveal everything, and so she did: from the moment she'd found out she was pregnant and told her mother, to when she'd woken in Brighton to find Eadie gone, to her police station visits. Sergeant Burns interrupted with questions about her failed search, and she scribbled notes and asked Alice to repeat the information about her brother's illegal adoption.

"Oh, and look at these," Alice said, as she brought out the birth certificates. Then she pushed a folded piece of paper across the table with her aunt's name and number and offered the police the opportunity to question Hope if they needed to.

It had taken a long phone call on the way there, and the relaying of the disturbing contents of her research, before she'd convinced Hope to change her mind and turn on her sister-in-law. "So, this will all help, won't it? This changes things." She was hoping that by the time she left the station, her statement would be lodged and Ruth would be brought in again for questioning.

Sergeant Burns pursed her lips as she finished taking notes. "I'm afraid not, Alice. We've spoken to your mother, and she's only told us what you already have. Unfortunately, there's still not enough here for us to investigate further."

"Why not?"

"Because we would have to charge her for child stealing under section 56 of the 1861 Offenses Against the Person Act, and it carries serious penalties. And she's the grandmother, Alice. I'm sorry, and I have looked into it, but does it really serve anyone's interest if we don't have enough evidence to bring a charge? It would only raise your hopes when I'm afraid there isn't any at this stage."

Alice's chest tightened. "I can't believe that. Family members are often the perpetrators in these cases. What good is it if you can't hold them accountable?"

"It's just very hard to prove your mother's involvement, and I'm sorry to say, but the descriptions that she gave don't really amount to anything." Her expression softened as Alice's face crumpled. "Weeks have passed, and I know you're not going to want to hear this, but we need to spend time and resources on cases we can readily pursue."

"But a baby is missing," Alice said, her voice cracking. "A

crime's been committed. Forget about my mother . . . just find Eadie."

"We've tried, Alice. I'm really sorry, but we have tried. Eadie will stay on the Juvenile Index, and if she's with baby farmers, as we suspect she is, there's a good chance we will get a lead at some stage."

Twenty-five

LONDON, APRIL 20, 1943

"Are you sure you're okay?" Theo asked, concern in his eyes and sympathetic smile.

"I'm fine, really," Alice lied as she watched the pages of Patricia Reece's novel furl through the feeder, certain that the last place she needed to be right now was in the middle of the countryside, out of contact with Penny, Olive and Sergeant Burns. And it was her birthday.

Under any other circumstances, seeing an Original Heidelberg printer would have impressed her. They had driven for over an hour to reach the printworks, one of only three left close to the capital since Partridge's regular printer, Latimer Trend, had been turned over to government books and stationery. Theo had driven cautiously, only twice veering onto the wrong side of the road, and on one occasion swerving just in time to avoid an oncoming truck. While Alice had felt strangely calm as she'd watched this unfold, she'd been unable to speak when Theo had pulled over to ensure she wasn't hurt. Now he stood opposite, talking to the foreman and casting frequent worried glances at her.

This wasn't their first outing together since the Foyle's luncheon. She'd taken him to visit the bookstores on Charing Cross Road, and they'd stopped to admire the Penguincubator, the book vending machine that Allen Lane had installed: cheaper books, conveniently located but so unexpected. "It's miraculous!" Theo had exclaimed as he'd placed a coin in the slot and watched the machine dispense a sixpenny paperback. They'd spent quite some time half-seriously speculating on how it might take off, before their conversation had turned to more serious topics.

The press gave a violent shudder, sending reverberations across the workshop floor, and Alice grimaced as she kept her eyes trained on the loader, watching the stack of printed pages grow, ready to be guillotined and bound, the smell of hot oil filling the air. It was an unpleasant sensation, her teeth chattering and her insides jolting around. Just when she hoped it would stop soon, the rollers abruptly ground to a halt and the machine gave a final judder.

The foreman looked up at them and shook his head. They had been having trouble with the press all morning, and it didn't bode well for their deadline. Not only were there bottlenecks in the production departments, but they'd been told there was also one in the bindery since one of its Seybold trimmers was broken, the other tied up for four days on a different publication. Even if they could solve that problem and Patricia's novel was printed, there was little chance they would get it to the distributors in time.

Mark Hughes, the master printer and general manager, had taken them on a tour when they'd arrived, first through the light-filled space at the front of the building that housed the commercial artist and typographer, then into the monotype department and compositing room. It had been interesting at first, and a good distraction from waiting to hear any news about Eadie, but now Alice regretted accepting Theo's invitation. She wished she could take control of her emotions instead of one minute thinking one way and the next moment the reverse. And she really should have stuck to her resolve not to spend any more time alone with Theo.

Mark's tour had taken them into the machine room at the heart of the building, and even to her untrained eye it was clear that the letterpress and offset lithography equipment had seen better days, so it was no surprise that there were problems or that the intense smell of burning oil was so overbearing.

Theo and Alice watched as the foreman tried to restart the stalled machinery.

"Shall we go outside?" she suggested.

"You go ahead," he replied. He stayed at the head of the machine, watching intensely, his hands balled into tight fists, as the foreman fiddled with the rollers.

Partridge couldn't afford another delay or a ruined batch of paper, as booksellers and readers were eagerly awaiting the next installment of the Mary Dray detective series. Alice knew the story inside out; in fact, she could picture one of the villains passing his victims through the jaws of the press, and the swirl of blood and ink that would ooze out the other end.

"I need some air," she said abruptly, and headed for the door.

Outside she leaned back against the wall, feeling the cold bricks through her dress as she gazed at the emerald fields that led to the horizon. She breathed in the comforting scent of freshly cut hay. Hertfordshire wasn't far from London, yet the countryside was as rural as any of the distant counties: rolling green hills flecked with the black-and-white dots of sheep and cattle, and vast hedges that hugged the road and train routes in every direction. Alice's eyes followed each artery into the distance, wondering if any might lead to Eadie.

The door jarred as it opened, and Theo appeared, looking around until he noticed her. "There you are. You sure you're okay?"

"Yes, I'm fine. I'm just not very good in enclosed spaces." She clasped her hands behind her back and leaned on them. "What's the news? Is the book going to live?"

"Sure hope so. They haven't been able to maintain the machinery properly, and there's been no investment. That's what's so frustrating—it's all avoidable, it just needs more oil and servicing."

"At least they know what's wrong with it."

"Doesn't help, though. They need to take it apart and clean it before they can get the press rolling again. Hughes says it will delay us by another day."

"A wasted journey, then."

"Not at all. Nobody's been up here to see them in months, not since Rupert left. Besides, I got to show off my driving skills." He kept a straight face as he lit a cigarette, and she tried not to smile either.

"You know," she said, "London's on the lookout for ambulance drivers."

"Pity I've already got a full-time job."

"Ah yes, well, there is that," she said, picking up a long stick and scratching a circle in the dirt.

There was an awkward silence as he watched her, then he joined in, adding a nose to the face she'd etched. After she embellished it with ears, they stood back and smiled at their unlikely creation.

"So, who is it?" Theo asked.

"Maybe George."

"The smile's too wide for him, surely. . . . I mean, George is more serious than that." Theo's lips tightened around his cigarette.

Alice realized Theo didn't know George all that well, and she studied him for a moment. *What kind of man is Theo Bloom? The best of men . . . or the worst of men, like Rupert Armstrong-Miller?*

She asked, "What are you *really* doing here?"

He didn't look surprised, just tilted his head up, smoke trailing into the sky before he returned her gaze. "What I told you in the meeting," he said. "Helping work through the mountain of rules and regulations. Every minute it seems as if there's a new guideline or practice."

"So you're not here to close us down?"

He took a beat too long to respond, and when he did, he didn't look her in the eye. "I'm here because with Rupert gone, George has got a lot to handle. Possibly too much."

"Maybe."

"You must all be missing Rupert."

It was all she could do to hold on to the stick and not hurl it across the yard. "Yes . . . of course we are. Although George and Tommy have taken on his workload so well that they haven't had to replace him."

"But maybe it would have been better if they had."

There was another awkward silence, and Alice couldn't collect her thoughts quickly enough to change the subject. She usually did a good job of keeping memories of Rupert at bay, but now they flooded back: the workplace flirtation, the brief rendezvous, and how he'd led her to believe they had a future together. It still seemed unbelievable that Rupert was one of Partridge's own, George's son, and yet the cause of all her misery.

"Were you friends?" Theo asked.

"Rupert and I?"

"Yeah. I heard you worked under him for a couple of years."

She flinched. "We were just colleagues."

"So you didn't know him well?"

"We were colleagues—nothing less, nothing more," she said coldly. "Now, shouldn't we get back inside?"

"Sorry, I was always told that I was too nosy. It's just, you're such good pals with Ursula, I hoped you might be with Rupert too. I want to know more about him and what he brought to your team."

"I'm sure George could tell you about that, or Tommy."

"Of course." A tractor started up in a nearby field, the rattle of its engine distracting them, and Theo held out his hand, frowning. "Friends?"

"Certainly," she said as she shook it and faked a smile. "I just think we'd better see how things are going, don't you?"

It was late afternoon by the time the printer jolted back to life, and the reassuring noise of the mechanism and smell of hot oil filled the machine room again. The foreman agreed to work overnight to help them get back on schedule, and by the time they'd finished their meeting it was too dark to drive back to London; Theo didn't want to risk driving on the opposite side of the road at night, and Alice was inclined to agree, even though she was desperate to get back. Mark Hughes directed them to the local inn and insisted on paying for their rooms.

"It's not too bad, is it?" Alice asked, glancing up from her pot roast. "Not like the kind of meals you're used to eating, I imagine."

He ate differently than she'd ever seen anyone eat before, holding his fork the wrong way up and in the opposite hand to hers. "It's good," he said, a note of relief in his voice as he speared another piece of brisket.

The dining room was half full, and it was just what she'd expected on seeing the dark-beamed exterior of the Swan: low ceilings and doorjambs you were guaranteed to bang your head against, lacy curtains on rods that ran like a petticoat around the window, and a vivid tartan carpet with tan-colored leather chairs, all somehow redeemed by a working fireplace that was nearly as broad as the bar. The smell of the place more than made up for the interior: the rustic aroma of food, the earthiness of smoking wood, the clamor of bouquets from the opened bottles and barrels fighting for attention.

Alice was trying to hide her anxiousness at being stranded. At least she would get to spend a night in a proper bed as opposed to the uncomfortable camping cot in Penny's attic, and she had her own bathroom. *It's just one day*, she kept telling herself. Perhaps a good night's sleep would give her strength and put her on track for all she had to do. This time tomorrow she would be back in London, hopefully with some news.

Her wine was still untouched, and she took a small sip, the alcohol unfamiliarly strong. With the next mouthful, an unpleasant sensation spread across her tongue—then it mellowed, and so did she, submitting to its power to slow things down and make her feel freer, and more tired, than she had in weeks.

Theo had already replenished his glass and nearly finished his meal, contentment settling over him like the glow of a firefly.

"How long do you think you'll remain in London?" she asked, watching as he brushed his mustache lightly with the napkin and leaned back in his chair.

"A couple of months. It's really to understand what's going on and come up with a solution. Walter is concerned," he added, growing serious. "And I can see why. If you take the war restrictions out of the equation, the business is still running at a loss and there's no singular reason for it. That's what I'm trying to understand—that and how to take advantage of the increased demand for books."

She could see he meant what he said: that he really did want to help. "I imagine it's frustrating."

"Certainly is. Especially when I can see that it wouldn't take much."

"Like what?" she asked, interested.

"Doesn't matter, I shouldn't be talking like this."

"I care too."

"Yes. I know you do."

They held eye contact, his gaze lingering until it dropped to her mouth and then returned to her eyes with a new intensity. She felt the need to look away. When she glanced back he was still staring at her, so she was compelled to break the tension. "Can you tell me a little more about your plans?"

"They're still only just ideas." He relented, telling her all about the strategies they had in the United States, and how he was meeting industry figures here in an attempt to discuss whether Britain could, or should, implement similar practices. It was fascinating, and she finished her wine as they talked, although when he was about to refill her glass she placed her hand across the top, remembering what had happened when she hadn't stayed alert enough to deny her attraction to Rupert, or strong enough to fend him off.

"And those books for the soldiers, tell me more about them?" she asked.

"The Armed Services Editions. There are several new titles each month; the first one wouldn't mean much to you, but to us Americans it's kind of a classic, *The Education of Hyman Kaplan*."

"What's it about?"

"This guy, an immigrant, trying to learn English in New York. He's not very good at it, that's what makes it so funny. It's about his exploits." Theo had laughter in his voice. "The writer is only a young guy who first published it as a series in *The New Yorker*."

"It sounds like a very charming and amusing tale."

"It is!" He leaned a little closer, turning serious. "The council I'm part of, the one publishing the ASEs, has a motto: 'Books are weapons in the war of ideas,' and it seems to have stuck."

"You're sold on the idea that books are weapons?" she asked.

"Certainly. And so is Roosevelt, it was his saying: 'In this war, we know, books are weapons.' Imagine it, you're on a remote island—Malta, for example—and all you can do is wait. The heat's intense, there's no food, the men are restless . . . What are you gonna do?"

"Swim?" she said teasingly.

He laughed. "Read!"

"I know, you're right," she said with a smile.

"They're hungry for information and ideals; truths they can hold in their hearts and minds. At the moment the men tear books into sections so they can share them."

It made her think of William and the letters they'd exchanged while he was serving. He too had described books as sustaining soldiers' lives in a way that nothing else could.

"Yes," she said, staring into the fire, "everything in their lives is rationed, or a secret, or sacrificed. They're bound to one another and their country, and the only freedom they still have is in the landscape of their minds."

"Which writer said that?"

"Just me." She would never understand what her brother had endured, yet she knew what characters he had for company, what settings would distract him, and what stories would sustain him when he most needed them. "Books might not always be a comfort, but they remind them of what it is to be human, and to love."

Theo regarded her with a small smile, and their eyes locked again.

The restaurant emptied around them and embers glimmered in the fireplace as Theo spoke passionately about his books and the council, then listened to her speak about her project. She understood exactly why he wanted to create these editions for the troops; it was no different than what she hoped to achieve for readers here.

"A reader can have a bond with a character as strong as any relationship with another human being," he said, his deep voice slowing to a drawl, his gaze intense.

Alice was drawn in, his words disarmingly sensitive, his manner so intimate that she realized she was feeling something for him that she couldn't fight.

At that point she made herself glance at her watch, saw it was nearly midnight and came to her senses. But she went to her room with a warm sense of contentment that she hadn't experienced in a long time. She tried not to think about what seemed to be a mutual attraction, but instead how a male colleague taking her into his confidence and treating her as an equal had restored something in her. She wished it could have been Theo that she'd worked with these past few years; he was decent and kind and behaved like a gentleman, not a predator.

In fact, by the time she fell asleep, she was fairly certain that Theo Bloom was the best of men.

Twenty-six

LONDON, APRIL 22, 1943

"Theo, Theo! Wait a moment!" a voice called from across the sun-drenched square.

When Theo swung round, George was walking briskly, wooden cane tapping the ground as he hurried toward him.

"Morning, George. No Nelson today?" Theo asked as the older man drew close.

"Tucked in his basket when I left. Dreaming of chasing ducks and swimming in their pond, I expect." His chin folded into jowls as he spoke, making him look just like his trusted Labrador.

"Good to see the weather finally brightening," Theo said, altering his stride to keep pace with George.

"I'm glad I caught you," George said, glancing sideways at

Theo as they continued toward the office. "I've been meaning to have a word."

Theo's fingers flexed inside his tight leather gloves, suddenly feeling trapped, and he tried not to frown. "What is it, George?"

"How long have you been here now . . . a month?"

"Just over."

The city had been a revelation to him in that short time; George had loaned him a small but luxurious apartment in Mayfair, and the treasures he'd discovered in the nearby streets and lanes were never-ending. He'd told Virginia, who'd briefly come on the phone line with Walter, about how he'd walked three different ways to the office, each time coming across centuries old churches and miniature timber-beamed public houses. But he had felt something shift in the past few weeks, and perhaps George had noticed it too—and seen how comfortable he was getting.

"Yes, that's right," he said, glancing at Theo. "It's certainly gone quickly."

Theo nodded.

"So, you've got a good measure of the place?"

"I'd like to think so." Theo slowed again since they were nearly at the gate and he sensed this was a longer conversation.

"And Walter's happy for you to stay for a while longer?" George said, as he turned to face him.

Theo wasn't sure if it was a rhetorical question. "Yep, I believe so."

"We're really starting to achieve progress. It's marvelous, really marvelous. There is just one thing . . ."

Theo could guess. He knew he was only here for a short time and that his allegiance was to the New York office. But he found it easy to feel at home with the Londoners, who had all been so welcoming. He'd had Tommy's errant twin boys crawl all over him at supper, and he'd met Emily's awkward fiancé, Timothy, who worked for a bank but dressed like an artist. And Theo had been embraced by George's family. He didn't want to play a part in closing the office down, nor did he believe it would make good business sense at this stage. He'd started to wonder if Walter might have another motivation, because as far as Theo could see, George was right: they were starting to achieve things. But perhaps not soon enough for George's brother.

Theo suppressed a sigh. "What is it, George?"

"It's Alice."

"What about her?" he asked, now trying to hide his surprise.

"I've known her for some time, but I've found her behavior recently very . . . well, very unpredictable. She's really not herself, and I've noticed the two of you have been spending quite a bit of time together. I'm wondering if she's said anything."

Theo was caught off guard; he hadn't known her long enough for her to confide in him or for him to make a clear judgment on her behavior. Except that he found her to be intelligent, thoughtful, surprisingly knowledgeable and charmingly understated.

"I'm afraid not, George—I can't say I've noticed anything out of the ordinary."

It was a half-truth. There were days when she'd been distracted, but he'd taken that to be out of concern for her family or anxiety over her book project. On a couple of occasions she'd disappeared with no explanation, but again he'd put it down to her personal circumstances with her cousin's baby. In any event, while there were lots of rumors of espionage within the media, now that he knew her, Theo didn't think her capable of any kind of subterfuge.

"I know the research she's doing for *Women and Children First* is taking her to some unusual places . . . and into contact with some unsavory characters," he said, thinking about some of the stories she'd shared with him. "You know what? Somebody should go with her, if we can organize that."

George crossed his arms and brought one hand up to his mouth, brushing his forefinger back and forth across his bottom lip as he considered Theo's words. "Hmm, well, we wouldn't want to put her in any danger, would we, but we don't really have any spare bodies. It's just an instinct, Theo, but keep an eye on her, would you?"

"Sure thing, George. Don't worry, I'll make sure nothing happens to her."

He thought back to their time in Hertfordshire a few days earlier. They'd talked long after everyone else had left, sitting close to the fire as it crackled down to embers, mostly discussing work until she'd asked about the council. Her mood changed, and she grew thoughtful then as she spoke about her brother, and so did he when he told her about Howie's death. They had a shared understanding and were quiet for a time as she rested a comforting hand on his arm, and the fire sputtered, and wind whispered through the trees.

"In Will's last letter home, he summarized the novel he'd just read," she told him, her eyes sparkling at the memory. "He was so surprised at the ending that he wanted to dispute it . . . see if I agreed with him." She turned toward the fire. "I sent him my reply with a new book, one I thought he'd find more satisfying . . . but he never got to read it."

Her face had looked so fragile in the subdued light; a delicacy to her features that he hadn't seen before. Even the loose strands of hair that fell across her face looked like fine threads of gold, and he imagined brushing them away.

"I'm sorry," he said.

"Thank you," she said with a brief smile.

"What was the book you sent him?"

"*Oliver Twist*. I thought it would give him fond thoughts of home."

"That's a coincidence—it's one of the books we're including in the ASEs."

"Really?" Her eyes were alight.

"Yes, I'm sure he'd have liked the ending."

Alice gave him the faintest smile, but it was enough to make his heart swell as he thought of Howie, and all the soldiers who were counting on their books.

"Which other books will your council send?" she asked.

"Some of the council members lobbied to send lesser-known authors and titles, but we decided to send a mix of fiction and nonfiction, classics and debuts. One title is *The Great Gatsby*—do you know it?"

"Yes, it's Fitzgerald, isn't it?"

"Let me think, who else is coming out in September. . . . Ogden Nash and John Steinbeck. Then there's *The Ship* by C. S. Forester, and of course your very own Graham Greene."

"Oh, which one?" she asked, with an interest so genuine it lit up her entire face.

"*The Ministry of Fear.*"

It was at that point he remembered he still hadn't told her about Virginia, and the fact that he had kept his engagement hidden worried him. But he couldn't just tell her out of the blue—he'd have to bring it up at a more appropriate time.

He focused back on their conversation and said, "Who else? Let's see . . . Ethel Vance, Joseph Conrad; there are thirty books each month—"

"Gosh, it sounds as if you've done a very good job. No wonder they sent you here to organize us too."

"How am I doing so far?" he asked, smiling at her.

"Not too bad. Although I'm not sure if the titles we're working on would compare to any of those. They don't exactly inspire the same level of bravery, even if they do count as propaganda!"

This wasn't the first time Theo had noticed how she understood concepts and ideas that he had to dissect for Virginia. Alice had an instinct, an acutely tuned emotional intelligence, which was why she'd become indispensable to Partridge.

"So," he said, "you see the business sense in the ASEs, even though they're free?"

"Yes, of course. You're building a whole new market for when the war is over."

"Yes! Men who've never picked up a book before, they're reading them in their bunks and shelters. We've opened up a new world to them. And when they come home . . ."

"They'll want to carry on reading."

"Exactly. So, you can see why this is so important in the long-term."

She frowned, eyes crinkling in a way he'd grown strangely fond of. "Then why doesn't Walter approve?"

"He thinks once they're available for free no one will want to pay for them. Ridiculous, I know, but between you and me, he can be a bit of a snob; he thinks that books should be for academics or entertainment, not for propaganda."

"Oh, I see," she said, frowning again. "How strange that he can't see how well placed Partridge will be to supply books in the United States once the war is over."

"And frustrating. But with your new books, we can do something just as special here in Britain."

Although they'd gone to their separate rooms shortly afterward, the imprint of her hand still tingled on his skin, and he'd spent most of the night awake, thinking of her.

"Thanks very much, Theo, I'm glad Alice can rely on you," George said, pulling him back into the present.

"Not a problem at all."

They reached the top of the steps to the office and were ready to go in when George placed a hand on Theo's arm. "There is just one other thing."

"What is it?"

"Sir Duncan said you went to see him recently—I ran into him yesterday. It's best if we take those meetings together in the future, united front and all that. You do understand, don't you?"

"Yes, George. Yes, of course," he said, returning his warm smile.

He was moved by the older man's generosity and glad that

it was out in the open, since where his loyalty lay had been weighing heavily on him. Theo decided that the time had come to talk honestly and openly about the conflicts and the real reason he was there, except that a couple of hours later, their offices received a long-distance call. It was his mother, and he would have to head back to New York as soon as possible.

Twenty-seven

NEW YORK, APRIL 26, 1943

The decorated billboards and vast brick walls of semi-industrial housing flashed past on the other side of the cab window: storage facilities, fireproof warehouses and car repairs, all there to serve the colossus that New York had become. Theo's heart swelled and he felt a beat of exhilaration, until he remembered why he was there: amid this vast metropolis, his father lay desperately ill, his mother keeping bedside vigil. When the operator had eventually managed to put the call through and his mother had informed him of his father's deterioration, George had insisted he leave right away. Through his personal contacts—and against the odds—George had secured him a flight out of Hendon Aerodrome, situated seven miles from the city and mostly used by dignitaries to fly to and from London. But there had been no time for a debrief, no time to say good-bye to Alice and barely a moment to send a telegram telling Walter and Virginia of his homecoming. He'd been warned against making the journey after heavy losses in the Atlantic in recent weeks, and it had been nerve-racking—a freezing draft had stiffened his neck and an overwhelming nausea had been brought on by the jet fuel—but the sickness and discomfort had done little to distract him from worrying about his father or any enemy aircraft that might be circling close by.

"Ya comin' home or visitin'?" the taxi driver asked as he caught Theo's eye in the rearview mirror.

"Coming home," Theo replied with a forced smile. "Can't ya tell?"

"One of the lucky ones."

The driver was right, and Theo instantly thought of Howie, and what an imposter he felt in civilian clothes—and as though he should explain his circumstances.

Howie's face was so clear to him, not as a man but as a boy. His energetic, straggly haired younger brother taking swings at a baseball and rarely hitting. Theo smiled at the memory, as he often did, but the hole inside of him always managed to take the shine off. Some people took a piece of the world with them when they left it, and Howie was one of them.

"Yep, one of the lucky ones," he echoed.

He had never before felt his noncombatant status more acutely. During his absence over the past several weeks, the United States had entered the war completely, their troops arriving in the Pacific and North Africa as well as European destinations.

It wasn't until the skyscrapers of Manhattan came into

view that Theo realized he'd barely considered seeing Virginia, that he'd been too preoccupied with Alice, and that this didn't bode well for the upcoming wedding. Not only had he not called her before leaving London, but he hadn't bought her a gift, as he usually did on one of his trips, although these were unusual circumstances. And what would Walter say about this sudden arrival? Would he understand, or would it give him an excuse to rebuke his future son-in-law? For a fleeting moment Theo contemplated his freedom from Walter if he didn't marry Virginia, but it would also mean he didn't have a job.

Hoping to distract himself, Theo caught the taxi driver's eye in the mirror again; he'd never met a New York driver who didn't like to chat, particularly now, when there was so much to talk about.

"So, you got family in the forces?" Theo asked.

"Younger brother and a couple of cousins. I got myself injured in a farmin' accident. What's your story?"

"I'm in the supply business. The government makes exceptions for some industries."

"What sort of supply—food, transport, guns?"

"Books."

"Huh?"

"Books, I'm in the publishing business."

"Right, gotcha, a man of words," he said, smiling. "Never been a reader myself—wife loves it, though."

Theo glanced out at the grid of tarmac and towers, and the bustling eateries, and thought about the moment that he first really knew Alice. It was a few days before the Foyle's event and they'd stopped for lunch on their way back from a meeting; they'd both been starving, as it had gone on late, and once they were eating her mood had changed. She seemed to relax for the first time, a barrier coming down.

"Which writers come from New York?" she asked him.

"How long a list would you like?"

"I'd start the list with Henry James," she said.

"What about Walt Whitman?" he asked.

"And Dorothy Parker. Who would be next?"

"Edith Wharton," they said at the same time and laughed.

He thought then how much he would like to show her New York, and how, like him, she would be as much at home on the Upper West Side as in the West Village, or the Flatiron District, or the Lower East Side. What would she make of the soirees on rooftop terraces watching the sun set over Manhattan, or the walks in Central Park, or the colossal size of the department stores compared to their London cousins? How could she not be impressed by the skyscrapers and the boldness of New York's architects? He smiled as he imagined taking her to the Waldorf Astoria, where they would eat off porcelain plates; then they would go up to East Fifty-ninth Street and visit Argosy, browsing the floors of the old bookstore. They would navigate the city together, and then—and then what? What was he thinking?

His father was in the hospital, and he was soon to be married to the woman he was planning on spending the rest of his life with. He needed to stop thinking like this; he needed to visit his father and then go to the office, distract himself with work. Then he would see Virginia, everything would return to normal and his life would be the same as it was before.

The driver was talking so fast that Theo couldn't follow, his Italian accent growing stronger by the minute, just like Theo's father with his Alsatian. They were immigrants in the American melting pot like hundreds of thousands of others, and Theo suddenly felt as though the differences between Britain and his homeland were every bit as vast as the ocean that separated them. The driver's voice droned on, and Theo turned his hands over, tearing at the quick then biting at his fingernails. It troubled him that he was so distracted by another country and a foreign woman. It didn't make sense—he'd planned his life, it had been following a trajectory, so why was he questioning it all now?

He wiped his hands across his face, the roughness of two-day stubble pricking at his palms. All he needed was a shave, a shower—something the English didn't believe in—and sleep, and then he'd be himself again.

But first he needed to see his parents.

The carved busts of founders and former surgeons guarded the lobby of the Brooklyn Methodist Hospital. As Theo bypassed the reception area and scanned the directory board, shoes squeaking on the gray linoleum, he hoped the bland walls and scratched skirting were a sign the hospital invested in treatments rather than décor. His father's ward was on the seventh floor, and he would usually take the six flights of stairs—he didn't want to give the diabetes gene an excuse to rear its ugly head—but today he was in a hurry.

He shared the elevator with a well-dressed couple, and the man acknowledged him while the woman hid her face in a handkerchief. The doors slid open on a near-deserted floor, disinfectant mingling with the stench of food and bedpans, and he waited a long time at the nurse's station before one appeared and directed him to his father. He followed impatiently, trying to hide his concern and irritation since he knew that while the war had ended New York's depression, bringing the docks and businesses back to life, it had also robbed them of their medical staff.

Flimsy curtains divided the ward into quarters, the overhead lights fizzed, and dark-painted lamps clung to the walls like crouching grasshoppers. Theo examined each bed closely before he found his father.

Samuel Bloom was lying motionless in the metal-framed bed closest to the window, two stands either side drip-feeding fluid into his bandaged hands. The sight made Theo's breath catch in his throat.

As Theo drew closer, he saw that his father's eyes were closed, not observing the green belt that spread out before him on the other side of the glass. Two bound feet protruded from beneath dull gray sheets, their white gauze protecting his father's agonizing ulcers. His bulk was a substantial contour beneath the blanket, reminding Theo of one of the causes of his illness. That and the diabetic ketoacidosis—a life-threatening condition, the doctor had explained to him after his father's last hospitalization. He supposed the fluids were for the insulin and the infection that Samuel had developed, and hopefully something for the pain.

Theo placed his small suitcase at the foot of the bed and moved quietly to stand by his father's shoulder, gazing down at his pale waxy skin, not the usual ruddy complexion of the diabetic. *No matter how well you know a person, there's always a mystery to discover,* he thought, noticing the deep creases at the sides of his father's mouth and the bony ridges of his eyebrows as if for the first time. It was the same with Alice's face, which offered surprises every time he saw it: a new expression, eyes lit in a different way, or a singular mannerism—

"What the heck are you doing here, son?"

Theo looked back down to see his father's blue eyes staring up at him. "How ya feelin,' Pop?"

"Fine. Still don't know why I'm here."

It felt as though a brace around Theo's thorax had been loosened, and he could breathe again. "Yes, you do, Pop. The denial thing won't work anymore, it's been fifteen years."

Samuel smiled. "You shouldn't have come. Madelaine was wrong to bother you."

"It's not bothering me, I wanted to come. Where is Mom, anyway?"

"She sleeps at home then comes back when visiting starts. She'll be here soon."

"How are you, really?"

"Honestly?"

"Honestly."

"Feels like someone laid me down on Madison and drove a truck over me!"

"That good, huh?"

"Yep. Don't tell your mother, though," Samuel added quickly, trying to haul himself up.

"Here . . . let me." Theo gripped him by the elbow and shifted the pillow further behind him while he shuffled carefully until he was sitting.

"So, what have they said to you?" Theo had an idea of what the doctors had said about his condition from his mother's hurried phone call, and he wanted to see if they'd shared the same information with him.

"They said what they always say: 'Samuel, lose weight. Get more exercise.'"

"Sure, but that's not why you're here. What did they say about the ketoacidosis?"

"Oh, that—trust Madelaine . . . I told her not to tell you. You're not to get involved, Theo. You've been here two minutes and look, you're already trying to take over. How did Walter ever let you go, or those London people? Tell me about London."

Theo was overjoyed and confused; the phone call had made out that his father's condition was dire, but Samuel didn't look like a man clinging to life. What was going on?

"Stop trying to change the subject, Pop. I want to know what the doctors said. How serious is this?"

"I'm in the right place, son, that's all that matters right now," he said, his tone more somber. "Sit down, will you?"

"Okay."

"Look, I know there have been some serious complications, but thankfully I'm recovering now. Your mother doesn't need to know about them, so it's best we just keep that between us."

Why did his father have to put a spin on things no matter what? "The truth, Pop, the truth."

"All right! I've been lucky, I grant you." He held his hands out in front of him, steady palms facing outward. "See, most of the symptoms have gone . . . and once the infection is under control, I'll be laughing."

Theo knew that wasn't the case. The doctor had once

explained how in some diabetics with infection there can be a resistance to the normal effects of insulin, and that his father was one of them. Unfortunately, this time it was too late to rely on weight loss or exercise as treatment; the doctors would need to find the right combination of drugs, and that in itself was problematic. Theo had witnessed his father's ongoing pain, and the vomiting and hyperventilation of an earlier attack, so there was little Samuel could hide from him. But he would go along with his father for the time being, just to keep him happy.

"And how is it here?" Theo asked, glancing around.

"You wouldn't want to bring your family here on vacation, but it's not as bad as it looks. Some of the nurses are pretty."

Theo smiled at him. He hadn't expected to see him in such good spirits, but it wasn't fooling him either—Samuel was worried.

"Would ya mind moving?" Theo asked.

"You're not taking me back to London with you—your mother wouldn't cope with the journey."

Theo couldn't help but smile again. "How about we move you over to the Mercy? It's got a great reputation. It would be a longer journey for Mom, but I'm sure she wouldn't mind if your treatment was better."

"You know we can't afford that."

"You wouldn't have to, Pop. But don't think about it right now. Just concentrate on getting better."

"Yeah, yeah," Samuel grumbled. Then he perked up again and raised his eyebrows. "Virginia came to visit yesterday."

"That was nice. How was she?"

"Fine . . . but haven't you seen her yet?"

"No, Pop, I came straight here."

Samuel placed a hand on his arm. "Thank you, Theo. You're a good son."

Theo smiled back, pleased his father felt that way but knowing what they were both really thinking: he might be a good son, but he was also an only son now, and he'd never be a hero like Howie.

Twenty-eight

Theo studied the mandarin skies as he walked up Fifty-fifth Street to the Blue Angel, hoping the fresh air would help wake him up. He was meeting Virginia at her friend's birthday party. After his grueling journey and the emotion of the morning with his father, he hadn't made it into the office; he'd been unable to face Walter, who he knew would want a detailed report on the London operation. Theo had been selective in what he'd shared with him so far, but he knew that Walter would be able to tell if Theo wasn't disclosing something important, like the recent problem with the Russell Square rent being hiked up—one of the much larger publishing houses had allowed Partridge to relocate there after the 1940 bombings and only charged a peppercorn rent until recently. He believed it was all manageable, and he wasn't deliberately deceiving Walter; he just wanted to buy the London team more time. In the next few months they'd know if their new titles were going to work—and if they'd get the paper rations they needed to publish next year's books.

As he entered the Blue Angel, Theo caught a glimpse of Virginia through the crowd, at a table surrounded by her usual fashionable group of friends. He didn't recognize many of them, perhaps the reason he suddenly felt awkward. She was deep in conversation with the woman next to her when she turned and caught sight of him, and she stood instantly and waved him over. "Look, everyone, Theo's back!"

Those who heard stopped talking and turned to look, and Theo's cheeks burned. It was unlike Virginia to be so exuberant and showy, and unlike him to feel embarrassed.

It proved tricky for her to navigate through the other partygoers and squeeze round the table, so she threw her hands in the air and blew him a kiss as he approached, which he caught and stopped shy of returning.

"I think you know everyone, apart from Arky and Felix—oh, and Alexandra. They're our new recruits." She smiled at the two men and woman she'd been talking to.

Theo could barely hear what Virginia said above the band as she leaned one hand on the table, champagne flute held high in the other. He didn't recognize the black velvet dress that hugged her figure, or the several strands of pearls that circled her neck and fell across her breastbone, barely concealing her cleavage. It struck him how starkly different she was to Alice, and how unsettled and conspicuous it made him feel.

A waiter appeared with a drink for Theo. Plates of lobster rolls, chicken wings and filled potato skins paraded past, and he realized how ravenous he was—and how obvious it was that the owner, Max Gordon, must have left instructions for the group to be well looked after.

Theo took his drink and sat in one of the nearby booths to wait for Virginia, the plush upholstery sinking under his weary limbs, and he closed his eyes. The musicians were doing improv, then songs he didn't recognize, until he heard the sweet and somber tone of a Charlie Parker number. He hadn't heard this kind of music for months, not since he'd visited an after-hours club with his friends in Harlem, where Dizzy Gillespie had been playing a set with Parker and Earl Hines. Virginia was taking her time coming over, so he listened to the music and reflected on how it had felt to fly home: seeing the fog rise off the Hudson and watching proudly as the city came into view, the rising sun gilding the Manhattan skyline.

He must have drifted off because the next thing he knew the seat next to him sank down and something brushed lightly across his cheek. He inhaled Virginia's distinct floral scent, and as he opened his eyes, her lips pressed against his. "Hello, sleepyhead," she whispered. "How's your pa?"

"No change since you saw him. He's putting on a good show of things, though, keeping the little staff they have busy."

Virginia glanced back at her group of friends, the birthday girl waving her over. His fiancée's profile was revealed in silhouette, her feline nose and her chin elongated under the harsh light, altogether stronger compared to Alice's gently sloping nose and heart-shaped face, features that now felt more familiar.

When she glanced back round, he was still staring.

"What is it?" she asked.

"Nothing," he said, except it wasn't, and no amount of

showers or shaves or sleep was going to change it. "You go be with your pals. I'll be over in a minute."

"And then we'll go off, just the two of us?"

"Of course."

They did, but it wasn't the reunion he'd imagined it would be. Virginia seemed too caught up with her crowd, and although she was still volunteering at the Red Cross station, she was surprisingly unfamiliar with the broader events of the war. Their conversation glided over the weeks they'd been separated—how everyone was and what they were doing—but she asked him very little about London.

At the end of the evening he felt dissatisfied; despite the abundance of food and drink, the champagne and easy laughter, there was something deeply unfulfilling about spending time with his fiancée. The experience was a stark contrast to what he'd left behind: to sheltering from the cold and rain in warm cafés, to the robust discussions around the Partridge meeting table, and to being welcomed into their homes to share hard-won meals from rations that had been queued for and carefully cooked. He suddenly couldn't relate to Virginia's world, even though it should have been his too.

It was almost midnight before he was able to prize himself away.

"Oh, you poor thing, you should have said something earlier," she said, giggling at his twitching eye. "What time is it in London?"

"Seven in the morning, so I've got roughly forty-eight hours of sleep to catch up on. And then some." He yawned.

"That's a shame," she said, stroking his face. "I was going to ask you to come back to my place, but I suppose we'd better call it a night and let you get some rest."

"I'll drop you off, if that's all right," he said, as she pulled him in for another kiss.

When their taxi turned on to Madison, her hand slid into his and squeezed his fingers. "It's divine to have you back—I've missed you," she said as she nuzzled her head into his shoulder.

He looked down at the soft smile playing on her lips. "Yes. I've missed you too."

But there hadn't been butterflies when he'd first seen her in the Angel. Desire, yes, a fondness and a longing, yes, but he hadn't felt compelled to take her in his arms—which was just as well, considering the large marble table that had stood between them.

He glanced out of the window at the lights of his city spinning by. After six weeks in London he no longer identified with these people, Virginia's people, and he found it hard to imagine spending the rest of his life with them. As the implications registered, an uneasy feeling settled inside his chest. Virginia hadn't changed, but he had, and he didn't think he could ever change back.

Twenty-nine

LONDON, APRIL 26, 1943

Alice pulled her collar tighter and braced for the downpour as the sky darkened, the air grew thicker and the first droplets began to fall. She hadn't slept again—she'd been unable to let go of the troubling thought that Frank and Beatrice Pritchard had been released from prison and were back preying on children. They could even be the couple who'd been in contact with her mother. So she'd tracked them down and was navigating as best she could with her scribbled map, passing row upon row of dreary interchangeable homes either side of the street. Most were empty, curtains pulled halfway across their cracked windowpanes. Leytonstone hadn't escaped the bombing raids, but even in the fading light the grimness of the area was evident in its run-down houses and disconsolate atmosphere. It was an area of northeast London she wasn't familiar with, and she counted herself lucky she hadn't had reason to visit before.

The rain grew more persistent, plastering strands of wet hair against her cheek, splashing in her eyes, but she was still a distance from the number she was looking for. It was strange: she should have been scared, but her breathing was level, her hands didn't shake and her thoughts were ordered. In fact, it now seemed the obvious thing to approach this head-on, and she struggled to think why she hadn't done it sooner—for everyone's sake. She'd been naive to think she could keep working and also look for her daughter, or rely on anyone to help.

When she'd discovered that Theo had left for New York, she'd known that things were dire. George explained it was for family reasons, but she felt she knew the truth: her book, and their days at Partridge, were numbered. Theo had been open and optimistic, full of ideas and enthusiasm, but he hadn't managed to hide his concerns from her, and now he'd gone running back to Walter.

A hundred yards further on, Alice found number seventy-nine: another slate-gray terrace house with boarded-up windows, splintered doorframes and no sign of life. She sheltered under the narrow doorjamb, listening out for voices, the steady beat of rain counting down the seconds. Then there it was—a child's cry. At least she thought it was, as everything fell quiet again.

Now she had to summon up the courage to knock.

She had imagined this moment so many times: the joy of finding Eadie, or a confrontation, or both. As a girl, she'd divided her books into categories: bravest heroines, best adventures, most romantic love stories. She had collated memories of other people's lives, albeit fictional ones, that she'd drawn on to help her through tricky situations. She'd wanted to emulate her bravest heroine now, but it suddenly seemed so pointless. The books, the stories, the characters—they weren't real, none of it was. She wasn't the same person she'd been a year ago, and her life might feel as illusory as any fiction she'd read, and her mother's actions and the truth about William's birth as impossible as any story, but this was real. She was here now, and Eadie might be too.

Alice was supposed to be at the book group, but she'd sent a note to Ursula asking her to go instead and take the promised books. She'd also left a message for Penny: a detailed account of everything, and list of contacts in case she didn't return, not to protect her so much as to ensure they would continue to look for Eadie.

She raised a clenched fist to the door, but it hovered in midair inches from the green flaking paint and the tarnished brass handle.

Perhaps it was madness coming to the Pritchards' home, given what she knew of them: they were convicted murderers, they'd starved children to death and left others emaciated, and she felt sick every time she thought about the conditions in which police had found the infants. But picturing them was enough to give her the rush of adrenaline she needed.

Alice knocked, glancing back over her shoulder in the hope that someone might be there to see her go in. It was too late to turn and walk away—this was her only hope—and she had to believe that no matter how wicked they were, no matter how evil this family could be, they might know where her daughter was.

The door scraped open, and a bulky man filled the space. He was backlit by the hallway pendant, and it wasn't until he stepped closer that she saw his hair, thinned to long wisps and combed across his crown. There was something birdlike about him, his fleshy cheeks divided by a long hawkish nose that threw his top lip into shadow. He was every bit as repulsive as she'd imagined him to be, but he wasn't one of the men her mother had described.

"Yes?" he said, glaring at her from beneath hooded eyes.

"I'm sorry to bother you . . . I hope you don't mind me calling in like this," she said, pressing her weight from one foot to the other. "It's just that I wanted to stop by and say hello. I'm going to be moving in soon, just down the street."

He continued to stare.

"And I thought it would be nice to meet the neighbors. Mr. . . . ?"

"It's not a good time right now. The wife gets a headache in the evenings." His voice was a small monotone. "Come back during the day."

"Yes, of course."

"Who's there, Frank?" a woman shouted from the front room.

"It's . . ."

"Grace, my name is Grace," Alice said, forcing a smile.

"Grace," he called back, "a new neighbor—"

"Well, don't be rude. Show her in!"

"You heard her," he said, taking a step backward. "You'd better come in."

Alice's hairs stood on end as she passed by him, stepping

cautiously into a hallway that stretched down a dark passage to the back of the house.

"Living room's just down there." He pointed to where a streak of light shone beneath a door.

"Come in, don't be shy," a voice sounded from the other side of it.

The floorboards creaked as Alice took one small step at a time, measured against her breathing, before the loud clunk of the front door being shut behind her made her jump, and Frank's heavy footsteps followed her in.

The living room was cluttered, too much furniture competing for space with too many ornaments, and a teenage girl sat on the sofa, half-buried in plush cushions. On the other side of the room, beneath the netted windows, a plump woman took up the expanse of a high-backed armchair, her skirt pulled up over her knees, swollen feet resting on a footstool. Her square face and short brown hair gave her a masculine appearance, and she watched Alice cautiously through dark eyes. "Come in. Don't be shy. Grace, is it?"

Even from where she stood, Alice could see the woman's face was scored with deep lines. "Yes. I'm sorry, Frank didn't tell me your name. . . ."

"It's Beatrice."

"I didn't tell you mine either," Frank said, as he came to stand beside her.

Alice's heart skipped a beat.

"You're such a prat sometimes, Frank," Beatrice said, and laughed. "She heard me calling you! Don't mind me." She grimaced at her puffy red ankles. "Things always get worse at night. It's a good job I've still got Annie here to help look after me, eh?"

Alice glanced at the girl on the sofa; her eyes were like saucers, and they were glued to her.

"Sit down, love," Beatrice said.

"I'm all right, thank you. I just wanted to say hello."

She could feel Frank beside her, an unwelcome presence standing too close, and he had a sour, unwashed odor.

"Tell me," said Beatrice, "what number are you moving to?"

"Two doors down, seventy-five."

"Really, the Robinsons' place, I didn't know they were moving," she said, glancing at her husband.

Alice let out a nervous breath. She'd never been a good liar—Ruth had taught her it was a sin—and now she wasn't sure she could convince the Pritchards if she couldn't even convince herself. "The truth is"—she swallowed—"I was looking for you."

"Looking for who?" the woman asked.

"The Pritchards."

The couple exchanged a look before the woman glanced over at Annie. "Can you leave us for a while, love?"

The girl rose ponderously and dragged her feet to the door, all the time with her eyes fixed on Alice.

"And stop slouching!" Beatrice shouted behind her.

The girl turned at the doorway to give Alice a small smile, then ducked out.

Alice took a deep breath and closed her eyes, trying to summon Eadie's face, her smell, her newborn essence.

When Alice opened them, the Pritchards were staring at her.

"What do you want?" Beatrice asked coldly.

"I need you to tell me about your activities since you came out of prison, about all the baby farmers you know in London . . . or anywhere, for that matter."

"Who are you?" Frank asked.

"It doesn't matter, I just need your help."

"And what's in it for us?" he said.

Alice didn't have much to bargain with. "Keeping your whereabouts a secret."

Beatrice gave a loud, throaty laugh. "That's not much of an incentive, love."

Alice thought she understood how far she'd go to find her daughter. She'd returned to her Dulwich home during the day when her mother was at work to get her father's gun. The trips with her father and brother had been to hunt for food, then when William was drafted he'd insisted she be able to defend herself. But as she fingered the pistol in her pocket and felt the cold hard metal beneath her skin, she didn't feel capable of using it on another human being.

Thirty

Regent's Park Road was in pitch darkness and the blackout blinds in all the houses were drawn by the time Alice stumbled through the café doors. The book group had finished, everyone long gone except for Ursula, who leaned against the counter, looking remote, and Penny, who threw her arms around Alice as soon as she appeared. "What happened?" she asked.

"I'll explain in a minute," Alice replied, "I just need to sit down." She sank heavily into one of the chairs, hands still trembling, while Penny scurried about, fetching her a mug of tea before sitting next to her. "How did you get on at the book group?" Alice asked, sipping it slowly. "Did Rex have any news?"

"Yes, he told us to remember the name Sidney Jardine," Penny replied, before exchanging a look with Ursula.

"What's happened?" Alice asked, glancing from one to the other.

"Ursula knows, Alice. I've told her everything."

"Everything?"

"Well, she guessed, actually."

So that was it; Ursula knew now. Alice was uncertain how she felt; a mix of relief and regret that she hadn't told her friend personally.

"I'm so sorry, Alice," Ursula said. "I can't imagine what you've been going through . . . what you must still be going through."

"Thank you. How did you guess?"

Ursula told her about the evening's events. They'd all sat in the usual horseshoe around the table: Helena, Rex, Marjorie, Terrance, Henry, Penny and Ursula. Terrance had propositioned Ursula. "As if I would contemplate a relationship with him," she said, sounding amused and appalled as she threw some humor into the conversation. "It's about as likely to happen as Churchill striding through the door and asking to join the book group!" She went on to explain how the group had argued about whose turn it was to open the box of books, and they'd waited patiently as Rex retrieved *The Body in the Library* and his eyes lit up. Everyone had seemed overjoyed—except Penny, who was gazing distractedly into space. "That's when I knew something was wrong," Ursula said, looking at Alice.

"Why?"

"I don't know, I just did—call it intuition. We were talking about the dramatic events of the book, when it struck me that the change in your behavior was akin to that of any literary heroine who has suffered great tragedy—and grown more distant and troubled." She raised her eyebrows. "Not only that, but there's the anxiety you've never suffered from before, the claustrophobia, the compulsive behavior, all of which we'd noticed. And they've all cropped up since you left to look after your cousin's baby."

Ursula's voice brimmed with emotion as she explained how she couldn't stop thinking about how everything had changed: Alice's disappearances, the secretiveness surrounding her cousin's baby, the falling out with her mother. And then how she'd heard Penny's children upstairs, their giggles and bumps and squeals as if they were jumping on the beds, and Penny's glance upward and the maternal frown followed quickly by a smile. It had clicked: the baby was Alice's. "I'm sorry, I forced Penny to tell me. But I wish it had been you."

"I know, and I'm sorry, Ursula, but at least now you know."

Penny had given her all the distressing details of the past six months—everything except for who the father was.

"And what about tonight?" Penny asked Alice. "Did you find out anything?"

"It was a waste of time—the Pritchards didn't know anything, and I couldn't wait to leave," she replied. She didn't want her friends to know she'd been too much of a coward to use the gun, or that she even had a gun at all. But she'd learned one thing for certain, that the Pritchards weren't any of the baby farmers who Ruth had described, and that they no longer seemed to be part of that world either, as Olive had thought they might be. "No, nothing at all. Now I'm back to square one, apart from this name . . . Jardine. I'll need to investigate that."

"Maybe, but you're not going anywhere on your own this time," Penny said. "One of us is coming with you."

It was a few days since her visit to the Pritchards, and Penny and Ursula had refused to let her out of their sight as they'd had no luck tracing Rex's lead.

"Hey, what do you say about going to the cinema?" Ursula asked. "*Women Aren't Angels* is on."

Alice gave a weak smile.

"It's a comedy. . . ."

"I don't really feel very much like laughing," she said flatly.

They were in Ursula's bedroom, standing in front of a full-length mirror. Alice stared at Ursula's masculine clothes: baggy trousers, white shirt with a woolen pullover and a striped Etonian tie, a jacket slung over her right shoulder.

"You know, Alice, I think you've possibly been approaching this the wrong way."

"What do you mean?"

"Well, it should be a couple looking for a baby, not a woman on her own."

"How does that make any difference?" Alice said grimly.

"Think about it . . . a couple are much more likely to be considered suitable, whereas on your own you tend to arouse suspicion."

"That's what Penny told me to do, with Michael's help," Alice said. "You're probably right. I did consider it, but I didn't want to inconvenience anyone. God, I've been such a fool!"

Ursula placed a hand on her arm. "Don't say that. You're not a fool—no one could be doing any more than you are now. I really don't know how you've coped for so long."

If only Theo were still there; if only she could have

confided in him and got his help, she thought. But that seemed silly now.

"I'm not giving up, you know," she said. "I'm going to keep on looking."

"Of course you are, Alice. And I'll completely support you." Ursula withdrew her hand and started pinning back her hair. "I don't think even my merciless family are capable of anything like this."

Alice forced a smile.

"Anyway," Ursula said, smiling at both their reflections, "the good news is that with me dressed like this, I think we'll get away with it."

Alice laughed for the first time in days.

"I'm serious!"

"You are?"

"Of course. If we make our approach as a couple looking for a child, it might be your best chance yet." Ursula selected a trilby from her dressing table and tucked her auburn curls underneath so that only wisps showed above her ears. "I think I look the part," she said, linking arms with Alice. "See, I told you, there will be no questions."

Alice examined Ursula's reflection and decided to acknowledge what had always remained unspoken between them. She knew that Ursula understood what it felt like to be an outsider, and to be judged and isolated because of it.

Their eyes met in the mirror, and Alice gave her a meaningful stare. "I know, Ursula."

"Know what?"

"I know why you dress the way you do, why you act as if you don't care."

"About what?"

"About not being like the rest of us . . . about not wanting to have a man in your life." Alice maintained eye contact. "But it doesn't matter to me. It doesn't matter in the slightest."

Ursula placed the trilby back in its place and shook her hair free, then she turned to Alice. "Is that why you didn't tell me about Eadie?"

"Partly. I didn't think that motherhood was something we could talk about so easily."

The bed was strewn with clothes, but Ursula cleared a space and indicated for Alice to sit down. "Perhaps with other people, Alice, but never with you."

Alice smiled. "Is there someone special?"

"Yes," Ursula said, smiling. "Her name is Bridget, and she's a wonderful companion."

"Does your family know about her?"

Ursula laughed. "Of course not."

"Are you going to tell them?"

"Why on earth would I?"

"Because . . . because . . ."

"Because they've never been there for me before, because they won't be there for me now. I haven't seen my sister in two years, or heard from my parents since I tried to visit them three Christmases ago."

Alice knew that Ursula was right; it was similar to what her experiences with Ruth had shown her.

Ursula told her the full story. She'd been sixteen when she read *The Well of Loneliness* and realized she wasn't alone, but she also realized that lesbianism was frowned upon by most of society, including her family. Her parents confiscated her book collection and packed her off to university, where she completed an English degree before moving to London, landing a job at a newspaper and embarking on an affair with a young male reporter. The six-week relationship proved to her that there was no place in her life for romances with men, and she sought out a new circle of friends.

Now she told Alice that she'd tried hard not to laugh when George had asked the team to "dig deep" into their personal lives; she was certain he wouldn't want to publish any of her or her friends' stories.

"But none of that matters anymore; what's important is finding Eadie. I'll do whatever I can to help you," Ursula announced. "And for everyone's sake, we need to finish this book and send it to print!"

Thirty-one

LONDON, MAY 2, 1943

The woman in front of Alice turned sharply and glared disapprovingly.

"Sorry," Alice whispered.

She'd caught the woman's heel as she'd joined the latecomers funneling into the red-brick church. It was a warm spring day, but the sun had done little to raise the temperature of the dark Gothic interior, and everyone still wore their hats and coats. Alice pulled her scarf a little tighter, for warmth and to hide her face. It had been two years since she'd been here for Will's memorial service, and she'd forgotten how vast the inside was, with its four-bay nave and double-pitched roof, and how unwelcoming the draft was from the cavernous crypt below. Alice glanced toward the nave where several aisles led away to arches and porches, and a staircase climbed to the tower and bell turret four floors above. On the south side of the chancel, the vestries and organ chamber occupied the space, and Alice watched as the organist readied herself ceremoniously beneath the tall vertical pipes.

Maybe this is why Ruth's grown so stony and cold—she's spent too long in this dark and ancient place, the chill seeping into her bones.

Father Mitchell was in the midst of delivering his sermon, his deep voice reaching far beyond the altar as his gaze swept greedily across the congregation.

Alice found a seat close enough to the back that she wouldn't be noticed, and looked around. The pews were nearly full, with some locals she recognized but mostly strangers. Then she spotted Ruth a few rows in front, head tilted up to nod as the priest talked.

". . . to all thy people give thy heavenly grace, and especially to this congregation here present—that, with meek heart and due reverence, they may hear and receive thy Holy Word, truly serving thee in holiness and righteousness all the days of their life."

But Alice wasn't there to hear the Holy Word; she wanted to watch Ruth. She still couldn't begin to understand how her mother could have chosen the Church over her family, especially since it meant she had no one now. Ursula's situation had made her question this attitude even more, and as she listened to Father Mitchell she struggled to work out what he stood for that would make a person sacrifice their family. Perhaps if their father hadn't worked every weekend, or if Ruth hadn't forced her children to accompany her for years, then she might have shared her mother's faith, but instead she'd stopped going as soon as she was able to.

She half-listened, concentrating on Ruth, on the strands of graying hair that brushed the collar of her worn coat; on the ivy-green of her sensible hat, the one she no longer needed in church but chose to wear. She and Alice had never shared the same taste in clothes, music, people—in fact, if Alice hadn't seen the birth certificate, she would have sworn she was the one who didn't share Ruth's flesh and blood, not William.

"And we most humbly beseech thee of thy goodness, O Lord, to comfort and succor all them, who in this transitory life are in trouble, sorrow, need, sickness or any other adversity," Father Mitchell continued.

Ruth bowed her head as the congregation joined in the general confession, their voices uniting in a chant that echoed across the transepts and sent a shiver up Alice's spine as she recognized his words.

"Almighty God, Father of our Lord Jesus Christ, Maker of all things, Judge of all men: we acknowledge and bewail our manifold sins and wickedness, which we, from time to time, most grievously have committed."

The priest's tone was loud and intimidating, and Alice struggled to see why anyone would choose to be bullied with these centuries-old words. But absolution was more important to Ruth than her daughter's forgiveness or trying to protect her grandchild.

Alice felt a gentle nudge against her right arm and turned to see an older woman looking at her solemnly, a white hand-kerchief scrunched in her outstretched hand. "Father Mitchell often moves me to tears too," the woman said, and smiled. "May the Lord be with you."

"Thank you, and with you," Alice forced herself to say before turning away. She hadn't even known she was crying.

As the chanting steadily rose, her heart began to race—but not in excitement, in panic. How would she ever find her daughter?

"For God so loved the world, that he gave his only-begotten Son."

Is that why Ruth could bear to sacrifice her only granddaughter?

"To you all my blessing. May the Lord be with you."

Where can I go now? Who else is there to turn to? I've run out of options.

The greeting reverberated through the congregation; she was drowning in the sea of voices, swamped by their prayers. Time was slipping away, as if she was standing on a peninsula watching water rise over the isthmus, cutting off the only escape.

Think, Alice, think. Think about the secrets people keep and the lies they tell. Who can be trusted?

Not Theo, unfortunately. She'd had no idea until Ursula told her that he'd returned to New York because of his sick father—and his fiancée, Walter's daughter. There had to be a reason he'd kept it hidden, and Alice could only assume he wasn't the man she'd thought him to be. The knowledge had thrust her into even more of a depression, a spiral of regret for the trust she'd placed in him and all that they had shared.

But she wouldn't allow herself to dwell on Theo Bloom, another man who'd deceived her; she needed to focus on who told the truth. Penny hadn't lied to her. Neither had Olive—

the journalist was doing all that was possible to help her . . . or was she?

"No, it's out of the question," Elizabeth said, adamant.

"It's my last chance. I wouldn't ask if there was any other way."

Alice had gone straight to the *Daily Mail* offices when they had opened the following day, and now she stood, hands braced against the counter, pleading with the librarian.

"Absolutely not. You don't know what you're asking, Alice. I could lose my job, not to mention getting Olive in trouble. She'd lose all credibility and trust."

"But my cousin could lose her baby. Forever."

Elizabeth dropped her head into her hands.

"Your paper ran the advert that led to her being taken, you know—"

A silence stretched out between them, and Alice let it settle, giving Elizabeth time to think. Then Alice reached over to squeeze her hand briefly. "I only need his name. And I'll be discreet, no one ever needs to know—not even Olive, if you don't want her to."

"Of course she'll know! Don't be silly, Alice. Do you think her informer is ever going to trust her again after you turn up? There'll be no more stories, no more information she can publish to keep the baby farmers in people's minds. We could be sacrificing thousands of other kids for your cousin's if I do what you're asking me to."

"But the law is coming in anyway. There's only a month to go. Yes, Olive's reports are important, but she's achieved what she set out to do—mothers and babies will be more protected. Her reports aren't going to make as much difference as they have in the past . . . not as much difference as they could to my cousin's baby and possibly others imprisoned by the same people."

Alice's intuition that there was someone else who had been helping Olive—a contact on the inside—had been right, but Elizabeth was resolute in her loyalty.

"Please. I wouldn't ask if there was any other way."

"You could wait until Thursday and ask Olive yourself."

"But I thought she wasn't back until the weekend."

Elizabeth grew silent again, her fingers playing across the edge of the desk, eyes trained down as if searching for the answer.

Their acquaintance had grown into a friendship over the weeks of visits, and Alice sensed that the librarian felt the same. Alice hesitated briefly and then followed her instinct and reached out her hand, placing it over Elizabeth's. "She's mine, Elizabeth," she whispered. "The baby that I'm looking for. She's mine."

The librarian looked up and her eyes filled as she bit her bottom lip, and Alice tried not to cry too.

"I don't know if it's even his real name," Elizabeth replied as she blinked away tears, "but I know where you can find him."

Alice squeezed her hand. "I don't know how to—"

Elizabeth gently withdrew her hand and picked up a pencil, scribbling on a scrap of paper, then pushed it across the counter. "It's best if we still keep it between the two of us, though. For the time being."

"All right," Alice replied, reading the hastily written name and address.

"And, Alice?"

"Yes?"

"Olive has good reason to want justice, and she trusts him . . . but be careful."

Thirty-two

LONDON, MAY 3, 1943

Alice was in a part of London that the world had forgotten. The East End slums and council housing had been razed and ravaged—and whatever the Luftwaffe and their Messerschmitts hadn't annihilated had been looted and vandalized, or so an older woman told her when she stopped to ask the way. "I'm not sure you should be wandering around here by yourself," the woman added in a hoarse voice. But Alice was long past caring for her own well-being, although she couldn't ignore her heart palpitations. Were they born out of anxiety or anticipation because there was a small chance Joe Stevenson, Olive's informer, would be able to help?

A raven-black cloud obscured the sun, throwing the street into temporary darkness, and Elizabeth's words reverberated in her mind: *Olive has good reason to want justice . . . but be careful.*

That was exactly what Alice planned to do, and she'd come up with a way to speak to Joe without risking herself or Olive.

The meeting place, a public house called the Black Swan, was on a corner site, the only business open in the row of closed shops. There was an ugly right angle of metal and glass to one side, and patched wooden hoarding on the other.

Alice couldn't see through the beveled glass door, so she moved inside the doorway, palms prickling as she gripped the handle. *Remember your story, Alice. Think about Eadie. Think about William and how brave he was, how brave and strong all soldiers are.*

There was a narrow bar at the back and upholstered stools, the rest of the room given over to a dining area of Formica tables and red vinyl chairs. A dark-haired man with a slight build moved back and forth behind the bar, serving customers: Joe. According to Elizabeth's description, he had eyes that never stayed still, and she'd also learned that the librarian had delivered and collected packages on a few occasions.

"What can I get you?" he asked Alice when she approached.

"Oh, just a soda water, please."

He leaned back on his heels and crossed his arms, a frown knitting his dark eyebrows together. "You can't have come all this way just for that."

"What do you mean?" she asked, her hands clenching.

"I can tell you're not from round here, and our egg sandwiches are notorious," he said with a grin.

"Yes, you're right." She noticed he wasn't from round here either: his accent was from the Midlands, or maybe further north. "I'll have one of your notorious sandwiches too," she said with a polite smile.

She observed him as he poured her drink and wrote the order down: average height, hair neatly groomed into a single wave and shirtsleeves rolled up—ordinary in every way, except that *he* could be the person who held the key to finding Eadie.

At one of the Formica tables, Alice finished the sandwich and a second drink, taking it slowly and reading a newspaper, her legs jiggling nervously as she waited for him to clear the empty plate.

"Can I get you anything else, miss?"

"I'm fine, thank you, Joe—"

Alice froze. She'd just risked everything with another stupid slip of the tongue.

He looked at her as if seeing her for the first time. "Do I know you, miss?"

"No, but—" She tried to replicate a smile she'd seen before, one Ursula used all the time to feign familiarity and put people at ease. "I've got some information that might be useful to you. Perhaps we could talk somewhere more private."

He glanced at the bar. "There's someone starting the next shift in about fifteen minutes. You could stay here or wait for me across the road."

She followed his gaze through the window to a playground opposite the pub. It was the only open space and appeared to be part of the housing development, but it would do.

No sooner had Alice settled on a bench than a group of children, accompanied by a teenage girl, arrived to play on the mangled equipment. Three girls rushed over to the roundabout; one of them, with auburn braids, lay across the bars, while another leaned backward, letting her head tip upside down, blond hair flying up as the roundabout whirled clockwise. The third girl pushed off with her left foot as the teenager waved at them frantically to slow down. Alice flinched at the memory of Ruth's face, rueful and pained, when she'd told Alice how much she and Freddie had wanted a child. As Alice watched the little girls at play, she realized that she understood the desperation that had driven Ruth to adopt William under dubious circumstances.

Alice released a breath and slumped back against the bench, the cold hard wood digging into her spine as she scanned the road for Joe. There weren't any trees to shelter under; the main features of the park were piles of shattered bricks that even the salvage crews had left. Dust and sulfur clogged her nose. Her first impression had been that the area was unsuitable and unsafe for a playground, yet daisies were poking their heads out of the dirt and bright yellow buttercups grew among the scrappy grass. It might be a wasteland, but it was also an oasis for the kids, and she felt sure there would be stories here for *Women and Children First* if she could only look.

Joe was true to his word and appeared fifteen minutes later, kicking up clouds of dust as he came toward her. She hadn't noticed in the pub that he walked with a slight hitch, his right leg making straight lines in the dirt, whereas his left leg created only a single footprint like Morse code. She guessed it must be from the war, and it lent him an air of vagrancy that seemed useful for his cover.

He sat next to her and promptly lit a cigarette, staring out over the playground as if purposefully avoiding eye contact. Alice desperately wanted to look him in the eye and see what

Olive saw, and to know that what Olive surely believed was true—that he was principled and decent.

"I expect you want to know why I'm here." Alice wished her voice wasn't so uneven.

"I'm more interested in knowing who told you where to find me."

"Would you be surprised to know it wasn't one person?" she said, sticking to her plan not to mention Olive. "That you've quite a reputation?" She'd decided to use flattery, as she'd often seen Rupert do—especially since it had got him exactly what he wanted, she thought with a flush of shame.

Joe turned to face her, brown eyes fixing on her closely. "And what's my reputation for, miss?"

"Sarah, please call me Sarah. And it's less of a reputation and more of a . . . let's see, a status. People speak highly of your ability to get things done." There was no going back now; she'd already decided that an honest request for help would likely be greeted with a flat refusal, and then where would that leave her? No, this way he would have to take her into his confidence and lead her to his contacts. Before he could ask any more questions, she carried on. "And, well, I've got rather a lot of things to get done that I hoped you might be able to help me with."

"Such as?"

"Girls in trouble. Friends, and friends of friends. Girls without boyfriends, girls with fellas who aren't coming home anymore."

He narrowed his eyes, understanding.

"And then there are those men who are just pigs," she said for good measure. "Ones who could do with a good beating if anyone caught up with them."

"And what is it you want from me?"

"I heard you know where they can get some relief from their little problems."

Joe ground his half-smoked cigarette beneath his heel, then ran his hands over his face. "Excuse me, I'm tired," he said, rubbing his eyes.

"That's all right, we're all entitled to a break. When are you due back at the pub?"

"No, that's me done for the day. I'm off to my second job now."

"And what's that?" she asked.

"Now that would be telling," he said, tapping the side of his nose.

"So, do you think you can help me?"

"Well, here's the thing." He laid his arm over the back of the bench as he shifted closer. "You don't seem to me to be the kind of girl who has friends with little problems, so I'm wondering what it is you really want."

Alice held herself steady. "I might not look like that kind of girl, but unfortunately it's true. And . . . well, I was told you have the best contacts in London." She looked at him with doe eyes, hoping she wasn't overdoing it.

His mouth twitched into a half smile. "And these little problems," he said, "when will they arrive?"

Alice swallowed. "A few are here already . . . and there will be others over the next few months. The girls don't have much money, and they want to know how much it is to take them off their hands."

"I don't know."

"But you must have some idea?"

"No, it's not my area of expertise."

"What is, then?"

Joe stared at her, then got up from the bench and started to limp away.

"What's wrong?" she asked, chasing him across the playground. Did he suspect something?

He turned, lifting his hands from his sides. "Do you want to come or not?"

"Where are we going?"

"I thought your friends were in a hurry. Do you want to meet the boss, or don't you?"

"Yes, but—" It was happening too quickly: the introduction had been too easy, and she wasn't armed. For the first time, she felt genuinely scared. "But I can't go right now. I wish I could, I just didn't know it would be so soon."

His gaze flitted over her. "Friday, then. I'll meet you here at midday."

Thirty-three

NEW YORK, MAY 5, 1943

Theo hurried the three blocks to his favorite diner on the corner of West Forty-sixth and Ninth. He needed coffee flowing through his veins before he faced Walter, particularly since it would be the first time he saw his employer—Walter had been away and was making a special trip from his New Jersey home.

Over a week had passed since Theo's return to New York, and he was still having restless nights. He lay awake listening to the clamor of garbage trucks as he wrestled with everything that was on his mind. There were concerns about his father and George, but most of the time he was consumed with thoughts of Alice. It wasn't just the guilt he felt at being disloyal to his employer and his fiancée, but also a deep-rooted panic at the very real prospect he would never see Alice again.

He usually enjoyed the walk through Hell's Kitchen, past the noisy banter of street traders and in among the tourists as they headed toward Times Square, but today he couldn't stop thinking about what to say to Walter.

Trying to distract himself, he crossed the street and looked up at the spaces between the buildings into avenues of cobalt sky. He was enjoying the fresh spring air, and it seemed the rest of Manhattan felt the same; they had descended on the Upper West Side and taken all the diner's outdoor tables.

Theo lit a cigarette and waited until a small table became available beneath the green vinyl awning. It suited him perfectly, and he ordered breakfast and spread his papers across the table so he could run through the figures one more time. He had to present a realistic picture of the British firm's predicament, while trying to make the accounts look as good as possible. He knew instinctively that the London office was worth saving—he just needed to be sure that this was a rational decision he could justify under Walter's intense scrutiny. He drained his coffee, relishing the taste after two months of Camp, the insipid liquid the British passed off as just as good.

It seemed that despite the odds, George and his team's blind faith and hard work had kept them going for all these months—and a bit of luck. What was that patriotic song that endlessly played on the radio? "Land of Hope and Glory." He couldn't help but smile as he realized he had to try to ignore the contagion of their foolish optimism. And to remember that this was his home—that he was a New Yorker—and his life here needed to go on.

When his food arrived it was a huge plate, not just fried eggs and Canadian bacon but also fried potatoes, tomatoes and rye toast, and he ate guiltily as he thought of the meager portions the British were living on. He ordered a coffee refill and decided to look through *Women and Children First* before he showed it to Walter.

When he reached inside his bag for the mock-up, he found an entirely different book instead, one that he must have taken on his hasty departure. This was a journal with stories and illustrations, newspaper cuttings and commentary, and articles of celebrities and politicians visiting London Zoo. There were margins of scribbled notes and drawings—and it was all in Alice's hand. The title page read: *The Zoo Chronicles: Tales from London Zoo*, and on the back cover there was an attractive black-and-white illustration, an advertisement for LATE NIGHT OPENINGS AT THE ZOO with floodlighting and music. He'd had no idea that London Zoo was still operating or that it was so vast; a map showed there were different precincts for all the animals. His time in London had been spent south of Marylebone Road, and he'd had no reason to visit, although he vaguely remembered it being popular with US servicemen.

There were several clippings about esteemed visitors and noteworthy employees, and he got drawn into reading one about Dr. Burgess Barnett, the "Snake Man," a former curator of reptiles who had been awarded an MBE for staying behind with refugees during the evacuation of Burma. Theo read about the hero who, as well as facing death by handling poisonous snakes, had endured treacherous conditions to march the party through an unfamiliar and hostile country until they reached safety and much-needed medical treatment. *And here I am worrying about facing Walter,* he thought. The next feature was about how the penguins' play-fights with the polar bears had brought them to the attention of the London papers, which commended their show as an antidote to the "jitters."

At the back of the journal was a suggested itinerary—"A Day in the Life of the Zoo"—also in Alice's distinctive handwriting. *With the doors open at nine o'clock there are a full three hours to wander at leisure and take refreshments in one of the cafés before the midday feed at the Penguin Pool. Then it is a choice between the polar bears at the Mappin Terraces and lions and tigers at the Lion House, and the sea lions or diving birds at three-thirty; one of the problems, or positives, depending on how you look at it, is that there is always so much to do.* He could hear her voice as he read, the emotion so very real, and he wanted to visit the zoo with her by his side. This appeared to be a labor of love: the vivid descriptions, the knowledge of the animals, the level of detail.

On the last page was a dedication: *For my father, Frederick (Freddie) Charles Cotton and his granddaughter, Eadie.*

Alice hadn't mentioned that her late brother had a child, so who was Eadie? And why hadn't Alice shown any of the team this journal before? It was inspiring and uplifting, an unknown part of British life on the home front, featuring animal rescues and human bravery. It was exactly the type of book they had discussed and agreed they wanted: "extraordinary stories of ordinary people."

"Good morning, Mr. Bloom," Kenny the elevator operator said, with a curt nod.

Theo felt a wave of nostalgia as he stood by the bank of brass elevators, their intricate panels of polished nickel and brass rivets giving the oversized lobby the appearance of a ship from the nearby Brooklyn yard.

"How are you, Kenny, and how's your granddaughter?"

"She's doing very well. Thanks for asking, sir."

"Very pleased to hear it."

"And how has London been treating you, Mr. Bloom?"

"She's been very kind to me, Kenny. I hope to go back—there's still a lot to do."

When Theo stepped out of the elevator, he thought of how he'd intended to stay in New York until his father's condition improved, and now he knew that it wasn't life-threatening; the doctors appeared to be satisfied that they'd balanced his medications. *The next time you see him he'll be at home,* one of the nurses had said cheerily. The issue now wasn't the need to move his father, it was Walter—and getting on another flight.

"Theo, great to see you," Walter said, as he jumped up from his seat and came around the desk to give him a vigorous handshake. "I'm sorry I wasn't here last week to welcome you. It's terrific to have you back. You can see everything's been piling up while you've been gone." He motioned toward the stack of folders on his desk.

"I thought the new associate was going to handle things in my absence," Theo said with a frown.

"Yes, the smaller pieces"—Walter took his arm and guided him toward the chairs—"but we wouldn't want him involved in any of the bigger deals, would we?"

Theo declined the cigarette Walter offered and took out a Piccadilly, George's brand, which he now preferred.

"How's your father?" Walter asked, smoke curling from his mouth.

"It's early yet, but he's doing better than expected."

"That's good, really good. Your family must be relieved."

"He's not out of the woods yet, but his condition is stable." Theo didn't want to tempt fate by assuming his father would be all right; the doctors had given them reason to be optimistic but with a note of caution.

Walter tapped his fingers on the side of the chair. "Come on, then . . . tell me all about it."

Theo spent close to an hour going into the specifics that the restricted long-distance phone calls hadn't allowed. He reiterated details of the wartime difficulties Partridge faced, but he also told Walter of the ingenious solutions they'd found, and about their new titles. Then he told him about the useful contacts he'd made and of the recent changes in the industry, including the opportunities for the Americans to supply books to parts of the Commonwealth and Europe, now that the British and their ships no longer could.

By the time Theo finished he was satisfied that he'd made it sound as if things were looking up, and that once the new titles were out, the annual paper rations would increase and allow George's team to continue to build their slate for the coming years.

"There is just one small matter; there's been an issue with the rent," he said, making the judgment not to keep a secret that his employer was likely to soon discover. "George has been paying for it out of his personal savings for the past four months, but Clare won't let him carry on."

"No, I can see that . . . I don't know many wives who would. I wish he'd told me himself, though," Walter said, puckering his lips.

Theo grimaced as he tried to think of a tactful reply, but Walter beat him to it.

"Still no profit, then?" he asked.

"Not this financial year, but it will improve next year," Theo replied. "The forecasts are promising."

"And how long are you proposing that we prop them up?"

"We're not. If you look closely at these figures, there's no debt. Not unless this year's books don't sell." Theo passed him the accounts. "There's no reason for that to happen, though. It's a simple case of supply and demand, Walter—there just aren't enough books to go around."

He'd hoped for a better reaction, but Walter just looked through the papers and made a few gruff comments. Yes, conditions were dire, but they had learned to cope; they were adjusting and improvising, and it was working, but it was hard to see that from the other side of the world.

"I really felt as if I was making a difference, and it opened so many doors being there," Theo said, leaning forward and stubbing his cigarette out in the ashtray. "You know, Walter, without their drive and their lobbying and initiatives, there would be no publishing industry to speak of. What they've done is really quite remarkable."

Walter remained uncharacteristically quiet, and Theo thought that perhaps he had shared too much. He knew his employer didn't approve of his work with the council, but he was convinced more than ever of how necessary it all was.

Walter rose and walked over to the window, his back turned. "Thanks for making the trip, Theo; I am grateful to you. I know it's been a sacrifice for you and Virginia. But the good news is, your work there is done." He turned to face Theo.

"I don't need you to go back . . . I need you to start looking for a buyer."

Hadn't Walter heard a word he'd said? He had to go back; he wanted to finish what he'd started. And he needed to see Alice.

"But they're doing all right. This isn't necessary, Walter."

It was as if his employer hadn't heard him. "Be discreet, though, don't talk to the big guns, Blackie or Collins or Heinemann, anyone like that. I need you to go through other channels. It would be very difficult if George got wind of it at this stage."

"But why do you want to . . . ? We don't need to sell."

Walter looked at him dispassionately. "Yes, Theo. I'm afraid we do. What you've just told me has made up my mind. We'd be crazy not to!" He'd grown more animated. "You say we're growing a new generation of readers, but that won't help us now—we don't know when the war will end. What will help is selling London and investing the money here. Britain might not be able to export books anymore, but we can. We'll be the ones to sell to the rest of the world."

The shock of what Theo had done slowly dawned on him, and he reflexively sat down while Walter spoke excitedly of his plans. George and the others would think that he'd betrayed them, that he'd known this was Walter's intention all along, when he had actually been trying to prevent it. And what of Alice's books and her career? He would be blamed for ending that too, along with any future they may have had.

"It's unfortunate, but you're a businessman, Theo. You know it's too good an opportunity for us not to take it."

"But what about George? What about his family?"

"They'll be fine. George has plenty of other business interests, and we'll make sure he gets a fair price. Publishing has never really been in his blood."

What a mug he'd been. Unknowingly, he'd become one of the architects of their demise. And he realized that he couldn't let it happen—somehow he would have to find a way to fix things.

Thirty-four

"Actually, I've changed my mind," Theo said, leaning forward so the cab driver could hear. "Take me down to South Street, take Fulton to the end and wait for me there. I'll only be ten minutes, and I'll pay the waiting fare."

"You're the boss," the driver answered.

It was lunchtime, and he'd been en route to the hospital to see his father, motoring down Bowery, about to turn on to the Manhattan Bridge, when the idea had struck and he'd decided to stop. He strolled east along South Street—it was where he'd spent much of his childhood riding bikes among the old steam plants and vast brick buildings in the "street of ships." His mood had turned grim after the meeting and he still couldn't believe that where he'd tried to help, he'd made things so much worse. *What you've just told me has made up my mind. We'd be crazy not to!* had been Walter's words. Theo knew a sense of freedom could be gained from standing at the water's edge—

that you could have a foot in two different worlds on the Atlantic Seaboard—and he needed to think.

He reached a wooden pier and took in the panorama of the East River: from the Williamsburg Bridge and the gigantic cranes of the Brooklyn Navy Yard across the water, to the floating docks and repair yards that clung to the waterfront like a special fleet. Ship horns blasted, and the staccato sounds of construction filled the air as steam spewed onto a horizon filled with machinery so gargantuan it dwarfed the skyscrapers. He looked to the right, the strong southerly nearly robbing him of his hat and depositing a fine spray on his expensive navy suit, forcing him to take a step backward.

A seaplane motored onto the sound then took off, banking to the right on the start of its journey; transporting one of the wealthy few who still took seaplanes from the Downtown Skyport to their Long Island homes, and it made him think again of Walter. His employer had placed him in an impossible position, but what galled him the most were Walter's comments before he'd left. "Think of the opportunities for America, Theo. We can send our greatest works to countries that have been under colonial control for far too long—places like Canada and Australia, South America and India. Think what it will mean for the company." And he'd told Theo again that it was his responsibility, as head of business affairs, to see that it was done.

He'd been naive to believe that Walter was ignoring the gathering demand for books, when it was obvious now that he'd been planning this the whole time. But what mattered was how Theo was going to put it right.

He took in the sight a moment longer, then carried on along the waterfront, the aroma of sea salt and Colombian coffee mingling in the air as the wharfies heaved sacks of beans from their freighters. The docks were quietening now, just the usual lighters steaming along the river, ferrying cargo from the larger freight ships to the piers, workers hauling the goods into waiting vans. In the hours before dawn the area would have been in a frenzy; it was then that Theo and his childhood friends had come to watch hardy crews unload their fishing boats and crate the catches with ice, ready for the Fulton Fish Market. Even now, dozens of trucks were still being loaded, destined for markets and restaurants across the city and upstate.

He knew he had better turn around soon—the taxi was still waiting—but something drove him on. His boots scraped across splintered planks while great gulls circled overhead, screeching their orders at the fishing vessels and their crews. After a few minutes, he found a sheltered spot and lit a cigarette. He was right to feel circumspect; this wasn't just about Partridge, it was about his work for the council, and about his father, and Alice and Virginia, and letting people down. He'd already failed to serve his country in the way he'd wanted to, and in the way that Howie had; he didn't want to fail again.

Theo glanced at his watch and took a final pull on his cigarette before grinding it into the plank; his ten minutes had passed, and he needed to visit the hospital and then attend meetings uptown before an early dinner with Virginia. He turned back along the boardwalk, churning with anger at himself and resentment toward Walter. He still had no idea what to do.

Samuel Bloom sat dozing in a high-backed chair, an open book in his lap, his glasses barely balanced on the end of his nose, and the sight of him made Theo smile. He could have been at home in his armchair, the radio blaring sports commentary in the background as his wife volleyed inaudible questions at him from the next room. Only he wasn't there, he was still here at the Brooklyn Methodist, thirteen days after his life-threatening episode. The two drip stands had gone from his bedside, and the table held transparent beakers of fluids, a basket of fruit and an assortment of cards. It was quiet, apart from the uneven snore of the patient in the bed opposite and the disconsolate whirr of hospital machinery.

The two other beds on the ward were vacant, mattresses eerily bare, a new pile of linen stacked portentously on the pillow, but Theo knew better than to ask what had become of the previous patients when Sister Dorothy arrived on the ward.

"How is he today?" Theo asked.

"Mr. Bloom is doing exceptionally well, considering . . ." Sister Dorothy had been on duty when his father was admitted, and she'd been encouraging about his improving condition. Her strong Irish lilt never made anything sound particularly bad—even serious conditions sounded like compliments—but today she was uncharacteristically stern. "Your father is an intelligent man, is he not, Mr. Bloom?" She pursed her lips and eyed him keenly.

"Yes, for sure." Theo didn't like rhetorical questions, but he assumed she was going somewhere with this.

"And he's well read, I understand."

"Very. Books have always been a big part of his life."

"Then why, in God's name, does the man not listen to what the doctors say?"

She was talking about their repeated requests for him to lose weight, and their other suggestions on lifestyle changes.

"Why does it fall upon deaf ears?" she continued. "Do patients think the doctors are comedians, that there's really a cure but it's a big secret that they're keeping from the rest of us?" She shook her head, her starched white cap remarkably staying in place. "There is no secret cure, no easy answer. They just need to do what they're told!"

Samuel stirred then opened his eyes, and it seemed impossible that he hadn't heard.

"Good afternoon, Mr. Bloom. Sister Rachel will be around soon to take your vitals," she said, before turning back to Theo. "And good day to you too, sir. Perhaps you can talk to him." She disappeared noiselessly, and he considered what she'd said. He had tried talking to his father before, so too had his mother; maybe Samuel didn't want to change—or maybe this scare would be the one that mattered. Only time would tell, and Theo wasn't going to spend the little time he had with his father lecturing him. Anyway, weren't sixty years of experience worth something? Hadn't he earned the right to decide how to live?

"Theo . . . what is it, son?"

"Sorry, I was miles away," Theo said, coming to stand closer. "How are you feeling?"

"Like it's time to go home."

The doctors had established that his infection had gone but that he needed a strict regimen of drugs and exercise to keep him stable, and possibly help him improve.

"How long have you been here?"

"Not long. I know Mom's on her way. I just wanted to check that you've got everything you need."

"I certainly have. I can even see Prospect Park Zoo through the window over there." Samuel pointed west to the collage of brown and green knitted in between the grid of Brooklyn's townhouses and tenements, and Theo could just make out the larger trees and enclosures. It made him think of Alice's book, her amazing pictures and stories.

"Maybe we could borrow a wheelchair to take you?" Theo suggested.

"I'll go when I can walk around by myself," he said, a typically stubborn note to his voice.

Theo laughed; it was good to hear his father determined again.

"Is Laura coming to see you?" he asked. He hadn't seen his sister for over a year, since she lived in Minnesota with her husband and three children, but it struck him that it would be good to take them to Prospect Park Zoo on their next visit. It was only a few years old, and he'd read that the brick and limestone buildings were decorated with sculpted scenes from Rudyard Kipling's *Jungle Book*. The "picture-book" zoo, *The New York Times* had called it, which again reminded him of Alice.

Samuel said, "I know she wants to, but I doubt she'll come any time soon with Raymond away. Anyway, the kids are too young to travel and not old enough to leave with anyone else."

"Maybe you could go see her . . . once you're feeling better. A vacation?"

"Are you kiddin' me? Your mother and I would last about

two days and then we'd be clamoring to come home. Nice idea, Theo, but keep it to yourself." He winked.

Theo moved closer to the window, searching the vast parkland to see if he could detect any animals, and he sighed heavily. If he was honest, he'd grown quite excited at the idea of publishing *The Zoo Chronicles*, and less inquisitive about why she'd kept it a secret, but it would never happen now. And he didn't know if *Women and Children First* would ever see the light of day either.

Something shook the treetops, a trail of brown shapes moving through the branches—the monkeys, perhaps—then the canopy settled back into place, shielding the creatures from view. Yes, *The Zoo Chronicles* was a book that people would want to read, and one that Partridge would benefit from publishing, and he needed to somehow show Walter that he was wrong.

"So, what's on your mind, son?"

Theo spun round to find his father propped up in his chair, staring at him.

He swallowed hard, wondering whether this was the right time to ask for his father's advice, or if he should wait until he was feeling better—but then what if that time never came? His father liked Virginia, both his parents did, so this wasn't going to be easy.

"You haven't always done what's expected, have you?"

His father laughed. "Lord no, that would have got me into a whole heap of trouble. You do what's least expected, and you've got to keep surprising people. Things would be a bit dull otherwise, you know that." His chuckle sounded hoarse. Then he looked at his son's poker face and grew serious. "Oh, you're talking about women."

Theo nodded.

"Ah, well . . . all I know about women is that when you've found the right one, you know, and you don't need to go looking anyplace else. If Virginia is the right one, then you'll know it."

Theo moved over to the bed, perching on the edge so he could look his father in the eye. "But what if she isn't? What if you think the right one might be someone else?"

"Hmm," his father said, pressing his lips together and looking down as he rearranged the bedclothes. "Well, then you're going to have to take a chance. You're going to need to tell the 'someone else' how you feel."

His father was right. He'd never told Alice how deeply he felt about her, because he already had a fiancée—although he'd never hid his feelings for her. Even here in New York he was doing things for her; he'd been to see Ike to make sure the Fourth Avenue Booksellers' Association had got their sidewalk bookstands back, and he'd spent the whole morning searching for a book for her. He'd come across an article in *The Washington Post* some time ago, about the mysterious Ethel Vance. She was the author of the bestselling novel *Escape*, but Ethel Vance was a pseudonym and her true identity was one of the publishing industry's most closely guarded secrets. It had caused quite a stir, and wagers were lost in literary circles when the real identity was revealed to be Grace Zaring Stone, the wife of a captain in the US Navy and the author of four previous books, one of which coincidentally was included in the first series of ASEs.

"I take it this 'someone else' doesn't live in New York?"

Theo shook his head.

"Then I assume she lives in London?"

Theo nodded, avoiding eye contact.

"But what about your job?"

"I don't know, Pop . . . I don't know if I even want it anymore." He didn't want to worry his father with the details, or his concern over what Walter had asked him to do, but they both knew it was unlikely there would be a job for him if he forsook his daughter.

"So, you're leaving us again."

His days in New York had passed so quickly—meetings with the council, long days in the Partridge offices and with his parents, and only a few outings with Virginia and her friends—but now he wanted to go back. He'd decided on the taxi ride over that he would try to convince Walter to give him another chance before selling: just three more months. He had told his parents that he wouldn't leave until his father was getting the right treatment and the best available team of specialists, and now he was.

"Only if you're okay with it," he said.

He didn't even know if he could get on a flight. There had been many delays or abandoned flights over recent weeks with increased fighting in the mid-Atlantic as the Allies tried to destroy the U-boats.

"If you're sure, Theo, then I am. You don't need to stay here on my account. Although they could do with your support up at Yankee Stadium."

Samuel smiled reassuringly, and Theo smiled back.

"Seriously, don't tell your mother I said so, but you go if you need to. I know you're not finished there. . . . But, son?"

"Yes?"

"Only if you're certain she's the right one."

"Yes, Pop."

Theo's heart was already racing, an adrenaline rush at the thought of getting back to London, of the fight they had on their hands to turn things around with Walter, and of seeing Alice. But first he had to find a way to talk to his fiancée, to tell her how his affections had changed, and that he now imagined a different future.

Thirty-five

LONDON, MAY 6, 1943

"So, this is it?" Alice asked, trying to hide her surprise.

She was staring down into a basement that could have easily been a bomb shelter, if it wasn't for the tremor through her feet or the huge man standing by the door.

Alice and Ursula were on a darkened street in Chelsea, and Alice's chest was already tightening, but her friend hadn't taken no for an answer. She had been simultaneously skeptical and worried when Alice had told her about the plan with Joe Stevenson—and concerned that Alice wouldn't be able to play her part convincingly. That was when Ursula had told her she knew just the place where they could rub shoulders with the sort of streetwise people she was trying to deceive: "Somewhere you're as likely to find a villain as a vamp," she'd said in her trademark ironic tone. Alice felt every bit the vamp now in the black crepe trousers and luxurious cream silk blouse that Ursula had saved all her clothing coupons for, just the type of ridiculously extravagant outfit that Ursula's heroine, Katharine Hepburn, wore.

"This is certainly it," Ursula replied, smiling with Elizabeth Arden's de rigueur red-coated lips. Then she fixed Alice with a purposeful stare. "Ready?"

Alice had barely recognized her own reflection in the mirror—but she could certainly imagine that woman on Joe Stevenson's arm.

She pressed her lips together, then remembered to breathe, and followed Ursula down.

The Gateways Club, or "the Gates," as Ursula called it, had long been a haven for the arty crowd. She'd said that you truly were just as likely to bump into a truck driver or a bus conductor here as a writer or a criminal. It was the meeting place for the Chelsea Arts Club but also for the homosexual crowd, as well as one or two scurrilous characters, and that was what Alice was banking on tonight.

"Good evening, Miss Rousson," said the muscle-bound doorman.

"Hello, Ronny," Ursula replied, smiling as he opened the door and they stepped inside.

Green velvet curtains opened to reveal a wall of smoke and dancers, and, off to one side, a jazz band, the four musicians stooped like musical notes. It was a small space—just thirty-five by eighteen feet—and Alice stood entranced. It had been a real worry that she might get panicked underground, but she quickly forgot about that because this was unlike anywhere she'd ever been. Clusters of people fanned out like a spinning roulette wheel in the center of the room. Men and women sat at scattered tables, while others leaned on the wooden shelf that ran around the edges, resting elbows as they drank, cigarettes lengthening fingers. Glimpses of the walls showed murals of London—fashionable Londoners, scenes from the Gates and vivid renditions of city icons, all painted, Ursula had told her, by students from Chelsea Arts Club. It was a kaleidoscope of music and laughter, of dancing and conversation, like a colorful cabaret in full swing, and for a moment she forgot the reason she was there.

She followed Ursula, squeezing through the crowd as they headed to the bar at the other side and waited to get served. Ursula moved out of the way to let a man in a trilby and patterned scarf squeeze past, balancing a tray of drinks, then she shuffled closer to the bar.

As Alice stood and waited, she noticed her friend watching a group at a nearby table. They were playing a boisterous game of cards, the two men and three women heckling each other, then shrieking as a woman won. The men wore gauche suits, and two of the women didn't appear to care that there was a luxury tax on cosmetics or a rationing on their clothes, still in fur jackets and glistening jewels. Their uproar died down and the winner collected her cards, slender arms and neck craned forward as she checked her fellow players had given up their money. Satisfied, she smiled and sat back in her chair, elegantly positioning a cigarette holder between her lips and turning sideways so one of the gentlemen could light it. The match flickered, illuminating her face, and she glanced up, catching Ursula's eye where she stood at the bar. They held each other's gaze for a second, then one of her companions said something to her and she turned away.

"Here you go," Ursula said, returning with two glasses. "You need to have more patience than Joan of Arc if you want to get a drink here."

"What is it?"

"Gin fizz."

"Thank you." Alice took a sip and winced at the bitter taste. "What do we do now, dance?" she asked uncertainly.

"Not yet. First, you've got to watch. See those two over there?" Ursula indicated the opposite corner. "What do you make of them?"

One was potbellied, casually dressed and wore a battered fedora, while the other was in an immaculate three-piece suit and kept his head down, examining his cuticles as his companion talked animatedly in his ear.

"The one in the suit is the crime boss and the other one's his henchman?"

Ursula rolled her eyes. "No, Alice. That's Ted Ware, the new owner, and I'm pretty sure the one in the suit recently lost the club to him in a poker game."

Alice grimaced. "What about those ones over there?" she asked, staring at three men drinking at the bar. "Are they crooks?"

"No. Isn't it obvious? They're policemen."

"Oh . . ."

Ursula leaned nearer as she explained. "Look how close together they're sitting, the way they're using their hands to communicate—it's evident they work together. And see the way they're glancing at each other and then around them? They're talking about something serious . . . but they don't want to be overheard."

Alice screwed up her face. "I don't see it. Isn't it just because it's noisy down here?"

Ursula sighed dramatically. "See, you're far too naive. I think this plan of yours is a really bad idea. And I'd have thought you'd have learned by now, Alice," she added worriedly, "that you can't trust anyone. Especially men."

Alice thought again, as she had a hundred times, about Theo, and how disappointed she was in him. But this was a completely different situation.

She let Ursula's frustration settle before she answered. "I told you, if Olive trusts Joe, then that's good enough for me."

"And you're certain you won't let Michael go with you?"

"Absolutely not, I'm not going back on my word."

It was touching that her friend was so concerned, but Alice really didn't think a crash course in character observation was going to help at this late stage. Yes, it might make her less nervous around the people Joe was about to introduce her to, and therefore less likely to give herself away, but as far as she could see, the people down here didn't look like hardened criminals anyway. She cast her eyes about for some shady characters, but all she noticed were people having fun. A group of nurses noisily celebrated a birthday, and onlookers cheered as first the birthday girl then other members of the group were propelled into the middle of their circle to dance. Alice couldn't help but smile as the crowd's excitement grew, the clapping building to a crescendo as the birthday girl's footwork got faster in response, threatening to topple her. *We could all do with a bit of cheer*, Alice thought; the week's news from Europe had been particularly disturbing. It was rumored that in Warsaw thousands of the Jewish community had been killed as they'd resisted deportation.

The dancers linked arms behind each other's backs and twirled clockwise, bumping into one another as their feet struggled to keep pace, the musicians playing ever faster. Then the song ended, and the dancers broke apart.

"They don't look like they're going to cause too much trouble," Alice commented, and downed the last of her drink.

While the band took a break, Ursula explained how to read a person's body language, from their nervous gestures and anxious energy right down to how you should shake hands when you met them—unless your palms were sweaty, of course.

"See that one in the red dress over there?" Ursula pointed to a young woman with a female partner on the dance floor. The woman swayed and bobbed with such easy rhythm that Alice guessed she hadn't only had one drink. When she placed her hands around her partner's neck and kissed her, Alice shyly looked away. "She's new to the scene," Ursula said as she continued watching their embrace.

"What do you mean?"

Ursula explained how more and more women were experimenting; women who, in the increasing absence of men, decided to try a relationship with another woman. Of course, the Gates was the ideal place for this.

Alice didn't ask how Ursula could tell; she wasn't sure she was ready for the answer. But she did know that the knot in her stomach had loosened and she was actually enjoying herself; she felt just like Patricia Reece's detective Mary Dray as she scrutinized everyone with Ursula's help. "You've surprised me," Alice told her, wishing she'd known how to do this before, as it might have been useful with Theo.

"What, twice in one week?" Ursula said, and they both laughed.

Ursula waved to a group on the other side of the bar, who waved back.

"You know a lot of people here," Alice said, "don't you?"

Ursula surveyed the room, her mouth curving into a half smile, then she grew serious. "Yes, I suppose I do. Although there are some individuals I'd never mix with on the other side of that green door, and I've seen things I would have preferred to avoid, but this unlikely group are the closest I've got to family."

Alice nodded. "I know."

"But I don't think you do." Ursula's cheerful bravado was replaced with candor. "It's the only place where people like me can really be ourselves, free of prying eyes and prejudice. The only place where we can show and receive affection, and not be judged."

"I'm sorry. You're right, I don't know, but I'm glad I came. And I'm glad you've trusted me enough to be yourself around me."

"Hmm, wish I could say the same to you!" Ursula replied and rolled her eyes in mock annoyance.

They were sipping their drinks, listening to conversations ebb and flow around them, when the card winner suddenly materialized.

Ursula smiled at her and kissed her cheek. "Alice, this is Bridget."

Bridget extended her hand. "I'm pleased to meet you, Alice," she said in a rich, velvety tone. "I've heard a lot about you." Her face was angular, a wide brow set above intense green eyes. She was taller than Ursula, by a good foot or so, and dressed conservatively: navy trousers and a cornflower-blue blouse with an exquisite diamond leaf brooch pinned near her collarbone. This outfit was in keeping with her medical profession, which Ursula had mentioned. *See,* Alice thought, *I am getting the hang of reading people.* "Pleased to meet you too," she said, then blurted, "We're on the lookout for criminals."

Ursula and Bridget exchanged a look, and Ursula whispered something to her before she placed a Sobranie between her lips.

Bridget leaned forward so Alice could hear her. "I'm sorry about your situation."

"Thank you . . . and that reminds me, I really should go," she said, looking at her watch; she was meeting Joe Stevenson in less than twelve hours' time.

Ursula rolled her eyes. "You can't go yet, we're not finished!"

"It was nice to meet you, Bridget," Alice said. "I'm sure I'll see you again."

"Likewise."

They shook hands, then Alice turned to Ursula. "Are you sure about everything I told you?"

"If I don't hear from you by four o'clock, I will go to Marylebone Lane Police Station and ask for Sergeant Mildred Burns—she knows everything."

Alice quickly nodded and gave them both a reassuring smile.

"You be careful, then," said Bridget.

"I will."

As Alice turned to leave, Ursula stopped her with a hand on her arm. "Remember, you need to look him in the eye and make sure your body language isn't defensive."

"How do I do that?"

"Accept your fear, don't fight it. Don't forget that anxiety is there for a reason, so let it work for you, protect you." Her lips quirked. "I should know. I'm good at pretending."

The band had come back on, and Bridget stood watching them, her body moving gently to the music. Ursula glanced over at her and smiled, radiant and happy in a way she could only be in private or here at the Gates.

"Are you as good an actor as Katharine Hepburn?" Alice asked.

Ursula kissed her on both cheeks and whispered, "Nearly."

Thirty-six

LONDON, MAY 7, 1943

"Thank you," Alice said, forcing a smile as Joe opened the car door for her to slip into the passenger seat.

When she'd arrived ten minutes early for their midday rendezvous, he'd already been waiting in the green Austin 8 two-seat tourer, yet he seemed preoccupied. Was he was having second thoughts?

"It looks like it might rain," she said, looking up at the leaden sky as her fingers toyed with the buckle on her bag—then she realized her fidgeting made her look agitated.

"Don't worry, the roof can go up if it does," he said, glancing at her clothes.

They headed west, picking up the A4 as they wound through Hammersmith and out toward Chiswick in a tense silence. The denser housing soon gave way to tree-lined streets and larger detached homes, and he stole another glance.

"What is it?" she asked.

"Well . . . I think you might have overdone it with the outfit," he said, eyes roaming over her navy polka-dot dress.

"What do you mean?"

It had taken her ages to get ready as she'd barely been able to close the zipper, her hands had been shaking so hard.

"You're just a bit . . . overdressed, that's all."

Alice turned away and caught her reflection in the window, her red lips gleaming. In her mind the image was replaced by Ursula's face, before it morphed into her mother's, and she abruptly looked away. "What shall I do?" She had taken a handkerchief from her bag, ready to wipe her lipstick off, when Joe's words made her freeze.

"I don't know, Alice Cotton. Why don't you tell me?"

She looked sideways and caught his eye. "How do you know my name?"

"Elizabeth called me . . . she mentioned you might come looking for some help."

He turned his attention back to the road, and she carried on watching his profile.

"Does Olive know?"

"Not yet."

The traffic was dwindling, the pavements becoming less populated as they headed into the suburbs. She had no idea where they were going, and Ursula was the only person she'd confided in this time and who knew what Alice was doing.

"What else did she say?"

"She told me that you're a good 'un."

Alice wondered if there might be something between Joe and Elizabeth, or even between him and Olive, or if there was another reason for the apparent bond between the three of them.

"What's he like, your boss?" she asked, her voice apprehensive as she considered the man she was about to meet.

"He's as slippery as they come," Joe replied, unsmiling. "But he'll be charming. Just tell him what you told me about your friends. Don't think about it too much or it won't come out as natural. And the less you say the better; then there's not so much to remember that might trip you up. He'll ask lots of questions."

"Will there be any children there?"

"No, of course not," he said, looking at her as they pulled up at a traffic light. "I wouldn't take you there."

She thought of the newspaper descriptions of the homes with dirt and maggots, and of Eadie lying in a similarly infested crib, and her skin prickled and grew cold.

"But you know where they are . . . the houses where they keep the children before the handovers?" she said, swallowing away her emotion.

"Yes."

The lights changed, and Joe crunched the gears before the Austin accelerated away in a cloud of exhaust, a horn blaring behind them.

"So," Alice said, "what do you know?"

"Not much. She told me about your cousin's baby, and that you might try to contact me."

"You could have said so to begin with."

"It was after we first met; besides, I'm just getting my own back," he said and smiled.

She relaxed into the leather seat, relieved to have one less pretense. "I appreciate your help."

"I figure if you're prepared to show up like this, well . . . then you must be desperate."

"If you've spoken to Elizabeth, then you'd know that I am. But not as much as my cousin." Olive still didn't know that it was her baby they were searching for, and there wasn't any reason to change that now.

Joe's thumbs drummed on the steering wheel as he drove, and she wondered if he too felt nervous. "I told her I don't know where your cousin's baby is. That's got nothing to do with my line of work."

They drove for another few minutes in a thoughtful silence, and Alice considered why Joe was prepared to take the risk to help.

"What exactly do you do for them?" she asked, noticing how tight his grip was on the steering wheel.

"I'm a driver, but never for the kids."

"Why haven't you gone to the police yet, with everything you know?"

"I have. But when you've done time, they're not inclined to believe you. And I figured I'm more useful to Olive this way. I've been giving her enough information to help, but not enough to make her an accessory," he said solemnly. "Besides, these people are cleverer than that—it will take more than me and a journalist to shut them down."

"But you've given her enough to get the law changed . . ."

"Yes, enough to do that," he said and sighed heavily.

She was still staring, thinking about her own experiences with the police, when he turned and caught her eye. A look passed between them, and she questioned again who Joe Stevenson really was: hero or villain, or something in between?

He slowed down and turned into a road where tall fences and overgrown hedges shielded the buildings behind, and only a few cars were parked in driveways. He pulled to a stop halfway down and turned the engine off, then leaned over the dashboard to survey the street.

Alice asked, "What now?"

"We go in, and I introduce you as Sarah Jones. Just stick to what we discussed."

"Do you think they'll believe me?"

"Let's hope so. For both our sakes."

"And you can't just find out where she is?"

"No, I can't. I've never asked about anyone before, and it will seem strange if I do it now. At least you have a reason for asking. I'll vouch for you, but that's all I can do."

"And what will happen if they find out that it was you who helped me?"

His hands traced around the edge of the steering wheel, fingers running back and forth along the leather seams. "They won't."

"But if they do . . ."

He held her gaze. "Then it could be time to move on." His expression didn't give anything away, and he made to get out of the car.

"Why are you helping me?"

"You need to ask Olive that."

"And what would she say?"

"She'd say that most children belong with their mother."

"I agree, but what do you mean?"

"I mean that Olive has more reason than most for wanting these baby farmers behind bars." His expression darkened. "She was a victim too as a child."

The housing block was set among overgrown gardens, and it seemed as if the building was deserted, the majority of its windows and doors boarded up—until they drew closer. A group of women were hanging washing as children played in the dirt, but they barely took any notice as Alice and Joe wandered past. Washing lines stretched across corridors on the upper floors of the tenements, like bunting from a forgotten party, and Alice's stomach twisted at the squalor she saw through the open doorways.

She glanced ahead at Joe as they climbed, relieved that he was now an ally and not another enemy who needed to be fooled. This was her last chance to run through her story, although she'd rehearsed until she was confident it was believable and not a work of fiction woven from truth and all her research. She paused on the landing to even out her ragged breath, realizing too late that there were blocked drains as her lungs filled with the overpowering stench.

Joe was ahead of her on the open corridor. A gust of wind drove leaves and litter swirling along the concrete floor, and he turned and motioned for her to follow. There were cracked windows and peeling doorways along one side, and with no walls the building was wide open to the elements on the other. Halfway along, a group of men in little more than trousers and undershirts stood smoking rolled-up cigarettes and fell silent as she approached. They continued watching until she and Joe reached a door that was in good condition except its wooden frame was scored with dozens of marks, as if someone had tried to hammer it down.

Joe locked eyes with her, and she couldn't see any of her own fear mirrored back.

"Ready?" he asked.

She was torn between bursting with expectation and bolting like a frightened horse, but she took a deep breath and nodded.

"Remember, just stick to what we discussed. You don't want to find out how unscrupulous they are."

Alice already knew exactly how unscrupulous they were, and what value they placed on human life.

Then he whispered, "And they can smell fear." His lips tightened, then he raised a hand and knocked.

It was opened quickly, and the man's stern expression broke into a smile. "Joe, what a surprise. I didn't know we had a meeting."

Alice tried to move her mouth into a placid smile, but her facial muscles wouldn't respond. It was only Joe's arm ushering her through the doorway that helped her move at all.

"I'm sorry to drop by unannounced, Sidney. I should have called first, but Miss Jones is only here for the day and, well, I didn't want either of you to miss the opportunity to meet."

Sidney's eyes flicked over to her, and she fought hard not

to look away. She could hear Ursula's voice reminding her to maintain eye contact, that it would gain his trust, but looking this man in the eye took all her nerve. He was Sidney Jardine, the man Rex had identified and whom they'd tried to find.

Joe introduced her, and as they followed him along a hallway lined with oil paintings and shopping bags, she listened as Joe did all the talking. Where she'd expected a filthy sitting room, there were clean floors and a tidy array of furniture and ornaments. Striped walls were hung with landscapes: snowy mountain peaks, tropical paradises and seaside rivieras, all places she imagined Sidney pretended that he'd been. He wore his dark hair long and slicked behind his ears, and dressed like someone who imagined a different life for himself, clothes worn like a costume rather than for function or practicality. Sidney Jardine was a wolf in suburban clothing, white eyes glaring from a weatherworn face.

"Please have a seat," he told them.

She sat next to Joe on the sofa, gas mask case on her lap, trying to remember not to hold on to the straps too tightly or look at the floor. She was Sarah Jones, a secretary from Ilford who had friends that needed help.

"Yes, I'm sorry to just turn up like this," she said, "but Mr. Stevenson knows there might be a business opportunity, one that's mutually beneficial, and he was kind enough to recommend you."

Sidney's eyes slid between them. "What sort of business?"

"It's all rather unfortunate, really—young women in my neighborhood who have become victims of this war," she said. "Under normal circumstances their babies would probably be looked after by the family or one of the adoption agencies, but everything's different now, with so many war orphans."

"And how do you think I can help?" he asked, narrowing his eyes.

"These women would happily present the gift of motherhood to someone else, if there was a reward for their sacrifice," she said, holding Sidney's gaze.

Here she was, a mother now, her life so immeasurably altered from a year ago, most likely face-to-face with one of the engineers of her suffering. Her throat tightened as she thought about where Eadie might be, and her fingers closed around the case that no longer contained her gas mask but her father's gun.

"Well, aren't you a one?" Sidney said, and burst out laughing.

Joe laughed too, and Alice shifted uncomfortably in her seat. A fear of failure, not of harm, suddenly overwhelmed her, but Sidney just offered them a drink and invited her to go into more detail. She told him how many girls she knew as well as when the babies were due, all the while trying to banish thoughts of maggot-infested houses. When she thought she'd shared enough, she picked up her teacup and took a sip.

"And they're all from decent families? I don't want any dummies or cripples—my customers wouldn't be happy about that."

It was all Alice could do to keep the tea in her mouth. "No, Mr. Jardine. They are strong healthy women." She forced a smile. "From what age do you take the children?"

"Any age—babies, toddlers, even newborns. Mothers who lose a baby are grateful for one they can have straightaway, takes away the pain . . . although it's not always a good idea."

She looked at him with a placid expression, hoping her contempt didn't show. "Why?"

"Some of them can be poorly."

"And what happens to them?"

"We had one on the south coast recently, only a few days old, and she got quick sick," he said offhandedly.

Alice grew cold as his words registered, and she had to stop herself from flying across the room at him.

"We've only ever had a couple that haven't made it, though." He frowned. "Here, you've gone quite pale, Miss Jones. Are you all right?"

"I'm fine. It's just . . . one of the babies," she said, swallowing a mouthful of bile, "the mother is family. My cousin, actually—it just brings it home, that's all," and she looked beseechingly at Joe.

"I'm sure that little blighter pulled through, Sarah," he said, focusing his attention on Sidney. "Mr. Jardine knows how to look after them."

"Not me, the carers. They're as good as gold. And yes, that little blighter pulled through. Don't you worry, we sent her to a safe place in north London. She's almost well enough to leave. Almost." He smiled.

It took all Alice's will not to swallow again or look away; instead, she forced herself to congratulate him on his good work, since flattery seemed to help loosen his tongue.

"That's marvelous, Mr. Jardine. You're doing a stellar wartime service, if you don't mind me saying," she said, smiling at him and then across at Joe.

"See, I told you," Joe said, his eyes crinkling as he smiled back, and she knew why he'd managed to be so successful at playing his role.

"Well," Sidney said as he glanced at his watch, "it was a pleasure to meet you, Miss Jones, and please give Joe your number. I'll be in touch—I think we can help that cousin of yours, for starters. Then let's see how we go."

Visualizing Ursula standing next to her was the only thing that stopped her legs from buckling as she shook Sidney's hand and said good-bye.

Neither she nor Joe spoke as they descended the stairs, and she floated like a phantom across the gardens to the car. It was only once the car door was shut that she finally broke down, sobbing uncontrollably as fear and disgust collided, and the stress and hopelessness of the past few months were finally released.

Joe slid his arms around her, pulling her closer in a comforting embrace. Her first reaction was that she wished he was Theo, and she felt ashamed of herself.

"It's all right. I think I know where she might be. Did you hear me, Alice?"

She opened her eyes. "Where?"

"There's only one handling house in north London, the rest are south or in the counties."

"What sort of godforsaken place is it?" she asked, wiping her face with the back of her hand.

"I don't know that, but at least I know where it is."

Thirty-seven

"The bloody printers burned down," George said grimly, after he welcomed Theo into his office.

It wasn't the reception that Theo had expected. Rupert had been killed in action, and Theo had thought George would raise that straightaway, but he hadn't mentioned the tragic news yet. Instead, he ranted on about the fire as he explained how one of their publications had been there for typesetting—on hot metal, as was the usual method—and the press had caught on fire; it had nothing to do with the Luftwaffe.

"At least it wasn't Alice's book," Theo replied, imagining how distraught she would have been, and how much he would have wanted to be there to comfort her.

"It's still a big setback, Theo. One we can't afford. At least no one was injured."

From his visit with Alice, Theo knew the printers hadn't been able to maintain the equipment properly, but it was a blow to lose another printing facility.

George sank down heavily onto a sofa and looked at Theo

wearily. "You don't need to tell Walter about this, though, not just yet."

"Of course not." He met George's melancholy eyes and gave him a sympathetic look. "I'm really sorry about Rupert, George. My deepest condolences."

"Thank you, Theo, and thank you for coming back. I do appreciate it—I need to spend some time with Clare and the girls."

The telegram had reached Walter while he was deliberating over whether to give Theo those three extra months to prove why he shouldn't sell; the news that Rupert had been killed had helped make up Walter's mind. Rupert's de Havilland plane had been on a reconnaissance exercise when it was involved in an accident and lost at sea, and while they hadn't recovered the bodies, it was believed that neither the pilot nor the navigator could have survived.

George sat with rounded shoulders and his head hung low. "We still can't fathom it, not really. It just hasn't sunk in, to tell you the truth. I suppose if you don't believe that it's real, then in a way it's not, is it?"

Theo could understand how refusing to acknowledge the truth might make George feel as though he could undo history, and why he was focusing all his anguish on a lesser target, one he could tolerate more than the death of his only son, which in this case was the fire. Theo also knew that only time would help George work through his grief, and not anything that he or anyone else had to say.

"I'm afraid you'll have to carry on dealing with the civil servants for a while, until we decide what to do," George said, exhaling heavily.

"That's fine, George."

"Rupert used to hate it, you know—used to joke that he'd rather come face-to-face with Goering than another bureaucrat," he said, and laughed awkwardly.

"Not his favorite part of the job," Theo suggested lightly.

"No—but then, of course, Rupert was used to getting his own way."

Alice had given Theo that impression too, even though she'd been reluctant to talk about him.

"And what about Alice's book?" Theo asked, hoping to change the subject.

"Well, the book is fine," George replied. "Emily is proofreading it at the moment. But Alice hasn't been here in days."

Theo was startled. "Does Ursula know where she is?"

"No, she doesn't, and we're all getting rather worried." He shook his head in a defeated manner.

It was worrying that not even Ursula knew where she was.

"I'm sorry, George. I wish I could have looked out for her like I promised you."

"It's all right, you had to be with your father." He sighed. "I had an inkling that Rupert had feelings for her—nothing he said, but I always thought he paid her special attention. I wondered if she might become my daughter-in-law. Only now he's not coming back."

Theo felt a stab of jealousy at the possibility of Rupert's feelings being reciprocated. Perhaps something had happened between the two of them that could explain why Alice was so reluctant to talk about him, and so insistent they had just been colleagues.

"And I'm particularly concerned about Alice," George

continued, "because she's been mixing with all sorts of unsavory characters in the past few months working on this book. It's become an obsession."

Theo felt as if all the oxygen had left the room. Things were far more desperate than when he had left: Rupert was dead, the printers and a whole publication run had been destroyed, and Alice was missing. He'd broken his engagement with Virginia before he'd left New York because of Alice, and now he would dedicate himself to finding her.

The two men regarded each other for a moment, and Theo wondered what it would do to George if he knew of his brother's treachery. Theo could have never done the same to Howie.

He'd developed a strong desire to protect George and his company. It wasn't about the business or the new titles anymore; it was about them—about George and Alice, and Ursula, Tommy and Emily, all the staff in fact—only Theo hadn't seen that before. He was certain that Walter wouldn't have him back, not just for his daughter's sake, but because he was sure that Walter blamed him for not selling when he'd first suggested it. But Theo hadn't considered that when George learned he'd known about Walter's betrayal, he wouldn't want him around either.

"It's so strange that she would disappear now," George said, "just when we're so close to getting it printed. All the publicity has been booked."

Theo knew he was referring to the campaign to capture public attention for the Adoption of Children Act on its passing through Parliament.

"After all she's fought for," said George, looking even more anguished. "What do you propose we do, Theo? We all agree she's been hiding something."

"You've got enough to deal with—let me handle it."

Theo knew that George was still in shock; once the reality of Rupert's death sank in, he wouldn't be able to function. It had been the same for him with Howie.

The telephone on George's desk rang, but he made no effort to answer it.

After several rings, Theo asked, "Do you want me to get it?"

"Yes. Thank you."

Ursula was waiting in the Friend at Hand, the pub they'd gone to on his first day in London. Two tumblers of whisky sat on the table in front of her, and she pushed one toward him as he sank down.

"I'm sorry for the cloak-and-dagger," she said, "but I'm not sure if George is ready for what I'm about to tell you, especially now."

Theo's heart was racing; he'd run the short distance to the pub, convinced that Ursula knew where Alice was, and the fact she'd had to keep it a secret didn't bode well.

"Where is she?" he asked. "What's happened?"

"She's all right, but I'm worried, Theo." Her eyes narrowed. "I know she was going to ask for your help before you left, so I'm asking you for it now."

He knew he'd been wrong to leave without speaking to Alice, he just hadn't known how wrong. "Tell me."

Ursula took a deep breath and looked squarely at him. "You know about her cousin's baby, the one she went to look after?"

"Yes."

"Well, it isn't her cousin's baby, it's hers." Ursula paused, letting the words land. "She wasn't going to come back to work—she was going to stay home, looking after her daughter and telling everyone it was her cousin's baby. But it all went wrong. Her mother took the baby as soon as she was born and gave her to baby farmers."

"You mean like the ones in the book?" Theo said, sickened. "How could she? Why?"

"Ruth is a very religious and troubled woman, not of sound mind. She believed it was in Alice's and her baby's best interests."

He felt as if he'd been punched in the stomach, a real physical pain. They held each other's gaze for a few moments.

Friend at Hand had grown busier, tables filling with lunchtime workers and tourists who had sought out one of Fitzrovia's oldest pubs. Theo stared into his tumbler, trying to imagine the despair Alice must have felt. And the courage that she'd shown. He ran his fingers along the edge of the glass, thinking about the pain she must have been in, trying to conceal it while still working on the book—now he could see it was partly a contrivance to help her find her baby.

"What's the baby's name?"

"Eadie."

A smile flickered across his face at the name inscribed in the zoo book. Then he grew serious again as another question came to mind—although he was sure he already knew the answer. "Is Rupert the father?"

Ursula pressed her lips together as she stared at the

tabletop, rolling her tumbler between her hands. Then she looked up at him, and he saw the answer in her eyes.

"Did she love him?"

"No! No, she didn't. I mean, she may have once . . . but he coerced her, and he deceived her." Ursula looked upset. "She never told him about the baby."

Theo realized he didn't feel disappointment or jealousy, only anger at this man he'd never met, at the pain he'd caused the woman he loved. He also felt a burning desire to protect her, the sensation so strong that it wrenched at his core. She'd been a victim—of Rupert, Ruth and the baby farmers—and whatever had been between her and Rupert didn't matter anymore. The important thing now was her and Eadie's safety.

"So where is she?" he asked.

"With Olive's informer. They've tracked down someone they think was involved in taking Eadie. I've got a name—the same one that another source gave us. And she told me to go to Marylebone Lane Police Station if she wasn't back by four."

"What time did she say she was meeting the informer?"

"Midday."

Theo looked at his watch; it was nearly one. They would be well on their way, perhaps even already there—and who knew what they were walking into?

"You did the right thing, telling me," he said. "Thank you."

"Will you go straightaway?"

"Yes—but look, George really needs to know. And I'd better be the one to tell him."

Thirty-eight

"Remember, Alice, just make sure it's her and come straight out," Joe said firmly, his hand gripping her arm. "I don't want you to get carried away."

They had sat in the car for several minutes watching the suburban house, but no one had arrived or left. After Alice's reaction to their meeting with Jardine, Joe had guessed that the baby was hers and she'd been forced to tell him the truth. He'd put his foot down hard and driven her in silence across town to the north London safe house.

"Then what?" she replied, as she pictured Eadie when she'd first seen her, skin covered in vernix.

"Then we'll decide. I don't want to show my face unless I have to. Especially if she's not even there."

Alice smiled tightly and stepped from the car. She'd never allowed herself to feel bereft. Sad, yes. Hollow, yes. A constant aching, yes. But she had never let go of the belief that she would see her daughter again.

It was a case of déjà vu: a tree-lined road, a homogenous row of houses, and the same fear and anxiety. She'd visited dozens of houses and flats over her weeks of searching while working on the book, and she'd been surprised and disappointed by whom she'd met and what she'd found: people surviving in appalling conditions, but no baby farmers.

This house was much larger than she'd expected: a mock-Tudor home with a steeply pitched roof, its half-timbered exterior infilled with herringbone brickwork. Sidney Jardine's handling house was in the kind of well-to-do neighborhood where she would have once imagined nothing out of the ordinary ever happened. Piano notes spilled from an upstairs dormer window; it was Brahms's "Lullaby," but the melody felt incongruous here, and disquieting.

Alice glanced back over her shoulder at Joe's outline behind the narrow windshield. She didn't blame him for not wanting to blow his cover, but it meant she was alone.

A scuffed carriage stood inside the pillared porch, half-blocking the front door, and a miniature set of broken gardening tools lay scattered across the tiles. Then a child's cry started from somewhere inside, overtaking every other noise so that Alice no longer heard the piano music or the squeak of the brass knocker as she raised it ready to hammer back down.

The cry had an uneven staccato rhythm; it wasn't the mew of a newborn or the sound of a hungry child—and contemplating the root of the child's unhappiness terrified her.

Thirty-nine

Theo's mind wasn't on the book, or on what George said to him as the older man leaned back against the police station reception desk, massaging his temples; all Theo could think about was why the police were taking so damned long. He'd known there was something seriously wrong, and he cursed himself for not returning sooner—and the others for not recognizing Alice's cries for help—because now it had come to this, and she was in real danger.

He and George hadn't waited until four o'clock but had gone straight to Marylebone Lane Police Station and found Sergeant Burns, who had quickly disappeared, vanishing into the bowels of the building. All this time Alice could already be at the house with those barbaric criminals.

Theo paced up and down, head inclined as he stared at the cracks in the tiles, trying to order his thoughts, and guessing that in all likelihood George was trying to do the same. It was hard to reconcile the kind, clever young woman for whom Theo had fallen so unexpectedly with the person whom Ursula had told him about, the one who'd been delving into London's criminal underbelly in search of her illegitimate child.

"It's all completely possible . . . even though it is bizarre," George said abruptly. "If everything Ursula says is true, it does explain all sorts of things."

Theo knew that he was referring to Alice's reluctance to come back to work, to her frequent disappearances and uneven moods. It did explain a lot, but if he was surprised by this, then what on earth was George going to say when Theo told him who the baby's father was? He had already had to quietly inform Sergeant Burns.

"*Women and Children First*," George continued, glancing up at Theo. "It must have been part of this." An admiring smile played on his lips. "My, she's clever. I always knew she was smart, but to combine the book and her detective work with finding her daughter, what a ruse! And what discipline and determination it must have taken."

Theo nodded. Then he stopped pacing, clearing his throat as he prepared for what was to come next. It was up to him to tell George, in the most sensitive way he could, that his dead son—a war hero—was also a scoundrel. He only hoped it would soften the blow for George to discover that he had a grandchild.

Theo offered George a cigarette and lit it before he took one for himself, trying to steady his mind while he blew the smoke upward, following its journey as its curled away into the glass roof-light. "George . . ."

"Yes?"

Theo shifted uncomfortably on his feet, one hand pressed

deep inside his jacket pocket as he held the cigarette in the other. "I'm not sure how to tell you this, so I'm just going to come right out with it."

The other man frowned. "What is it, Theo? Has something else happened?"

"It's about Alice's baby. There's something you need to know—"

The office doors swung open, and Sergeant Burns hurried back through with two other police officers. "We've got the location," she said. "Local officers are on their way."

"But we need to go too," Theo said.

"I'm afraid that's out of the question. The police can handle it, I assure you."

"But no one knows what's happened to the baby. We hope to God she's safe, but can you imagine if she's not?" The thought of it made Theo ache. "She might not even be there."

"Perhaps it would be best for someone to be there whom Alice knows," George said brusquely, addressing the older of the uniformed men.

The policeman looked at George. "I suppose since you're the grandfather, that counts as family," he said, weighing it up. "But you still have to stay in the car."

And the officers strode toward the door.

"What did he just say?" George asked in bewilderment.

Theo clapped him on the back. "Come on, I'll tell you on the way."

Forty

Alice was about to knock, but the door was already open, and there was no one behind the panel of diamond-patterned glass. *Accept your fear, Alice*, she could hear Ursula say. *Don't fight it. Let it work for you.*

It only took one gentle push.

Inside was dark and empty, and a red carpet swept away to the rear of the house where a gray linoleum kitchen and the green horizon of a garden beckoned.

Alice stood on the threshold and listened, the breeze from the garden rushing through the hallway, scented with honeysuckle and grass. Fragments of conversation drifted with it, and she cocked her head to listen—but the voices were too distant, so she eased cautiously into the living room.

It was sparsely furnished in muted colors that gave the place a transient feel, as if no one had spent any length of time there, or laid down any roots.

The crying resumed overhead, and Alice swiftly investigated the other downstairs rooms then headed for the staircase.

At the bottom of the steps she looked up—the house was as hollow as a skull, and her hand trembled as she laid it on the rail. Inwardly she was calm, moored by her self-belief, even though she wanted to scream her daughter's name.

Then she followed the sounds up to the next floor. Steps veered to the right, bringing her out opposite a room at the back of the house that overlooked the garden. She was possibly only feet away from where Eadie might be sleeping, and the thought drew her on, across the landing and through the glossy white door.

An animal mobile swung above the empty crib, and there were pastel walls and a rocking chair stuffed with pink-and-white gingham cushions. It could have been her own nursery—the lullaby, the decorations, her baby sleeping soundly—only she knew it wasn't, because she would never place the crib beside an open window.

And there wasn't any piano music, she realized; it was in her imagination, her subconscious weaving the lullaby into the present.

As she headed back onto the landing and toward the second door, she believed she could feel Eadie close by. Her heart hammered in her chest; she promised her mother's God that she would forgive her if Eadie was here, safe and well.

A boy of about five lay asleep on top of a single bed, the curtains drawn and the room in semi-darkness. She tiptoed out and along the hallway until she was outside the only other bedroom.

Her fingers pushed lightly, and the door creaked inward.

Two small hands poked through the bars of the cot, and a toddler with a pacifier in his mouth pulled himself up to standing and stared at her with flat brown eyes. Then he grasped hold of the guardrail and shook it hard as he tried to cry.

Alice quickly brought a finger up to her lips. "Shush." Then she whispered Brahms's "Lullaby." "Good evening, good night, with roses covered, with cloves adorned—" He stopped his rattling and sat down in the corner of the crib. She waited a few moments for him to settle before she retraced her footsteps downstairs.

The rooms were neat and clean: no filthy clothes, no festering lice or maggots, but no sign of Eadie either.

She leaned against the wall, weak and trembling with disappointment, about to sink to the floor when she noticed three silhouettes through the sheer dining-room curtains. They were standing in the garden: two men and a woman, her back to Alice—her hand resting on a baby carriage handle.

Alice's heart thudded, and anticipation rippled through her as she crept soundlessly along the hallway, then stopped at the threshold to steady herself; she would only have one chance at this.

They didn't notice her at first as she emerged from the shadows of the house: the men with their mugs and cigarettes, the petite blonde with her arm extended, rhythmically rocking the carriage, and the afternoon sun shrouding them in a surreal yellow haze. They were only young, probably not much older than Alice, one man in the khaki serge jacket and trousers of the Home Guard, the other in civilian clothes and a battered trilby.

The wind dropped, and everything seemed to slow to half-speed.

The air was soft and welcoming, whispering for Alice to come and take her baby back. The last time she'd seen Eadie, her daughter had barely opened her eyes; she'd been an armful of pale marbled skin and fine silken hair. She had only slept, as she probably was now, her tiny tongue protruding ever so slightly through lips like a miniature strawberry, her hands laid lightly across her chest. She hadn't even had the chance to wrinkle her nose like babies did—in fact, the few times she had opened her eyes, she'd stared straight past Alice, unable to focus.

Her heart galloping, Alice walked steadily onto the terrace. The conversation stopped as the three heads turned toward her.

She wondered if her daughter was asleep or awake, and if she still slept noiselessly as she had in her first few hours. That scarce time had been so precious: watching her, bending close to check her breathing and, when she couldn't, moving even closer to feel the warm breath on her ear. Such a small memory, only hours—a fraction of the life that was to come.

The woman's eyes widened as she saw Alice and she gasped, lifting her hand off the carriage, and its gentle motion stopped.

"Who are you?" one of the men asked.

Alice would see Eadie any moment, know if she was asleep or awake; she just needed to get her away from them. Except the one in uniform came toward her.

"Stay where you are!" she shouted.

But he kept coming, passing in front of the woman and the baby carriage so that neither of them were visible to Alice. "What do you want?" he asked as he drew nearer.

Alice's throat tightened, and her mouth wouldn't form the words: *I need to get to the carriage. I need to rescue Eadie.*

She'd always felt safe and secure with her father, and she remembered what that kind of love was like—the right kind of love—as she took a deep breath and reached for his gun.

Forty-one

The police car stopped at a level crossing to let the train pass, the uniformed troops inside the carriages flashing by as the train sped away from the city. Then the warning lights stopped blinking, the barrier rose, and the police car accelerated across the tracks, George and Theo sitting silently in the back. Theo had let the police explain everything to George: all of the details from the report that Sergeant Burns and the A4 Women's Branch had shared with them before they'd left the station. Now George sat unblinking, something constricting behind his eyes as he digested the news about his grandchild, and his son.

They drove north for another five minutes, passing shops and houses, schools and churches, Theo drumming his fingers against the inside of the passenger door as he wished he was behind the wheel and could make the damned car go faster.

He caught a glimpse of George's face, pale and immobile, and wondered what the man could be thinking in the aftermath of such news: shame and disappointment, but also possibly excitement. Or perhaps he was still in shock.

George must have felt Theo's gaze because he turned, and they exchanged a compassionate look.

"How much further?" George asked, watching the driver who looked at him in his rearview mirror.

"Not far, a couple of miles."

Trees and pedestrians sped by as they overtook cars and buses. Theo's thoughts were moving just as fast, images of Virginia slotting in beside Alice like a film reel. He reflected on how his life had changed so markedly in just a few short months, and how sickened he felt at what had happened to Alice and her child.

"All right, we're here," the officer announced as they turned into a road and made an abrupt stop. Then he leaned over his shoulder to give them an order. "You two stay here. We'll call if you're needed."

As the officers left the vehicle, Theo's gaze panned across the parallel rows of parked cars, and he noticed there was no sign of any other police.

There wasn't anyone standing between him and the door; between him and a chance to mend his broken promise to keep Alice safe.

Forty-two

Alice held the gun out stiffly in front of her.

The metal glinted, and the man's face twitched. "What do you want?" he asked.

She was close enough to see his jet-black hair and acne-scarred skin, and other shiny red scars on his forearms. The fact he wore the regimental badge and cap of the Home Guard sickened her even more.

Alice nodded toward the woman. "I want her to push the carriage over here."

He dropped his cigarette on the floor and ground it out slowly with the heel of his shoe. "And what if I say no?"

Alice turned her attention to the other two, and the other man slowly backed away.

"I want you to give me the baby."

The woman edged away too, shrinking further behind the uniformed man.

"Stay where you are!" Alice shouted.

The woman froze, her hands pressed against her sides.

"How do we know it's loaded?" the man in uniform asked as he inched forward. He was close to her now, barely six feet away.

She had nervously checked the mechanism several times in the privacy of her room at Penny's, but there was no denying the power she felt holding the weapon, or her lack of fear. "You'll know it's loaded when the bullet hits you," she said, moving the gun away from the woman and aiming it straight at him. "Don't come any nearer."

His laugh was exaggerated before it abruptly stopped. "So, how do you see this working?" he said, stretching himself taller. "There's three of us and one of you . . . and we've got the baby . . ."

"Just give her to me, and I'll leave you alone. I won't bother you again. No one knows I'm here."

"If we do that, we don't get paid. What are you going to do about that?"

"I'll get you money. Just push the carriage over here."

The woman's eyes darted nervously between the two men. "What do I do?" she asked, voice trembling.

"Why do you want her?" the volunteer soldier demanded.

She didn't answer, and he exchanged a look with the other man.

If only she could get between them, separate the woman from the men, then she would have a better chance of reaching the carriage. The gun wavered in her hand, and she steadied it, pointing it directly at the uniform across his heart.

"Now don't be a silly girl. You were already silly once before, weren't you? It's your baby, isn't it?" He laughed. "That's what got you into this mess."

The other man joined in, mocking her as the woman stood by, bristling with fear.

After an interminable moment, Alice stepped forward. She didn't care about their ridicule or what they thought of her. All she could think about was holding Eadie.

Forty-three

Theo was on his feet and running as soon as the two policemen disappeared through the front door. He cut through the side gate, heading toward the back of the house, George's slow footsteps echoing behind him.

A gunshot sounded.

Then he heard raised voices and, as he rounded the corner, three strangers and a pram came into view.

And Alice, pointing a gun.

There was no sign of any gunshot wounds. He sighed loudly, relieved he wasn't too late.

Her eyes darted over at him, then the others turned to look. For a second, he thought she was going to fire the weapon. Except that the man closest to her lunged, while the other one took off running toward the end of the garden.

Alice stumbled backward, still pointing the firearm as her attacker advanced with a strange, unreadable expression.

Theo hesitated. The man was in a uniform, albeit one he

didn't recognize, and it confused him. Still, he immediately hurled himself at the aggressor as he'd done on the football field countless times.

The man fell, and Theo wrestled his arms behind his back and held them as the man yelled obscenities. Just then, the two policemen came running from the house.

It seemed as if the second man was going to get away, but one policeman chased him as he tried to scramble over the back wall, and the second officer handcuffed the captive as he continued to shout and curse.

Sirens sounded in the distance, and Theo guessed that the local police were finally on their way.

He couldn't read Alice's expression as he helped her up off the ground and slid the gun from her fingers. Everything had happened so fast, and she was probably in shock.

"Alice. Are you all right?"

She gave him a thin smile.

He didn't blame her; he hadn't been there when she'd needed him, none of them had except for Ursula, but at least they'd made it just in time. He dared not think what would have happened otherwise.

Forty-four

"She's safe, and she's as good as gold," the woman said, as Alice inched toward the baby carriage. "I've looked after her, honestly."

It didn't matter to Alice that this was probably the wet nurse—the woman who had nursed her baby—because after all the days and weeks, here was Eadie, only an arm's-length away. Wasn't she?

Alice swallowed the thickness in her throat and bowed her head to look inside the hood: a soft cotton lining, buttercup-colored blankets, and a baby swaddled in white muslin.

Theo approached slowly, then George.

She looked up at them, her eyes brimming with tears.

"Is it her?" Theo asked.

Alice swallowed hard. "I think so." She leaned down, her curved arms gently scooping the baby out. The girl's face was still familiar in sleep, and Alice checked the birthmark on her shoulder before she clutched her as tightly as she dared and began to cry.

Alice closed her eyes, remembering to breathe. When she opened them again, it was as if time had folded in on itself, the past months disappearing until there was only today. Time hadn't robbed her of her daughter; she'd faced her enemy and survived, and she'd placed her trust in other people.

Eadie stirred in her arms, and Alice held her out so they could see each other. Her daughter made a small sound as her mouth stretched into a wide yawn, and she opened her eyes.

Theo's eyes glistened, and George smiled broadly.

"I'm sorry," Alice whispered to her daughter. "I'm so sorry."

More police arrived, spilling from the house. Officers in uniform searched the garden, while a couple of detectives stood a distance away, glancing at the strange trio and the baby. Alice was grateful they were giving them some time.

"Come," Theo said, and guided her over to one of the outdoor chairs. "You have nothing to be sorry for. It's us who should be sorry . . . sorry that you couldn't tell us. Sorry that we weren't able to help you."

It was a comfort to feel his arms around her shoulders, to know that she hadn't been abandoned, that he'd come back.

Theo and George watched as the handcuffed men were marched back through the house, but Alice never once took her eyes off her baby.

George looked sadly at Eadie, then his gaze settled on Alice, his hands motionless by his sides. "I must make my own apology, Alice. I don't know what to say to you—how to ever make it up to you for what you've been through." His expression was benign, all emotion sapped away, and his voice heavy with sorrow.

"I should have come to you," she said, "but I thought you might take her away."

"It's all right, the police explained," he said. "We just want to help you now. Rupert can't make amends for what he did. I don't expect that you know this . . . but he's been killed in action." Anguish flashed across his face, and a tear escaped his eye.

Alice let out a deep sigh—of sadness, relief, pity, she wasn't sure. "I'm so sorry for you, George."

"You don't need to do this on your own, though. We're here for you, if you want us to be . . . and for Eadie." He reached out to gently stroke the top of his granddaughter's head.

Now Alice was crying helplessly, but she wasn't helpless at all. She didn't have to pretend anymore; she'd rescued Eadie safely, and she'd been rescued too.

"I'm so glad you're here—both of you," she said, managing to stop sobbing for a brief moment to look at Theo, just long enough to smile.

Forty-five

LONDON, OCTOBER 1943
FIVE MONTHS LATER

Eadie's eyes widened, glinting with delight as she stared overhead where bunting fluttered like magnificent Amazonian butterflies. The multicolored flags stretched from the rooftop of the cafeteria all the way across the outdoor terrace where they were secured to the trees. Alice stared too, seeing the world through her daughter's unblinking gray eyes, as she held her close.

Dusk was settling, creating golden crowns on the birch and oak of the surrounding gardens where a band accompanied visitors taking tea beneath the leafy canopy. Fairy lights illuminated the animal houses, floodlighting made brilliant spectacles of the Mappin Terraces and the Penguin Pool, and a patchwork of grass plots featured clusters of light from the unique glow-worm displays.

"Do you want me to carry her for a while?" Theo asked, a soft pleading in his voice.

Alice involuntarily clutched her daughter tighter. "No, she's not that heavy."

"That's not what I meant," he said, and smiled fondly. "I thought you might like to walk around, meet some of your fans."

She could see he was itching to carry Eadie, and so teasingly said, "No, I think I'll just enjoy being here a little longer."

A thread of lights spun overhead like a spiderweb, creating a magic that had never felt as strong, and a spark of that energy passed right through her.

"Lots of guests want to talk to you, you know," he said with a raised eyebrow. "You need to make sure you do the rounds—you wouldn't want George complaining about poor marketing."

She still wasn't sure if he was serious or teasing, but that was part of the excitement of getting to know each other better. Their friendship had evolved slowly over the intervening months, and it was obvious now to everyone how they felt about each other.

Five months had passed since she'd been reunited with her daughter. The 1939 Adoption of Children Act had finally come into force, and Alice knew that the work of Olive Melville Brown, Joanna Swift and the welfare sector had been instrumental in the change. Olive had forgiven Alice and Elizabeth since Joe had been able to keep his identity secret, and Olive had told Alice a little about her experiences as a victim of baby farming.

Ever since *Women and Children First* had been released, it had been a huge success, thanks partly to it being so topical.

Sidney Jardine and his associates were in custody awaiting trial. While Ruth could have been prosecuted for abduction, Alice had dropped the charge, although she still couldn't bring herself to see her. Hope kept Alice up to date since she was regularly in touch with both Ruth and Alice.

Theo had stayed in London to oversee *The Zoo Chronicles* himself as it had hurriedly gone to press, doing a marvelous job of sourcing good-quality paper and including enough lithographs to keep the sensibility of the menagerie of characters alive. The Zoological Society of London had been delighted with the publication and insisted on giving a reception to mark its launch, and so here they were—the various committees, staff and public—as well as the Partridge team, enjoying twilight refreshments along with the human entertainment and animal encounters. There were a number of high-profile people involved in the Zoological Society council, including the Duke of Devonshire, Colonel Monckton Copeman and J. R. Norman, Esquire, as well as three sirs and two professors, so it was no surprise to see the large contingent of gathered press, or that one of the zoo's employees was filming the event on a Dekko camera.

The book had only been in the shops for a few weeks, but it had already been well-received by the public and the critics, and with zoo visitors who were able to buy it as a souvenir.

"So, Alice, what are your plans for the sequel?" George asked, with a half smile.

He was joking, of course; she'd already told him there wouldn't be one for the time being, that Eadie was her priority now, and he'd not tried to convince her to stay at Partridge—or claim custody, as she'd feared he would. Whatever feelings George had about his son, he kept to himself, and Alice knew that at least he and his wife found some comfort in their granddaughter.

Theo nudged her and indicated to where Julian Huxley, the director of the zoo, stood on the top step, gazing out over the terrace as he straightened his jacket and prepared to speak.

Alice scanned the crowd too, and she shivered, as she often did in public places, when she thought she caught sight of Rupert's tall, dark-haired image. They'd had a memorial service for him, and he had been mourned, but a body had never been found, and the idea clawed at her that one day he might reappear.

"Ladies and gentlemen, welcome to London Zoo, or Regent's Park Zoo, as some of you know it . . ." The director waited until the crowds had quieted down and he had most everyone's attention. "It's not often that we assemble in groups, for good reasons these days, or above ground—"

A murmur of laughter rippled through the crowd.

"—so, it is with absolute pleasure that I stand before you tonight to congratulate the zoo community—and by that, I mean everyone, the workers, the visitors and the animals—on the magnificent achievement of taking us through this wretched war thus far. It's your stories in here that are a reminder of what we can do when we set our hearts and minds to it."

An animal gave a screech of approval in a nearby enclosure, and another wave of laughter swept through the audience. Penny, Michael and their children stood at the front listening, and Olive, Elizabeth and Joe Stevenson were there somewhere too. Tommy, Ursula, Emily and other Partridge employees were scattered through the crowd, as was Mr. Vinall, the penguin keeper. Even the book group had turned up—apart from Marjorie and Terrance, who'd stopped attending meetings when they'd discovered Alice's status as an unmarried mother. It hadn't mattered; new members had joined the group, and the esprit de corps had remained, as had Rex, charming as ever and without showing any prejudice, or that he was put out at being part of the subterfuge, which Alice suspected he had rather enjoyed.

"We know that these stories are resonating with young and old, and I'm told that the public have enjoyed reading about the exploits of our new arrival, the mona monkey, and hearing how Joseph the python has recovered from pneumonia. And I'm sure you will all be relieved to know that the four escaped parakeets have returned."

A cheer went up, and he waited until the noise abated before he carried on.

Alice knew every story and every page by heart, and she'd read them all to Eadie. She'd told her about Peter the brown bear, who put on rather unusual physical displays, and Pollyanna, the only reindeer in the zoo, as well as the ever-popular Ming, the panda who had returned from Whipsnade.

The book had reportedly already created favorites among visitors, with some enclosures particularly crowded, including that of Peter the five-foot alligator. He was initially a temporary guest, on account of being moved from the Hammersmith apartment he'd shared with his owner, Miss Thelma Roberts, and an Amazonian crocodile. Apparently they were quite the socialites, featuring regularly on shopping expeditions as well as fundraising at charity events, but judging by his popularity now, he might have to become a permanent exhibit alongside the aardvark called Adolf and the axolotl named Mussolini.

"Of course, it's not just the animals we are grateful to," the director continued. "There are many, many, zookeepers and staff, past and present"—he caught Alice's eye—"who have helped over the past few years. Directors, curators, researchers, superintendents, surgeons, clerks and gardeners, accountants and secretaries—too many names to mention, but all of whom carry out very important tasks. Without their help and dedication, we would not have been able to keep our gates open, or keep the animals safe."

Alice glanced at the display of books, thinking back to all the stories that had been included, far more than she'd intended to, but they were all so extraordinary, from the sixteen-year-old boy-keepers, barely more than children themselves, to the full-page photo of Mr. and Mrs. Churchill at the zoo with one of the cubs from his pet lion, Rota.

"And now we have this wonderful book to treasure, to extend the pleasure that our visitors get from our zoo. It's important to carry on giving people some much-needed escape from the cruel realities of war. So, I extend my thanks to Miss Cotton"—he smiled broadly at her—"and to Theo and George, and the team at Partridge Press for giving us this testament to the importance of the animals and their keepers. I extend those thanks to the public too. Without your patronage, your donations and your sponsorship, none of this would be possible. So, thank you all," he said, eyes traveling across the crowd, "from me and our staff and our wonderful menagerie."

There was a long and rapturous applause, and Theo had to wait for the noise to die down before he could whisper in Alice's ear, "Aren't you glad we mixed those books up now?"

"Yes. Yes, I suppose I am. And I'm very glad you came all that way to bring it back." She smiled, even though inside she felt anything but calm. Theo had been due to return to New York, but he'd come up with a proposition that Walter had approved, and now it seemed she wouldn't have to imagine her life without him for the near future.

She stared at him in the moonlight, until he turned and caught her looking.

"Excuse me a moment," she said, blushing, as she noticed Ursula standing under a tree with Bridget. Alice hadn't told her friends the good news about Theo yet, and she made her way across the lawn toward them.

She'd nearly reached them when Mr. Stilwell, the ex-naval sign-writer, stepped out in front of her. "Miss Cotton, might I have a word? I just wondered if there was anything you might do to help us. You see, there is a downside to all this publicity."

"Oh, really, what appears to be the problem?" she asked, as she stroked Eadie's back.

"Well, apart from the cockatoos and parakeets showing off and taking to the woods at Hampstead, there are ongoing problems with people damaging cage labels and noticeboards—and stealing the nameplates. They are taking them as souvenirs!"

"Oh, dear, I see what you mean. That would be a problem.

You wouldn't want to mix up your animals, would you?" She tried to hide her amusement as she thought about all the chaos that could ensue. "Well, I really don't know what I can do to help."

"When you reprint the book, can you put in a note, something asking people not to take things when they visit?"

"I could try, but wouldn't it be best if you put up a notice at the entrance?"

"We did," he said, glancing down at his shoes, circumspect.

"And what happened?"

"Well, someone stole it."

"Oh, I see," she said, struggling not to laugh.

"Yes," he said, looking at her and smiling. "That's my problem."

"I'll see what we can do."

"Thank you, Miss Cotton, and you make sure you bring Eadie back when she's old enough to ride the camels."

"I certainly will, Mr. Stilwell. Please excuse me, I just need to catch a friend before she leaves."

When Alice joined the couple midway through their conversation, Ursula was saying, ". . . you know these keepers really are a mine of information. One was just telling me you can hypnotize a lobster. Alligators too, apparently."

Theo appeared from the crowd and came to stand beside Alice.

"Did you know that they're using the webs of black widow spiders to manufacture precision instruments in the United States now?" he said.

"That's remarkable," said Bridget, "but how?"

"The strands are as strong as steel or platinum wire, so they can use them in telescopes," he said, smiling.

"They wouldn't have much luck here at the zoo—all the poisonous insects and reptiles were destroyed on the first day of war," Alice replied.

"Well, now that we know it's safe . . . can I have a cuddle?" Ursula said.

"I thought you'd never ask," Alice replied. She lowered Eadie into Ursula's arms. Her daughter was asleep, ebony lashes resting on her rosy cheeks, air whistling through lips puckered into a bow.

"Would it be terribly selfish of me to say I'll miss you?" Ursula said, looking up at Alice with moist eyes.

"I'm not going anywhere! You're not getting rid of me that easily."

"But I thought"—Ursula glanced at Theo, then lowered her voice—"didn't he ask you to go with him?"

"Yes, but he's changed his mind. We're staying."

There hadn't been the chance to tell any of them about Theo's agreement with Walter, and the plan to buy him out. According to Walter, three thousand miles away wasn't far enough for the man who had jilted his daughter.

"That's wonderful," Ursula said with a grin. "You wouldn't want to deprive the publishing world of such immense talent."

"I know. And besides"—Alice looked at Bridget and back at her friend—"you do get to meet such interesting people." Ursula gave Eadie an affectionate squeeze and handed her back to her mother.

Theo moved closer to Alice, placing his arm around her, and when she turned her head toward him, he kissed her tenderly on the lips. When he pulled away, she gazed longingly into his eyes and smiled, then they both looked out over the zoological gardens at the sun-burnished trees and the citrus skies.

Alice clutched Eadie tightly, her skin pricking with happiness, and knew that at last they were safe. And as the night pressed away the last band of gold on the horizon, she felt Theo's hold tighten, and she shivered as a feeling passed through her, a sensation she barely recognized: one of yearning, which filled her with such overwhelming force that she couldn't have prevented it if she'd tried.

AUTHOR'S NOTE

If you're anything like me and you like to know the truth behind a story, then you are probably reading this before you've read the novel—except on this occasion, you really should turn back and read the book first, as it contains spoilers!

There is a belief that stories find you, and that was the case with this novel. It started with a family secret from a few generations ago that I needed to try to understand. How could someone sell their own flesh and blood? What I discovered was that selling babies was much more commonplace than I'd thought, and although I vaguely knew about the baby farmers from the turn of the twentieth century, I'd had no idea that the practice of selling and trading babies and infants had carried on for so long—or that the wartime conditions made it so much worse. Discovering how the legislation to protect them was postponed because of the outbreak of World War II just confirmed my belief that it was a story worth following.

While researching my previous novels, *Maggie's Kitchen* and *Eleanor's Secret*, I came across fascinating material about the role that books played during wartime, as well as the challenges faced by the publishing world. Books became more important than ever: for soldiers to read while waiting, to distract the public during raids, and for readers to understand what was happening to their world, as well as for escapism in general. But the industry faced a battle to overcome the shortages and challenges to produce these books as demand grew.

A great deal of truth and real events are woven through my story, from the bombing of the publishing industry in Paternoster Row in 1940 and the fact that the larger publishers really did offer affected smaller publishing houses peppercorn rent, to the book schemes in the United States and the United Kingdom, such as the Armed Services Editions and the Forces Book Club.

Much of the detail about London Zoo—or Regent's Park Zoo, as it was often called—is based on real events, animals and people. It really was a miracle that the zoo survived as well as it did, and that it provided a respite for visitors and servicemen. I've used some of the animals' real names as a way of honoring them, from the well-known ones such as Rota the lion, who was given to Mr. Churchill as a gift, and Peter the alligator, who was rescued from his Hammersmith home after a bombing raid and removed to the zoo for safekeeping, to the aardvark called Adolf and the axolotl named Mussolini.

As well as the institutions I mention in the Acknowledgments, I visited locations in Brighton, Bloomsbury, Fitzrovia, Primrose Hill and Chelsea, as well as London Zoo.

The "Gates," or the Gateways Club in Chelsea's Bramerton Street, really was a hub for LGBTIQ+ people to socialize during the 1930s and '40s, and it has a fascinating history during wartime and beyond.

And while I didn't make it to Book Row in New York, it is also an authentic location. Although it's now reduced from seven blocks of bookshops to two, it's still full of a million stories—and ink, dust and promises—and I can feel a research trip coming on!

ACKNOWLEDGMENTS

Once again, many fiction and nonfiction books have played key roles in my writing process, as well as libraries, museums and archives, and I'm indebted to each and every one of them and to all the individuals who helped. Among them were the State Library of New South Wales, the UK National Archives, the Museum of London, the Foundling Museum, the Brighton Museum & Art Gallery, the Victoria and Albert Museum and the Metropolitan Police Heritage Centre.

I'm particularly grateful to Ann Sylph and Sarah Broadhurst, librarians at the Zoological Society of London, for opening up the magical and dusty world of their wonderful zoo. Thanks also to Wiktoria Uljanowska at the Ditchling Museum of Art + Craft, and to Mick Clayton, the print workshop manager at the St Bride Foundation, Fleet Street, London, for sharing his printing secrets and his wonderful demonstration, and to Dan Robertson, curator of local history and archeology, Royal Pavilion and Brighton Museum.

Some of the books I consulted in writing this novel include: Diana Athill, *Stet: An Editor's Life* (London: Granta, 2000); Mary Cadogan and Patricia Craig, *Women and Children First: The Fiction of Two World Wars* (London: Victor Gollancz Ltd, 1978); Toby Faber, *Faber & Faber: The Untold Story* (London: Faber & Faber, 2019); John Feather, *A History of British Publishing* (London: Croom Helm Ltd, 1988); Lara Feigel, *The Love-charm of Bombs: Restless Lives in the Second World War* (London: Bloomsbury, 2013); Andreas Feininger, *New York in the Forties* (New York: Dover Publications, 1978); Robert Hewison, *Under Siege: Literary Life In London 1939–45* (London: Weidenfeld & Nicolson, 1977); Valerie Holman, *Print for Victory: Book Publishing in England 1939–1945* (London: The British Library, 2008); Molly Guptill Manning, *When Books Went to War: The Stories That Helped Us Win World War II* (New York: Mariner Books, 2015); Marvin Mondlin and Roy Meador, *Book Row: An Anecdotal and Pictorial History of the Antiquarian Book Trade* (New York: Carroll & Graf Publishers, 2004); Alan Munton, *English Fiction of the Second World War* (London: Faber & Faber, 1989); Iain Stevenson, *Book Makers: British Publishing in the Twentieth Century* (London: The British Library, 2010).

Background research and context came from countless newspaper and magazine archives, including *The Times* (London), *The New York Times*, *The Bookseller* and the *Daily Mail*. The character of Olive Melville Brown was inspired by the *Daily Mail* journalist who followed the baby-farming stories, and the headlines on pages 134 and 153 are borrowed from articles she wrote in 1943. Extracts on page 125 are adverts or notices from local newspapers of the time, and the report on pages 199–201 was taken from an actual newspaper article for authenticity, but the names have been changed.

I would also like to acknowledge the Library of Congress, Prints and Photographs Division/Mary Evans Picture Library for the use of the Franklin D. Roosevelt quote in the front of the book. The quote on page 30 is from *Alice's Adventures in Wonderland* by Lewis Carroll.

I am grateful to Gillian Green for recommending the memoirs of Diana Athill, who was an inspiration for Ursula, although not her sexual orientation, and to Kristine Pack for helping with Americanisms. Thanks also to Dr. Rebecca Overton, general practitioner, and Clare Jordan, clinical midwife consultant, for medical information on Alice's physical and mental well-being following the birth and trauma.

Sincere thanks to Christa Munns for her encouragement and to Kate Goldsworthy for her thoughtful editing, both of whom helped me write the best version of this story. Heartfelt thanks to Annette Barlow for putting her faith in me for a third time. Thanks also to the rest of the team at Allen & Unwin who, like the team at Partridge Press, all play such an important role in creating and selling books. I owe huge thanks to Danielle Dieterich and all those at Putnam who have worked so hard to produce this novel for US readers, as well as for the divine cover.

My love and thanks to Tina Cook, Lisa Blacklaw-Taylor, Jacqueline Beecham and John Lydon for reading early drafts of the manuscript and for their valued feedback. A final thank-you to my glorious grandmother Ellen Mary Taylor, who passed away on November 30, 2019, at the age of ninety-eight. She was an inspiration for my writing and the keeper of our family secrets, and will be dearly missed.

POPULAR BOOKS FROM THE ERA

Some of the most popular books of 1942–1943 in the UK and US, according to *The New York Times* and *The Bookseller*, include:

A Tree Grows in Brooklyn, **Betty Smith, Harper & Brothers, 1943**

The Provincial Lady in War-Time, **E. M. Delafield, Macmillan, 1940**

The Battle of Britain, **Ministry of Information, 1941**

Bomber Command, **Ministry of Information, 1941**

Coastal Command, Ministry of Information, 1942

Five Little Pigs, Agatha Christie, Dodd, Mead & Company, 1942

Five on a Treasure Island, Enid Blyton, Hodder & Stoughton, 1942

Frenchman's Creek, Daphne du Maurier, Victor Gollancz Ltd, 1941

No Orchids for Miss Blandish, James Hadley Chase, Jarrolds, 1939

The Ministry of Fear, Graham Greene, Heinemann, 1943

Mrs. Parkington, Louis Bromfield, Harper & Brothers, 1943

Put Out More Flags, Evelyn Waugh, Chapman & Hall, 1942

The Body in the Library, Agatha Christie, Dodd, Mead & Company, 1942

The Screwtape Letters, C. S. Lewis, Geoffrey Bles, 1942

The Myth of Sisyphus, Albert Camus, Éditions Gallimard, 1942

The Song of Bernadette, Franz Werfel, Hamish Hamilton, 1942

The Robe, Lloyd C. Douglas, Houghton Mifflin, 1942

West with the Night, Beryl Markham, Houghton Mifflin, 1942

The Moon Is Down, John Steinbeck, Viking Press, 1942

The Scarlet Imposter, Dennis Wheatley, Hutchinson, 1940

When We Meet Again

Caroline Beecham

A Conversation with Caroline Beecham

Discussion Guide

BOOK ENDS

PUTNAM
—EST. 1838—

A Conversation with Caroline Beecham about When We Meet Again

What is your novel about?

When We Meet Again is the story of a young woman, Alice Cotton, who shows extraordinary courage and determination when she cleverly combines her search for her missing child with the challenge of creating much-needed books during wartime. The novel starts when her baby, Eadie, is stolen and Alice's search takes her into the dark and frightening world of baby farming in the 1940s. (Baby farmers were people, often couples, who took infants and children for a fee under the pretext of looking after them but in most cases did the opposite.)

Though a tense and moving story, there's also a lot of light in the book, which comes from the fascinating world of book publishing during the Second World War. Alice works as an editor at Partridge Press, where they are struggling to keep up with the demand for books with ever-increasing paper rations. Everyone is reading more; in the shelters, in their blacked-out homes—for entertainment and escapism—and more books are also needed for the troops and servicemen. *When We Meet Again* is a story of love and hope, about the importance of friendship, of loyalty and forgiveness—and the belief that books have the power to change lives.

Discuss your inspirations for the novel. Were there any personal experiences that drew you to this plot?

I discovered a long-held family secret from a few generations ago; that a relative's baby was sold to a childless couple in a nearby town. I was quite shocked until I started looking into the circumstances and found out how common it was for unmarried mothers who were desperate to find a way of taking care of their illegitimate children. Unfortunately, they were often pressured into going through illegal adoptions and turning to baby farmers. I went through a number of stages trying to understand the desperation that could drive you to part with your own flesh and blood, and I realized how complex it was, and that it wasn't a new social problem. When I discovered that a law that was supposed to be passed to protect children and stop unlawful adoptions was shelved because of the outbreak of war—the exact time it was needed more than ever—I knew that it was a story worth following.

There were also a number of individuals who inspired me; social activist Clara Andrew, fought to get the Adoption of Children Act passed, and journalist Olive Melville Brown followed the story and kept it in the public eye. Diana Athill was another pioneering woman who had a distinguished career as an editor and worked in the industry throughout the war and was one of the stimuluses for the character of Ursula.

A couple of settings also provided inspiration for the story; London Zoo and Book Row in New York. As soon as I learned how London Zoo, or Regent's Park Zoo, as the locals called it, remained open during the war and grew in popularity, becoming a refuge to visitors and servicemen, it became a sanctuary for Alice too. There were also such wonderful real stories about the animals and their antics that I had to include some of them too. Once I knew about the important role books played in wartime—the US had a Council on Books in Wartime and a very successful books scheme for their troops—it was great to then discover Book Row. This area in New York had seven blocks of bookshops back then, and although its reduced to only two blocks now, I really hope to visit one day!

One of the novel's most salient messages is the transformative power of books to unite and inspire during periods of hardship. Which books fill that role for you, either in your personal life or in your development as a writer?

I think there are books that you discover at different times and sometimes you find that perfect one. As a teenager it was the brooding romances of *Wuthering Heights* and *Tess of the D'Urbervilles*, or scaring myself with Stephen King. I've read a range of fiction and nonfiction since but now really enjoy fiction that shows me something new as well as has compelling characters and unusual settings, like Sarah Perry's *The Essex Serpent*, Bridget Collins's *The Binding* and Delia Owens's *Where the Crawdads Sing*. I don't turn to any specific books during challenging times but find that historical fiction can be so distracting and offer the world through a new lens.

As a writer, it makes a huge difference if I'm reading a book that really inspires me, and I find that reading established writers, like William Boyd, Maggie O'Farrell or Isabel Allende really helpful, as they are such accomplished storytellers with enviable vocabularies and the writing is so assured. I love British author Rachel Joyce for her wonderfully quirky characters and have enjoyed getting to know the work of American authors such as Kristin Hannah, Kate Quinn, Fiona Davis, Paula McLain and Meg Clayton White. And of course, there are exceptionally talented Australian historical fiction writers such as Natasha Lester and Kate Morton, whose books are inspiring and a joy to read!

Books are transformative; they do unite and inspire and remind us of our shared experiences. You only have to look at the millions of books groups and online clubs and sites around the world. Historical fiction in particular shows us that there are many who have gone before who have experienced harder times, and it's important to remember that. In the same way that books were so important during wartime, many people have found the same to be true during lockdown. In wartime people read to understand, to entertain and for escapism and I think the same is true of why we've read so much more over the past year; and are reading still. It was fairly surreal editing the novel last year, when we were in lockdown and thinking that here was history repeating; you weren't allowed to congregate in public places in groups of more than two hundred in wartime London, and there were similar restrictions again some seventy years later. It's another way that historical fiction can be thought-provoking; reminding us how previous generations endured and carried on.

Many readers will be astonished to learn about the practice baby farming and its wartime prevalence. How do you think this practice fit in to societal attitudes toward motherhood at this time?

Unfortunately, there have always been people who will take advantage of others misfortune and sadly, unwanted babies fed an industry; the practice of baby farming. As I've already mentioned, baby farming was the practice of taking money for looking after a baby but not doing that, and children were often underfed and mistreated. There were also a lot of illegal adoptions that took place; adverts in British newspapers with babies and children for sale, although luckily, there were also people that wanted to help legalize the industry. It's not surprising there more unwed mothers and more illegitimate babies during wartime given there was so much uncertainty about the future and the temptation to live each day as if it were your last. I'm sure society was shifting its attitude about motherhood during this time because of war, and because so many men weren't returning, and there was probably a renewed feeling of the sacredness of life. People may have turned a blind eye to it before and banished unmarried mothers to convents and babies to foundling hospitals, but there was social change thanks to women like Olive Melville Brown who pursued the cause in her newspaper stories, and Clara Andrew, who worked for the National Adoption Society.

In what ways does the current iteration of the novel differ from the novel you initially intended to write? In what ways has it stayed the same?

Initially I didn't know how I would combine the stolen baby storyline with the publishing one, but as soon as I found out about the practice of baby farming and had the idea that Alice would combine her search for her missing child with creating these much-needed books, it gave me the engine of the story. The introduction of the real settings of London Zoo and Book Row, and the competition between the British and American publishing industries created a fascinating canvas for the story too. Given how essential books were during wartime, and how significant the struggles of the industry were then, this became an important storyline. By including the competition and collaboration between the US and British, I was able to include some of the fascinating detail about the publishing industry in Britain and the US during wartime.

The developing relationship between Alice and Theo stayed the same as I'd intended, but the character of Ursula had a much larger role in an earlier draft, and while it was right to reduce it because this really is Alice and Theo's story, I am tempted to go back to Ursula one day . . .

Though this is your American debut, you have also authored two previous works of historical fiction in Australia. How did the writing experience of your current novel compare to that of your past novels?

The writing process for this novel was quite different to my debut novel, *Maggie's' Kitchen*, which I spent four years researching and writing. It's about a cook who struggles to open and run one of the Ministry of Food's British Restaurants to feed hungry Londoners during the Second World War. My second novel, *Eleanor's Secret*, about a young female war artist who wants to record the war overseas the same as her male counterparts do, was quicker to write, as I had developed more of a memory and research bank about the era and life on the Home Front. The novel is a mystery and has a contemporary storyline that solves the wartime mystery, so it was exciting trying something new as well. Writing *When We Meet Again* was more straightforward in one way, as I knew what I needed to do because of the experience on my first two books, although it was challenging because I made higher demands of myself; I wanted to be braver, create more drama, find ways of using different language and avoid cliched metaphors. It's a bit like the saying: The more you learn, the less you know. Writing is a craft, and I can't imagine that you ever stop learning, or wanting to try new ways of doing things, pushing your boundaries and hopefully creating memorable stories.

Each of your novels is set during World War II, albeit focused on civilians' wartime effort on the home front. Why did you want to write about this era, and what do you hope your novel helps readers understand about this moment in history?

I came across the story of the British Restaurants that the Ministry of Food set up during the Second World War and found them intriguing and was surprised that I hadn't heard of them before. Lots of other people hadn't either and that's what gave me the idea for *Maggie's Kitchen*; what could be more important than giving people this most basic need in wartime, and food is so restorative. As I researched this story, I found other great untold stories in the archives and thought they were also worth sharing. Before that I worked as a TV producer so it was a whole new way of storytelling but there seemed to be more possibility with fiction, although now I think *Maggie's Kitchen* would make a great drama series too!

I hope readers find these stories entertaining and that they shed new light on this well-documented era and give a different perspective. It was such a fascinating period of social change when women had to suddenly take on roles that had previously been in the male domain and this was cause for celebration and upheaval, especially when the men came back from war and wanted their jobs back! There are so many interesting stories about life on the home front, and it's inspiring finding out about these pioneering women. There seems to be a new wave of women writers who are putting women at the center of these wartime stories and giving them the action and adventure that men previously had; it's probably because these stories have been hidden for so long that they are coming to the surface now.

What's next for you?

I'm working on a new novel inspired by the real life of a British woman who helped rescue thousands of Jewish refugees from Europe in the 1930s and '40s. There are some fascinating stories about the diaspora and the amazing legacy she helped create. It's an exciting novel to research and write, but it's also a very different way of working; I usually come across an untold history and create fictional characters to weave the history around. Creating a story inspired by a real character does come with the additional pressure of remaining true to their spirit while also creating an engaging character, and, of course, plenty of drama and romance. This is a challenge, but I feel that she sacrificed so much of her personal life to help others that it's a great opportunity to give her something back and create the love life she never had. I just hope I do her fighting spirit and incredible legacy the justice it deserves.

Discussion Guide

1. Alice shows fierce bravery in her search for her child, overcoming physical and emotional obstacles, pain and discomfort and showing courage in facing the dangerous baby farmers and venturing into unfamiliar places. Where does Alice find her strength? How far would you go to rescue someone you love?

2. How does the wartime setting impact the events of the novel? Discuss the ways that war affected different areas of life in London during this time.

3. Compare and contrast the relationships between mothers and daughters in the novel, looking specifically at the connection between Alice and Eadie and that of Alice and Ruth. In what ways is Alice's parenting style similar to or different from her own mother's?

4. At the heart of *When We Meet Again* is the idea that books can change lives. Has a book ever changed your life? If so, what was it? Why did it have such an impact? Why do you think that books were particularly important during wartime?

5. Both Alice and Ursula face immense stigma in society. How does Alice's status as an unwed mother change the way those in her community treat her? How is Ursula's sexuality perceived by others?

6. The basis for *When We Meet Again* was rooted in the author's own family secret—a relative of hers had an illegitimate child, who was sold to another family. Were you surprised to learn about the history of "baby farmers"? What else surprised you about the history of this time period?

7. Many characters in the novel increasingly rely upon their friendships as their family loyalties are tested. Why do you think these friendships were so powerful? Can you think of a friendship that sustained you when perhaps family did not?

8. Theo is dismayed when he learns of Walter's disloyalty to his brother, George, but also could himself be considered disloyal based on his broken engagement with Virginia. Do you think Theo made the right decision? Where should his loyalty lie? How are different kinds of loyalty—romantic and familial—contrasted in the book?

9. Is there a "villain" in *When We Meet Again*? If so, who do you think it is? Why did each of the antagonists make their decisions, and can you empathize with any of them?

10. What do you imagine happens to Alice, Theo and Eadie after the novel's end?